Happy Valley USA

Michael Mary,
You have your own Happy Valley!
Glad to say it-Finished!
JPL (Jim) Jul Ann

J.R. FISHER WITH HIS FATHER CARL

Happy Valley USA

J.R. Fisher

EVENT HORIZON PRESS

HAPPY VALLEY USA

A Novel

Copyright 1997 and 2013 J.R. Fisher

Designed and Produced by
EVENT HORIZON PRESS

This book is dedicated
to the memory of my parents,
Carl and Thea Fisher

Preface

I'VE ALWAYS THOUGHT OF THIS NOVEL as my father's book. Like the Carl in *Happy Valley USA*, my dad's name was Carl, Carlton actually, but he was nothing like this Carl. Instead of being prejudiced, my father was the first manager in Long Beach to integrate his department with Proctor and Gamble by hiring an African-American. He was also a lifelong Lutheran, a person of great faith. Somehow, I've always thought of Frank Hessel as being more like my father, but in this novel, Frank ends up being Catholic and a teacher, neither of which apply to my dad. I became a teacher in my second career but not a Catholic, so how does anything in this book fit my father?

The novel is set in 1999, the year of the Y2K scare, when all the computers in the world were supposed to shut down. It is also the dawning of a new millennium. Frank, Carl and Jonathan, the main characters, are all in their seventies, so they witnessed some of the Depression, but were too young to fight in World War II, although they certainly witnessed it in papers and newsreels. The time-frame is very close to my father's. The action of the novel takes place in a German farm valley, similar to the one in which my father was born, outside of Appleton, Wisconsin. It was so "German" in fact, that my father did not speak English until he started school. Like Frank, my father lost his wife, my mother Thea, and then later remarried, happily, in his senior years. He and my stepmother made several trips to Germany, where they visited Claire's cousins. My father spent the last years of his life in remission from cancer.

As for prejudice, my father told me that their church, The First Evangelical German Lutheran Church of Long Beach, California, was smeared with yellow paint and fire-bombed during World War I, when Americans had little use for Germans. The name of the church was changed to the more neutral First Lutheran. Even the Germanic C was dropped from my family name, Fischer, during World War I. My uncle's wife, Peggy, was Jewish, so I learned about antisemitism from her. All in all, then, this novel is my father's book because it matches the span of his life, it mirrors the experiences he had growing up German-American, and it is written from the point-of-view of a good man, someone like my father. Like any novel, it is also my book, his son's, because my own experiences appear throughout it. I grew up confused about being German-American, wondering how we could be proud of Martin Luther and yet be ashamed of having even remote ties to Adolph Hitler, the man responsible for the Holocaust. Like Frank Hessel, I became a teacher, but I also became a poet and a writer.

In short, this book is my father's book and my book. It is our family's book, but it also belongs to the many German-Americans who grew up confused about their heritage. My father's name at birth was Carlton Frederic Fischer. His younger brother was born between the wars and christened Gaylord Lansing Fisher. Out of the shame of being German, we became English. By the time America got into World War II, German-Americans fought in the European Theater, unlike the Japanese-Americans who were confined in the camps. Today, I am in my seventies and have witnessed and experienced much of what is in this book, even though I've chosen to set the scene in my father's era.

The prejudice explored in this novel, whether religious, racial or ethnic, is real. It was real then and still exists today, though hopefully it is being reduced with every new generation of Americans. Having lived through the Civil Rights Movement, I can say that racial prejudice is much reduced from what it was, but it still exists. Unfortunately, in the aftermath of 9/11, we have a new target, Muslim-Americans. Human nature is human nature. We hate what we fear. Hopefully, we can all remember the founding of this nation and the words, "All men are created equal."

— *J.R. Fisher*

Introduction:
   Happy Valley USA

ASH WEDNESDAY

SEVENTY YEARS OLD and still dragging your heels, I told myself as I walked out of the church. It was the first day of Lent, always a thoughtful time for me, but even more so now, with everything else going on. I had tried to pray, asking God to remove this affliction from me, but the concentration wouldn't come, nor, it seemed, would any answers. Father Einsphar had preached on Y2K and the coming End of the World, tying it in to Ash Wednesday and the long wait until Easter, none of which helped my mood. Since I had stayed for a while after taking communion, the church was mostly deserted when I walked out the side door and into the bright sunshine.

"Is that you, St. Francis?" The words washed over me from out of the light. It was a voice and a name that I hadn't heard in years.

"Yes, it's me," I said, holding up one hand to shade my eyes. I tried to focus on the figure emerging in front of me, while I sought to place the voice. It had to be someone from the old days because St. Francis was my nickname way back in grade school. By high school, it had mostly been dropped. The clearer the figure became, the more familiar the man looked, but I still couldn't place him at first, even when he spoke again.

"You old codger," he said, "it really is you."

I could see the man clearly now, but for a second or two, I didn't fully recognize him because he'd gotten so old. His hair was pure white, but his skin was tanned like always, now with several new wrinkles. Still there was no hiding the smile and the jaunty way he stood, the same as he did sixty years ago when we were kids together.

"Carl Marx," I said, delighted to have solved the mystery. "How long has it been?"

His name is really Carl Markdoffer, but the nickname of Marx had stuck ever since I can remember, just like St. Francis had for me.

"I don't know, Frank. Thirty years maybe? When was that last high school reunion I came in for? Wasn't it our twentieth?"

We stood there shaking hands and then hugging and darn near crying. Lord, it had been a long, long time. Lots of water under the bridge.

"Here," Carl said, offering me his handkerchief, "you've got dirt on your forehead."

"It's ashes," I said, surprised and even a little offended that he wouldn't know the importance of the ritual. "This is Ash Wednesday. You know, the first day of Lent."

"Good grief," he said, "I've forgotten all that religious crap."

In just a brief, two-minute conversation, I learned that Carl hadn't changed one bit, not in all the time he'd been gone —he was as irreverent and prejudiced as ever. He had been raised Lutheran, and I, Catholic. The arguments we used to get into back then—well, suffice it to say, they contained all the passion of our youth.

"Don't get yourself all worked up, Frank," he said, seeing the expression I couldn't hide. "I apologize for shooting my mouth off. Nothing personal."

"I just walked out of the church a minute ago—" I started to explain, in justification for my reaction.

"Hey, Frank, I said I was sorry. Let's forget it and go someplace where we can talk. What do you say?"

He made a feint at punching me in the stomach with his right hand but just tapped me on the shoulder with the other hand, instead—exactly the same games he used to play when we were kids. I jerked in surprise, but then I couldn't help smiling as the years rolled away. Good Lord, we shared a lot of history, Carl and I! Never have been able to stay upset with him for very long.

THE PARK WAS ACROSS THE STREET, so we headed over and sat on one of the empty benches, not in the shade of the oaks, but out in the warmth of the sun. It was early spring, but mornings could still be on the cool side. The irises were already popping out of the ground, but Carl didn't seem to notice.

"I'm moving back here, Frank," he said.

"You're kidding me? After all these years?"

"Yeah, I'm living in the Lutheran home on the other side of the river. Hung up my clothes this past weekend. God, I always said I'd die before they ever got me into a place like that, but things change. It's close to my boy's house, and I absolutely refused to move in with them, though they offered. You know that I lost Karen last year?"

Hearing her name aloud jolted me, making my arms tighten, even though I'd already formed several mental pictures of her as Carl and I talked. Karen had been his wife for many, many years. Before marrying Carl, Karen had been my girlfriend. Even after all these years, the memories still hurt. Now she was dead.

"Your son told me, Carl. Sorry I missed the funeral, but I was in the hospital myself that week. I sent you a sympathy card, but it came back to me a month later, marked address unknown."

"No surprise there," Carl said. "I just closed up the house and turned it over to an agent. Sold it, lock, stock and barrel. Stayed drunk for damn near six months. Scared my son, Jim, half to death … but I suppose he told you all that?" Carl asked, looking at me closely.

"No, he just said you were living in Philadelphia."

"For a while," he answered, seeming to relax a little, "till I got tired of it. Hell, Frank, I guess I just got tired of living, but I figure if I'm going to curl up and die, it might just as well be here in the valley."

"I'm glad you're back, Carl. Really glad."

"Thanks, Frank. It's good to be home, I guess. I've been away for a long, long time."

"You can say that again. So, what've you been doing all these years?"

"Hell, Frank, you know all that stuff from the Christmas cards. I've never been much of a writer, not like you, but we always tried to put in a note and a picture or two."

"Sure, I know *where* you've been, but not what you've been doing. That's what I want to know."

"Yeah, I see," he said. "Wish I could write a Christmas letter like you do, but I just never seemed to find the time. I like getting yours, though—"

"Oh, yeah?" I said.

"What's that supposed to mean?" he asked, looking at me defensively, until he remembered. "Oh, I get it." Then he started to laugh, and I joined in.

The one time Carl had come home for our class reunion, he'd made fun of my Christmas letters, parodying them at our table, and doing so at length. He implied that I was stuck here in a do-nothing town, while he was off having real-life adventures in the big city—that kind of thing. Everybody laughed but me.

"Jesus, I was a jerk back then," he said. "I'm sorry."

And just as profane, I thought to myself, but aloud I said, "Hey, that was a long time ago, Carl. Don't worry about it. Did you notice that I never stopped writing those letters?"

"You know what? I've still got every one of them."

"You're kidding?"

"Honest to God. I never knew it, but Karen kept the letters in a drawer, all in order."

"She would," I said, thinking back to how she'd been when we all went to school together. She was the perpetual class secretary, keeping everything neat and tidy. Everything in order. And now? Another of my friends dead and gone. I couldn't help wondering if she'd kept those letters out of some old feeling for me, but then I caught myself—here I was feeling sorry for myself over losing a friend, even if she was an old girlfriend, when Frank had lost his wife. "You must've been married close to fifty years," I said, reminiscing aloud.

"Would've been fifty in a couple of years. We celebrated forty-seven, through all the pain she was in from the cancer, and then she apologized for not being able to make it to fifty, the 'big one' as she called it. Can you believe her, apologizing to me for dying?"

"She was like that," I said simply, while my head spun with memories of Karen and thoughts of how she must have died, the pain of it all.

IT HAD TAKEN ALMOST FIFTY YEARS for us—me and Carl—to be able to talk about Karen. Maybe she had to die first, if that makes any sense, but I guess it does, somehow. You see, Carl took her away from me, long ago. Everyone in town assumed that Karen and I would get married one day because we'd gone together, on and off, all the way through high school and the summers between my early college years. It was a nice, friendly relationship. We never made love. Hard to believe something like that today, with sex so free and easy, plastered all over the TV, but it's the honest truth. Things were different back then, I guess.

Carl never came home during his college years, not even once. He'd gotten a sports scholarship to UCLA in California, while I struggled my way through our local college, Worten, working part-time the whole while to cover tuition. It took me six years to graduate. Carl never made All-American like he'd hoped, in fact, he spent his last year injured, but the whole valley was proud of him anyway, and everyone saved the clippings and talked about him in the barber shop. Carl just breezed back into town the summer after he'd finished up and swept Karen off her feet. She'd thought about going to college for a while, but things were different then for women. She'd actually been accepted to Worten but never started, going to work instead to help her folks out. World War II was over, but times could still be tough. Besides, there wasn't the same push in those days for women to graduate college, nothing like today with all the ERA and equality.

CARL AND I SAT THERE IN THE PARK, making small talk and losing ourselves in memories, until I just blurted out, "You know something, Carl? Karen and I—we—we never even—"

"I know that, Frank. She told me. I'm sorry, but I didn't believe it back then. My own jealousy came between us," he said, turning to look at me.

"You were jealous of *me*?" I asked, hardly able to believe it. How could that be possible when he was everything I'd ever wanted to be? Smooth, handsome, a football hero, and Karen's husband.

"For years and years, I almost hated you. Years and years. All of that after us being so close when we were kids," he said, shaking his head as if to clear out all that lost time.

After we'd each said what we needed to, we sat and talked for over an hour, most of it Carl telling me about his career in sales and how he'd closed some pretty fancy deals. Just when he'd been in line for a vice-presidency, the company had been bought out, and he'd been forced into retirement. Carl talked and talked, just as funny and witty as ever, until he finally started to wind down. All of the sudden he seemed to remember something he'd been saving up.

"You'll never guess who lives right down the street from me."

"Who's that?" I asked.

"Jonathan Green he calls himself now."

"Who?"

"Little Johnnie Greenbaum—you remember him?"

"Sure, I do," I said, as the memories flooded back, many of them pleasant, up until that final day when he'd left the valley. That day had been anything but pleasant. Of course I remembered Jonathan.

THE LAST TIME I SAW JONATHAN, we met in the playground, and he told me that he was moving away from the valley to live with his aunt and uncle.

"How come?" I asked him.

"My father lost his business—" he started explaining to me as several other kids drifted our way, Carl included. Jonathan didn't finish the sentence once he became aware of the other kids.

"Hey, Carl," I said. "Jonathan's leaving."

"Yeah, I know," Carl replied, the words coming out flat, but with a sneer hidden in there, someplace.

"Good riddance," one of the other guys said. To this day, I can't remember who it was because things started happening so fast afterwards that I recall it as a blur.

"Dirty kike," someone else hollered, someone standing in the back. I'm not sure who. "Stinking Jew," another of the boys said.

Suddenly, Jonathan had his fists clenched and acted like he was going to take on all five or six of them. I just stood there, not able to believe what was happening as the other kids started to circle Jonathan.

"What's going on, Carl?" I asked. If anyone knew, it had to be Carl, always my leader and my friend.

"Nothing, Frank. He's just going home. Isn't that right?" he asked Jonathan, looking straight at him.

The tension was almost more than I could bear. No one answered any of the questions I asked. The kids on our side of the yard formed a half-circle facing Jonathan, but they seemed to be waiting for Carl's lead, watching to see what he would do. Jonathan and Carl just stared at each other for a long, long moment. I looked at Jonathan and saw his hands slowly begin to unclench, not completely, but they relaxed a little.

"Jonathan, what—?" I started to ask, taking a half-step toward him, before he interrupted me.

"Go back to your goy friends, Frank. "You're all alike, every one of you."

Jonathan backed up a couple of steps, then turned and walked away, neither slowly nor quickly, just a steady walk away from us, out of the playground, and out of the valley.

WITH THAT PICTURE OF JONATHAN'S EXIT still fresh in my mind, I tried to continue the conversation with Carl. "What were we then? Fifth grade or so?" I asked him, haltingly.

"About that, near as I can recall," Carl answered me, with the strangest look on his face. I tried to read the look. What was it? Scorn? Anger? Yes, Carl had been there, too, in the playground, the day Jonathan left.

"You say it's Green now?" I asked. "I wonder why?"

"Lots of Jews changed their names after the war, trying to be more American, I guess."

"How long's he been here?" I asked.

"I don't know, but it must be a while, a few weeks anyway, because they seem pretty much settled into their house."

"You've been inside?"

"Sure, my son Jim pointed him out to me on the street. Knows him from City Hall. It seems he's a retired judge. I didn't recognize him right away, but I put two and two together—Jonathan Green, Jonathan Greenbaum, same person. Had to be. Well, Monday morning I was walking into town when I ran into our Mr. Green and his wife right there on the street, in front of their place. He introduced me to her and all, though I could tell he really didn't want to. Guess he didn't have much choice, though, because I forced the issue. She's the one that invited me in. You can bet that he never would have. She's lots younger than him, but good looking, if you like the type."

"What type is that?" I asked, trying to take in all he'd told me about Jonathan but only succeeding in focusing on the last word.

"Dark and mysterious. You know, he may be Jewish, but she is *really* Jewish."

"What do you mean?" I asked.

"The look of her and the way she dresses, plus they've got one of those candle things on the table, a menorah I think they're called, and a shawl with tassels. Prayer shawl, I guess. Hell, you know how they are—Jews, I mean."

I looked at Carl and saw that I'd been right—he really hadn't changed much in all these years. The profanity and the prejudice were still there. His foul mouth was something I'd never gotten used to. As handsome and popular as Carl had been, I could never understand why he needed to swear all the time. It was almost as if he deliberately swore to shock you. Similarly, he was just as prejudiced now as he'd been when we were kids. Jon and I had always been pretty good friends—that's the way he spelled it, Jon from Jonathan, but it had always been Johnny in school, never Jonny or Jonnie, probably because that would look like a girl's name, I suppose—anyhow, Carl never could seem to forget that Jonathan was Jewish, even when we were playing together.

"Strange that no one ever told me he was here," I said aloud.

"No one knows," Carl answered me back. "You and I are probably the only ones here who would remember him, or figure out it was him."

"Wonder why he's never come over to see me?" I mused aloud, but even as I asked the question, I knew the answer. It had to go back to that last day, and the guilt I still carried.

Sixty years ago, on that afternoon, I lost a friend, one of my best friends at the time, but instead of going after him and shaking hands, or hugging him, or telling him I'd miss him—instead of any of the *normal* things you'd expect—I just stood there with the kids who had said good riddance and called him a dirty kike. What a terrible thing to do, I thought—meaning that I'd done nothing, a sin of omission, when I should have done something, anything—but then I was jolted back to the present when I realized that Carl said something I'd missed.

"What did you say, Carl?"

"Just that he knows you're here. Mentioned seeing you in the store once or twice."

Jonathan saw me and never said a word? The thought struck me like a blow. I could feel my head jerk back. Why would he do that? After all these years, is he still that upset? The memory of what we'd said to him cut through me like a knife.

"Does he look the same?" I asked Carl, not willing to tell him what I was really thinking.

"The same?" he said, starting to laugh. "Hell, no, he doesn't look the same. He's sixty years older now. Looks just like you and me—a couple of doddering old fools."

"Speak for yourself," I said, automatically joking back at him, just like the old days. This time without much humor.

"Just kidding, St. Francis, just kidding. In fact, you'll recognize him right off the bat. He knew me, too, once I introduced myself." Again Carl had that silly smile on his face, almost like a smirk.

In that moment, I knew that I had to see Jonathan. At least, I had to try to set things right. It was another piece of unfinished business hanging over my head like the Sword of Damocles, suspended by a hair, or the Pendulum in Poe's Pit, swinging over my body. Time was running out.

THAT EVENING, AS I THOUGHT ABOUT the afternoon I'd spent with Carl, I got to looking through our old high school annuals. They had disappeared for years, into a box, stuck in the far corner of the garage, two different garages really, never being unpacked after our last move twenty-seven years ago. One day, inspired by some unknown and long forgotten project, I dug around in the garage looking for something else and came across those books, four years' worth of them. The Fidelians our class was called, the Faithful. I sat in the dusty garage for hours, even back then, looking, reliving, imagining, remembering, and that was years ago. This time, I knew right where to find them—on the shelf, in the hall, where they'd been gathering dust for another twenty years and more. You can only go poking around in the past every so often.

Gray, red, black and green. The covers had faded, getting sticky in spots. From what? Ant spray, maybe, or mildew. They were already arranged in order of years, but I started with the last one, our graduation annual. Inside the front cover were dozens of messages, hand-written things from the past. From the grave in many cases. Some still clear as if they'd been written yesterday, others faded so bad I could hardly make out the words. Different inks, I suppose, not all of them being the Sheaffer's permanent blue-black that I preferred back then.

The first message was from a girl who had a crush on me. As soon as I saw it there, in the upper-left-hand corner of the first page, I remembered how she ambushed me in the hall on the first day the books were handed out. Not only did she ask me if she could sign my book (the reverse of the usual protocol for such things), but then she took the best spot, the page and position usually reserved for best friends and true loves.

"I wish we'd had more time to know each other better," she wrote. "This year has been wonderful, sitting next to you in Geography. I hope we can see each other over the summer, maybe take in a movie or something?" There was some other stuff that I won't bore you with, something about how she'd always liked my eyes. You get the idea.

Brazen stuff for a girl to write in that era. Looking back on it now, the words were an open invitation. Like the call of a

Greek siren from prehistory, they reeked of sex, flesh and the devil. Who was she? I knew the name, of course, but there was no clear mental picture of her on file in my mind, other than her being a little overweight and having straggly brown hair. Annette Klueggen—a combination of French and German. I remember thinking about her two names when Mr. Vorderhausse talked about the traditional borders between those two countries. I whispered something to her then, something to the effect that she was both those places in one, France and Germany.

I suppose that was when she fell in love with me—when I talked to her. For the rest of the school year, I did everything I could to avoid her, Annette, and her best friend. Now, what was the friend's name? That's the worst part of getting old—trying to remember the names. All I can recall of the friend is the thick glasses she wore. She'd looked at me through those glasses with huge, magnified frog eyes, and asked if I liked her friend, Annette. Kids did such things then, indirect, second-hand approaches.

"My friend likes your friend. Does your friend like my friend? If so, would your friend like to go to the dance with my friend?"

How innocent and obtuse we were then. Why not just ask directly? For instance—"Do you like me?" Seems to me that would be a lot simpler.

Kids are probably still doing it, though, being indirect, I mean. They were back when I was teaching. No reason to think they've stopped, even if they do dress and act like—well, no sense getting me started on what the younger generation is up to, them and their MTV dance videos.

Anyhow, I'm getting way off track here. What I intended doing was looking up our old pictures—Carl's and Karen's, especially, because I already knew what I looked like. There they were, on the same page of the annual. Markdoffer and Mertz, just a column apart. He was your typical athlete—confident, smiling, brash. Karen was just as I always remembered her—pretty, sweet, a little shy, even demure, but eager to taste life, to experience things, full of hope. Dead and gone, now.

At the bottom of the page, under their senior pictures, I read the brief biographies. For Carl it was: All league two years in Football, Basketball and Baseball. Junior Class President. Student Council, freshman and sophomore years. Humph, I thought to myself. He was popular all right, but when the chips were down, he stopped running for student offices and just concentrated on the sports. Got out of politics just before everyone realized he wasn't any good at it. He was a salesman right from the start, but he didn't have much follow through. For Karen it was: Student Council, freshman, sophomore, junior and senior years. Class Secretary, freshman and sophomore years. Student Body Secretary, junior and senior years. Varsity cheerleading, freshman, sophomore, junior and senior years. Then a jillion clubs and social groups.

Karen had signed her name in the blank space right above her picture. I almost shivered to see her handwriting like that, especially now that she was gone, dead and buried. Every letter was carefully, perfectly formed. Smooth and flowing. Turning to the back of the book, I searched for where she had written her longer, senior message to me. I found it, ironically, on the same page that Carl had used. His was something about what a good guy I was and to have fun over the summer. Nothing personal, just the stuff one boy writes to another, even if they are good friends.

Her message was warm and sweet but careful, too. After all, we were just dating then, not engaged or even pinned. "Dear Frank," she wrote, "Well, here we are seniors, ready to graduate and go out into the world. We've been friends for a long time, now, and we always will be. I have so many memories—the senior prom and our picture together, your looking so handsome in your suit. All the hayrides and our lunches together on the lawn. Now it's on to college for you at

Worten. I'm so proud of you for sticking to your goals. You will make a wonderful teacher. Don't forget me while you're off to school. Love, Karen." She signed her name followed by a heart, neither too big nor too small. That was it. I read the message once more, then went back in the book to look at her picture, again. So young, hopeful and vibrant. Carl was young, too, but he was cocky and confident. I just sat there staring at the page for a long time.

Eventually, when I got tired of looking at their pictures and reminiscing, I turned back two pages to the H's and looked at the me of fifty years ago. Francis J. Hessel. Chess Club, Student Council, Future Teachers Club. Good Lord, what a nerd! It was those wire-rimmed glasses that made it all so bad. In those days, you had zero choice in frames. They were wire, no matter what. Make that two choices—you could have silver wire or gold wire. I reached up to adjust my current pair of glasses, thinking, Here I am, after fifty years, gone right back to the same wire-rimmed frames. Coming full circle, I guess. Just like life itself.

No sense trying to find a picture of Jonathan Greenbaum, or Green as it was now, I thought, *because he'd never gone to the high school here*. Nor would I find my wife's picture, either. Ruthie was exactly four years behind us in school, and now she's been gone these past ten years. Over the course of our marriage, we'd lost her class annuals, no telling where. In one of the moves, I suppose. I could dig out one of our old scrapbooks, if I really wanted to see a picture of her back then, but I just don't have the energy right now. Anyway, all I have to do is close my eyes, and I can see her face, as if she were still sitting right here with me.

THE NEXT DAY, CARL DROVE AROUND to my side of the river, and we had lunch together at the Italian restaurant. Sometimes Luigi's spices aren't exactly what my stomach needs, but it sure was good being with an old friend again, no matter what we did.

"What did you give up for Lent?" Carl asked me, out of the blue, the question jolting me.

"What makes you think I did?" I asked.

"Because I know you, that's why."

"You remember all that stuff? How we used to argue all the time?"

"Sure, I do," Carl answered. "You were a mackerel snapper and I had the truth directly from Martin Luther. It was my sacred duty to straighten you out."

Carl said this straight-faced, just the way he used to tease me all those many years ago. Lord, I can still remember some of our "talks" and how we almost got into fistfights over important theological differences. I told him that Martin Luther was just an alcoholic priest who'd got thrown out of the church, and he countered with saying that we Catholics were all going to hell for worshiping plaster saints.

"Well?" he asked again. "What did you give up for Lent?"

"What's there for a man my age to give up?" I asked him, trying to dodge the question. "There's not much left that would be a sacrifice."

"One year you gave up chewing gum."

"I remember. For six weeks, you offered me a stick of Juicy Fruit every time I saw you."

"Yeah, and a couple years later it was cigarettes."

"And you never even smoked because of sports, but you carried a pack of Lucky Strikes around all through Lent."

"Just trying to keep you honest."

"That's what you call it? Seemed more like you were playing the devil's role," I teased him back.

"Who, me?" he answered, looking absolutely shocked. "All that devils and angels shit was your thing. Us Lutherans knew better. Man is his own devil … or angel." Then he fell silent for a minute, lost in his thoughts, before saying, "Karen was one of the angels."

"That she was, Carl." For a while we were both quiet, until

I asked him, more to change the subject than anything else, "Do you ever think about the war?"

"What do you mean?"

"Oh, that angels and devils thing you said—it reminded me of Hitler, I guess. You know how people always thought him a devil."

"Sure, I think about the war sometimes. It just killed me that my mother wouldn't sign for me so I could get into the action. By the time you and I were eighteen, it was all over. Shit, I still wish I could've gone."

"What in the world for?"

"Damn it, Frank, it was a war. We should've been there."

"You really think you could've shot someone, another German even?"

"You bet I could," he answered, with fire in his eye. "Nazis or Japs—all the same to me." Carl turned to look at me directly, seeming to remember something. "Jesus, Frank, you don't still think of yourself as a German do you, after all these years?"

"I'm American, Carl, just like you."

"Maybe so, but you always had that German thing too. Does the valley still go nuts during Oktoberfest?"

"Yes, just like when we were kids."

"Great," he said, the word dripping with sarcasm. "I can hardly wait."

"You always made fun of the festival," I remembered aloud. "I never could understand why."

"It was a crock of shit, that's why. We're supposed to be Americans, so what's wrong with the Fourth of July?"

"You're sure getting grouchy in your old age."

"Wait till October if you want to see me get grouchy. Shit, I'll bet they still have the damned parade, don't they? With the tubas, and those stupid shorts and suspenders."

"Um huh, just like we used to."

"Thank God, I was always on a sports team, so I didn't have to be in that damned band."

Carl must've forgotten that, unlike him, I was always in the band, back then, right up front, playing my clarinet. I didn't remind him, even though I'd always been proud of the band and our parade. Maybe it was a kind of a nerdish thing, but I liked it, still do, though now I just watch.

"Don't be so negative, Carl," I said. "Just go and have fun. You'll love it."

"I'll bet, and you still haven't told me what you gave up for Lent," he reminded me.

"I'm going to give up having lunch with my friends," I said, reaching for another piece of Luigi's garlic bread.

Soon, we were both laughing again. "You haven't changed a bit in all these years," he said, "not one damned bit."

"Neither have you, Carl. Neither have you."

WHAT DID YOU GIVE UP FOR LENT? Carl had asked me. What a question! One that might just take a minute or two to explain. It has to do with something that's been on my mind for a long time now. A little over a year ago, I was feeling so tired that I finally went to see my doctor.

My appointment that afternoon was at four-thirty, making me the last patient John would see. John Gunther, MD, hard as that is to believe. He'd been a student of mine years ago, then gone on to college and medical school. The whole valley was proud of him, especially when he opted to come back here and set up a practice. He's a good man. I'd gone to see him when the troubles began.

"So, you're just tired?" he asked. "That's it, nothing more specific?"

"More than tired, John. Exhausted is more like it, and all the time, now."

He and I had long since resolved the formalities of the Mr. Hessel, due to a former teacher, and the Dr. Gunther, due to a present MD. We agreed that it should be just plain Frank and John.

"You're not a kid anymore, Frank," he offered up in his

most kidding and least authoritative manner after listening to my complaints.

"It's more than that, John. I've been tired before, but this is really different."

"Okay, you just had a physical last year, but let's take some blood tests now and see what we can find out."

LEUKEMIA IS WHAT THEY DISCOVERED. Sweet Jesus, if you ever have to go through a diagnosis like that, you'll understand how it hit me. Good as being dead, that's how. Like a hammer blow to the head. I'd been through cancer once with my wife, Ruthie, and I sure didn't want to go through it again.

Well, that's all been a year ago. I told everyone that I was going away on vacation, but instead I went to the city for two weeks of tests and treatment. The hospital got me stabilized and started me on a series of new drugs that my own doctor could administer. It wasn't until I got home from the hospital that I learned of Karen's death and that she was already buried. After a few weeks of local treatments, John told me that everything seemed to be working out well. I could already tell because I was feeling much better. Since the chemo had worked so quickly, I never even lost my hair. After a few more months passed, he told me with even more confidence that everything was good—super, in fact. The good news is that I'm now in remission. I take a few pills every month to keep it that way. The bad news is that I still have leukemia. It'll kill me eventually, I suppose, just not today. Thank God for that.

Just a few months ago, I was back to feeling as good as ever, but I was still having difficulty living with the knowledge of what was happening inside me. I took a few pills every month, but it was like my body had betrayed me. Physically, I was doing fine, but mentally I couldn't shake the idea of cancer. When I saw John Gunther for another periodic examination, he started poking around in my personal life.

"How're you feeling today, Frank?" the doctor asked me as

he walked into the consultation room. He moved to the sink and washed his hands, like he probably did every time he changed rooms.

"I'm good, John. Very good."

"I don't mean morally," he kidded me. "You can still kick up your heels, you know?"

"Thanks for the advice. How are the blood counts today?"

"They're strong, Frank, very strong. You may outlive us all. Plenty of energy?" he asked, making a feint at my kneecap with his rubber tomahawk gizmo.

"Not bad for an old geezer," I answered, "and one heck of a lot better than a year ago."

"Good," he said, making notations on my chart. "You still seeing Sarah Bruene?"

"Yes."

"She's a nice lady," he said, nodding, and then started to ask me something else, but held off. He just pursed his lips and looked back down at the chart in his lap. "I hate to see you moping around, Frank." He didn't say anything more, though I could tell he wanted to. "Well, continue with the medicine, and I'll see you in a month."

Good God, I think he was actually on the verge of asking about our relationship, mine and Sarah's! John and I shook hands, and he walked me to the front door and closed it after me. Thank God, he hadn't asked. That would have embarrassed me no end. Some things don't change. He might be a doctor now, but I can still remember him as a pimply-faced freshman with a crush on Lucy Schroeder. Some questions you ought to leave alone.

I'd just gotten some good news, about the continuing remission, but it was still a long and lonely walk home. Sometimes it's just too darned late to do anything about anything at all.

NOW YOU CAN UNDERSTAND THE MOOD I WAS IN the other morning and why I tried to pray in the church. A long time ago, T. S. Eliot wrote a poem called "Ash Wednesday." It is a devout but deeply depressing work that opens with the line, "Because I do not hope to turn again," and continues with one I've always remembered, "Why should the aged eagle stretch its wings?" I assigned the poem once in a literature class, but it was a disaster. My students were too young and inexperienced to understand it. They just thought it was depressing. Ash Wednesday, a time of sorrow, a time of grief. The opening section to the poem concludes with the familiar line from the Hail Mary: "Pray for us sinners now and at the hour of our death, / Pray for us now and at the hour of our death."

When you're looking your own death right in the eye, you do tend to get a little down. Take it from me, no pun intended.

FRIDAY NIGHT, SARAH BRUENE AND I went to the movies, like we've been doing for a good while now. We had a quiet dinner at Luigi's first. Sarah had the eggplant, and I had my usual seafood pasta. Catholics are no longer required to eat fish on Fridays, but once I settle into something, I usually stick with it. Sarah wore the powder-blue sweater that sets off her eyes so well and a black skirt. She has light grey, almost white hair that looks perfect with her skin. I found myself staring at her throughout the meal, as if I couldn't get enough of looking at her.

You see, in the back of my mind, I thought this was going to be the day I would break up with her, letting Sarah go her own way, maybe to find someone she could settle down with. It wasn't fair for me to keep on tying up her time now that I was a lost cause. Somehow, I had rationalized this decision as being a Lenten sacrifice on my part. I would miss Sarah, but she would be better off without me. And the answer to the question you're thinking is, No, I haven't ever told her about the cancer. After my experiences with Ruthie, the very word *cancer* just puts me into a freeze.

My half-baked plan of breaking up with Sarah didn't work

out because Carl's return and his telling me about Jonathan had distracted me so much that I never got around to talking seriously with Sarah. Of course, I'd already told her over the phone about running into Carl and what he'd said about seeing Jonathan. She remembered Carl all right, even though she's a lot younger than we are. I know, I know. Call me a cradle robber if you want. Yes, I've been dating a younger woman. I'm seventy and she's sixty-two. It's no surprise that she remembers Carl. Everyone in the valley knew him, because of his being a big-time athlete. She didn't remember Jonathan, but that didn't surprise me any because he left when we were still pretty young. Heck, Sarah would only have been four or five years old when Jonathan still lived here.

"Why are you so quiet tonight, Frank?" Sarah asked as we walked to the theater.

Why were so many people asking me such tough questions lately? I wasn't ready to tell her what had really been on my mind, so I told a little white lie.

"Oh, just thinking about Carl and Jonathan, I guess. It's been so many years since we were kids together that I'm getting all nostalgic."

"Old friends are the best kind," she said, sliding her hand into the crook of my elbow.

"True enough, Sarah," I said, patting her hand with my free one. "True enough." *What will I do without this woman?* I asked myself. The rest of my life looked bleak enough, as is, but without Sarah in it, my life looked like a gravel road, with me being destined to walk it barefooted.

We didn't say much else on the rest of our stroll, but I was thinking what you are probably wondering right now—*Why haven't we ever gotten married?* Not now, of course, because of my cancer, but sometime over the past ten years or so? Well, there are lots of reasons, I suppose, but I'm just not up to going into them right now. There's too much else happening for me to write about that.

Here we are, right on the verge of a new millennium with all the Y-2k scare about computers shutting down and the lights all turning off. The alarmists are calling it the End of the World. Father Einsphar had spoken on it in his sermon that very morning. I can remember nodding as if I understood it completely, as if I were an expert on computers and world disasters. Getting sick can do that to a man. Blame me for being moody, but all week long I've been thinking about the good friends I've lost over the years, including and especially, the major women in my life—Carl's wife, Karen, and my own wife, Ruthie. Right now, I just can't handle anything more, like thinking about losing Sarah, even if it would be for the best. And now, all of the sudden, two old friends move back to the valley. What's that all about? Enough's enough, and this has already been a pretty full week.

Chapter One:
First Sunday in Lent

THE INVOCAVIT

THE LATIN TERMINOLOGY is pretty much gone from use, now, along with all the beautiful Latin phrases that I liked so much in the liturgy, the words adding a mystery to the ceremony. For example, *Kyrie eleison*—doesn't that have a ring to it? "Lord have mercy" is what the words mean. Some rock and roll band used them as a refrain a few years back, so I'm not the only one who remembers.

As usual, I went to the early mass at St. Ignatius, sitting in my regular pew. The handout listed this Sunday as *The Invocavit*. As it turns out, every Sunday in Lent has a Latin name. I know because I found all of them listed in the back of my Bible when I got home. This first Sunday has a simple enough name that I could figure it out. "To invoke" is to call up or to summon, so I took the words as a sign and did just that— I got on the phone and called my old friend, Jonathan Green. Getting the number was easy, nothing more than a simple check with the operator for their new listing, but dialing the number was a different story because whenever I thought of calling, I got nervous remembering back to the last time Jonathan and I had spoken. To tell the truth, I was ashamed of myself. Kike, nigger, spic, and gook are such hateful words. I never tolerated language like that in my classroom, but as a child, I had tolerated such a word's being spoken to one of my best friends. For us Catholics, sins of omission can be just as haunting as those of commission, maybe even more.

Idly, I sat by the phone, trying to drum up the courage to pick it up and dial the number. Out of the blue, I remembered a parent's argument from years ago, back when I was just starting my teaching career at the high school. I had sent the man's son to detention for using just such language.

"So what if he used the word *nigger*? That's what they are," the man had argued.

"It's a hateful word, Mr. Schaucher."

"Were you in the war, Mr. Hessel?" he asked me.

"No, I was too young."

"If you hadda been, you wouldn't be so delicate. A gook's a gook, and a nigger's a nigger."

"What in the world does the war have to do with —" I started to ask, but he'd already stomped off.

He hadn't been the only example over the years, just the most memorable. Actually, that kind of bigotry isn't much of a problem in the valley simply because we're all so uniform. The vast majority of our people are German, on both sides of the family. The occasional Pole shows up, and we do have the token Italians running Luigi's, but they're Tyrolean, from way up north, making them closer to Germans than to Southern Italians.

I wonder why the terms, Polack and Wop, are not as hateful as nigger, kike and gook? Maybe they are if you're the one being called by one of those names, but no, I doubt that's true. The first group is a form of national slander while the other goes to whole racial types. There does seem to be a difference, even if slight. Heck, I had been called a blockhead in college, but I didn't even know what it meant or that it had to do with being German. What if someone had called me a Nazi, though? What then?

Without further thought, I found the phone in my one hand as the other reached toward the keypad. I still miss the old dial phones, if you want to know the truth, but you can't do a thing with them anymore because of the new computer technologies, unless you like sitting forever on hold, that is. After one last glance at the slip of paper, I punched in the number and waited for the ring. Once, twice.

"Hello, the Greens' residence," said a woman's voice in a slight accent which I detected but couldn't identify. I'd expected Jonathan to answer, so she caught me by surprise.

"Um, yes. Could I speak with Jonathan Green, please?"

"Could I say who's calling?"

"Frank Hessel."

"Just a minute, please." Again the slight accent which I couldn't place.

Voices in the background, then footsteps.

"Is that you, Frank?"

"Hello, Jonathan," I answered with a surge of pleasure. His voice *was* the same, just as Carl had warned me, exactly the same as from years before, which I told him. "Good grief, it's been sixty years, and I think I could still recognize your voice. It's almost spooky."

"You sound quite a bit different, but I can still recognize you in there, someplace."

Of course, I would sound different. Out of our whole class, I'd been just about the last boy whose voice changed. In fact, I was still singing soprano in the choir when Jonathan left the valley. In contrast, Jonathan's voice had been the first to change. He'd already been shaving by then, too.

"So, how have you been?" I asked.

He started to laugh but cut it short. "What a question! Up and down. Some years good, some not so good."

"I guess it was a little silly. We've got a lot of catching up to do."

"Yes, we do," he said. Coldly, or was it my imagination?

"Shall we get together for a visit?"

"That would be fine, Frank."

"Do you remember Bucher Lane?" I asked, facing the usual problem of directing people to my house on a dead end street that had no sign. One of these days, the city will put one up, but I've been saying that for who knows how long?

"Why don't you come here, Frank? I'm in the old neighborhood, just a block behind your folks' house. The address is 543 Maple."

"Sure, that would be great."

"Tomorrow morning?"

"Yes, I'm free."

"How about ten o'clock?"

"Fine, see you then."

THAT EVENING I SAT AROUND THINKING about the valley and our lives here. October is just about the only time of the year that we have any real excitement, and that one month's worth is thanks to Oktoberfest. Since the current month is February, you can understand why I was surprised to have all of these unusual events happening—the meeting up with Carl, and learning that Jonathan was here, too. Most of the time, our valley is pretty quiet. Let me describe it to you. Black's Woods runs through our side of Happy Valley, paralleling the river. The woods continues on to the other side of the water, but the name changes over there to Cotter's Woods. Why? I haven't a clue, and I'm seventy years old—every one of them spent in the valley, except for my time at college—so if I don't know, who does? My father was born here, too, and spent every one of his eighty years in the valley. His father immigrated from the Old Country, but once arrived, he never left, either. We have roots here that go deeper than the oaks. This valley is our home, our land, the land of our fathers.

Now don't get me wrong. I am proud to be an American, but when we celebrate Oktoberfest, I do remember my German heritage. You can bet on that. Sauerbraten, hot potato salad, chocolate torte, and good bock beer—all of my favorites. For that one month of the year, people flock in here from both ends of the valley, but don't get the idea that we have a major highway running through the valley connecting us to the world, not by a long shot. We are so far off the beaten path that the roads through the valley sometimes look just like paths, one two-lane main road on each side of the river.

We could be near Appleton, Wisconsin, or anywhere in the Midwest, even all the way to Washington State, anywhere that Germans chose when they arrived in flight from the potato famines of the 1800s in the old country, take your pick. To the east of us is Boston, where the Founding Fathers tossed the tea into the drink. To the south of us is Texas, where Americans died defending the Alamo, to the west of us is Hawaii, and to the north is Canada. We could be a farming valley almost anywhere Germans settled. *Why am I being so evasive?* you ask. Well, we have enough changes going on in the valley, without having tourist buses coming through, night and day. Now, you *can* get to a major city by driving through the valley, but you sure wouldn't want to, unless you have a couple extra days to kill. The roads are just that bad—rough and winding. At one time, we had a railroad through here, actually the main line was in the next valley over, so we just had a spur line, but not any longer. Most of the tracks have been ripped up now, but you can still see traces of them in spots down by the river. For a while, maybe sixty or more years ago, it looked like we might get put on the map and develop into a real city, but it never happened. Most of us are just as glad. We like it here pretty much the way it is—quiet and peaceful.

We used to have a bridge across the river, right in the middle of the valley, but it got washed out in a flood years ago, for the second or third time in a generation, so now people just drive to one or the other ends of the valley to get to the other side. It isn't even that big a deal, the whole valley being no more than twenty miles long. The most traffic we get from one side to the other is on Sunday mornings when all the Catholics on the other side of the river drive over to our side, and all the Lutherans that live over here drive to the other side. Those are the only two churches in the valley—St. Ignatius and Our Redeemer. You'd think that by now all the Catholics would've moved to this side of the valley and the Lutherans to the other, but it just doesn't seem to work out that way. At my age, I'm just happy that my church, St. Ignatius, is right here, just down the street. It makes my life a whole lot easier.

The bridges at either end of the valley are single car varieties, where you have to wait for your turn, so on a Sunday morning it's one Catholic coming this way and one Lutheran going the other, the two lines taking turns every other car. It's the closest thing we ever come to a traffic jam, but mostly it's tolerated with good humor. The only problem is with Jeb Schmidt who is perpetually late and every third or fourth Sunday tries to sneak ahead of the traffic coming to our side. Every now and then someone will give him the finger for jumping his turn, and once it led to a fist fight, but that was back quite a few years ago. Now Jeb is just tolerated. Heck, we can tolerate pretty much anything in Happy Valley.

Like I said before, the only real excitement we get here is during October, when the city folk flock in to buy up the ladies' crafts and drink the beer, which is made in the local brewery over there on the Lutheran side. They might have the beer, but we have the only decent restaurant in town, the Italian place I mentioned before, Luigi's. Been here for years. Go figure that one out if you can—Italian food in a German valley. I've been eating there for seventy years, and I haven't solved it yet.

You notice that I called it *town*, singular, as in "one town," even though we're split down the middle by the river. Our side is West Himmelberg, and the Lutherans live over there in East Himmelberg, most of them anyhow. Oh, what the heck, we're all the same people, and it used to be one city, one town anyway, when the main bridge was still up and working. Now someone from the West side of town can stand and talk to an Easterner right across the river because it's only ten feet at the widest, except during flood season, but if they wanted to shake hands, somebody would have to drive the twenty miles around or take the ferry. I told you this place isn't for everyone. Even I can see how comical the whole situation is.

Interspersed with all the nostalgia was the question to which I had no ready answer. Why had Jonathan returned to the valley? *Well*, I thought, as I started to get ready for bed, *I'll find out tomorrow, I suppose.*

THE NEXT MORNING I WOKE UP QUICKLY, already looking forward to seeing Jonathan again, yet dreading it, too. I got to the river early, hoping to catch Ernie Warden on this side, but no such luck. Ernie runs our local ferry service, if you could call one boat a service. His dory was still over there, rocking up against the small pier, empty of course, which meant he could be most anywhere—having coffee, running errands, or just fooling around.

Ernie is no kind of businessman. Now I don't mean that he doesn't take his duties seriously. He does do that, maybe even a little too seriously, or a lot too seriously, depending on whom you ask. He is the Charon for our River Styx. For a buck, Ernie will pole you over to the other side. Now that is a serious duty, a matter of life and death, and eternity, which is just about how Ernie approaches it—deathly serious. He and he alone is the final judge. You almost have to prove your business before he'll haul you over. There isn't any choice for it but to go along with his rules.

When Ernie finally saw me waiting, he waved but then disappeared into his shed for another five minutes. Now, he could've come over here, got me and been back on the other side in under two minutes, but he must've had something important to tend to, like a cup of coffee, or a donut. You have to understand that things move to a different drummer here in the valley, nothing like the pace of a big city, and yet people are all the time trying for "progress," as they see it. The latest idea is to put the bridge back up so East and West Himmelberg will be just a thirty second stroll apart, instead of a twenty minute drive by car, or who knows how long of a boat trip over the ten foot river. Seems to me it would be a lot simpler just to get Ernie into gear instead of thinking about the expense of putting up another bridge that could get wiped out in the next spring flood.

As you probably gathered, I don't drive any longer. Gave up the car the last time I ran the thing into the ditch. Just about two years ago now. There was no getting around it any longer—my vision was getting worse and worse. My eyes are still fine for reading, thank God, but I have lots of problems making out anything past twenty feet away. If I couldn't see a ditch coming up, how was I to see a kid on a bike? Sold the old Ford to Pete Wagner for two hundred dollars. Good riddance. But without a car, there I sat, still waiting for Ernie. It gave me a chance to think back on that last time I had seen Jonathan, almost sixty years ago. This time I recalled more of the details.

"I'm leaving, Frank," he told me.
"You're leaving the valley?"
"Yes, to live with my aunt and uncle in Trenton."
"What happened to your dad?"
"Like you don't know."
"What do you mean?"
"He lost the business, after what this valley did to him."
"What are you talking about?" I asked.
"Don't play innocent with me —" he said.

That was the last thing I could remember before the other kids drifted over and the fight almost broke out. What was it that Jonathan thought I knew? I didn't know back then, and I just barely know now, as I sat there waiting for Ernie.

After that day in the school yard, I never saw Jonathan again, never even heard of him, in fact, until Carl told me he was back. But after Jonathan left the valley, I did learn some of what he was talking about that day. Apparently, Jonathan's father had abandoned the family after he lost his business. He was a silversmith who had a shop in the central area of East Himmelberg. Back then, nobody would tell me the whole story because I was just a kid of ten or eleven years, and this was adult business. Carl just shrugged his shoulders as if he didn't know a thing.

None of my other friends knew much either, just some vague rumors about Greenbaum's being a lousy businessman and going broke. The kids repeated what they overheard the parents saying. "Damn shame that he just up and left the family that way, but everyone knows how Jews are," someone told me. "All they have to do for a divorce is say the words three times—I divorce you, I divorce you, I divorce you—and off they go to the hills with another wife. Most likely that's what happened to the Greenbaums," someone else said. "The father was a funny duck anyway, always wearing that silly little cap on the back of his head, a yamook or some such thing (that's what one of my friends called the yarmulke). Feel sorry for the kids, but that's the way it goes with those Hebrews." That kind of talk. Kids can be cruel, but so can their parents.

ERNIE FINALLY MADE HIS LONG-AWAITED reappearance and pushed off from the other shore, breaking my reverie. He had a cable rope strung between two trees, one on each side of the river, and then through an eyebolt in one gunwale, so his hands were free to pole the boat across. I decided to time him just for the heck of it. It took all of thirty-six seconds. I tried to make sure that Ernie saw me looking at my watch, but he pretended not to notice.

"How are you doing, Frank?" he asked, soon as the boat grounded on my side of the shore.

"Pretty good, Ernie. Business all right?" I asked him back, trying for a little dig, but he wouldn't bite.

"Not bad, Frank. Could be better, but things will be picking up a might now that spring's almost here."

"Suppose so, Ernie," I said, getting into the boat and sitting down.

So far, he hadn't made a move toward pushing off. The man did have his traditions. I decided to wait him out, just to see how long he could stretch the thirty-six second trip. Mum's the word, far as I was concerned. For a long time, neither of us said anything. I wasn't about to say the first word, so when Ernie broke the silence, I felt like I had won a minor battle.

"Going somewhere, Frank?"

"To the other side, Ernie."

Well, you might've thought he could get a message out of that, but not good old Ernie. He just nodded, real thoughtful like, and reset his old hat. It was one of those Greek fisherman caps with gold braid set all over the bill. God only knows where Ernie had found it.

"Got some business, do you?" he asked, eventually, like it was any of his concern.

"Just a visit."

He nodded again and readjusted the cap, like he was trying to make sure I'd seen all that gold braid, the symbol of his authority, as if I hadn't seen that stupid cap a million times already.

"A visit, you say?"

"That's right."

At that moment, I made up my mind that there was no way in hell I was going to tell him where I was going or who I was going to see. If he could be stubborn, I could be twice as stubborn. If you know any Germans, you already know what I'm talking about.

"Can't remember the last time I took you across just for a visit."

"Is that so?"

"Yep, it might've been when Ron Burbank had that heart attack. How long ago has that been, do you suppose?"

"No idea, Ernie. Are you going to start the boat up?"

"Nothing to start up, Frank. There isn't a motor, but I have been thinking about adding one. Not getting any younger, you know."

"None of us are, Ernie, especially not sitting here like this."

"I believe it was in November," he went on, as if he hadn't heard a word I'd said. He still made no move at all toward getting me to the other side.

"What was in November?" I asked.

"Ron's heart attack," he said, glancing at me like I was retarded for not being able to follow the conversation. "You know, the last time I brought you over for a social call. I've taken you across plenty of times for shopping or business, but not much for social reasons.

"Uh huh."

"Just going over for a visit, are you?" he said, going back to staring off into space.

"Is that okay with you?" I asked.

"Heck, Frank. You don't need my permission for something like that."

"I was starting to wonder."

Still he made not the slightest move whatsoever toward getting me to the other side. I was darn near starting to fume, but all Ernie did was continue to stare down the river while occasionally adjusting that hat, his badge of authority.

"Yep," he started up again with a quick nod of his head, "I thought we were going to lose old Ron that time —"

"Ernie, I'm going over to see Jonathan Green," I said, finally giving up, acknowledging that I had been beaten by a better man.

"Well, why didn't you say so in the first place?" he asked, suddenly getting into action as he pushed the boat away from the bank and started to pole. "Changed his name, you know. Dropped the ending, I mean."

Thirty-six seconds later, I was standing on the other side of the river in East Himmelberg.

"Thanks, Ernie."

"You're welcome, Frank. That'll be a dollar."

Old Ernie had won the war. There was no way to deny it.

EVEN THOUGH I HAD JONATHAN'S address memorized, I still pulled the slip of paper from my pocket to check it one more time. I had allowed myself plenty of time. No sense being in a big hurry, not after waiting sixty years for the reunion. On top of being nervous about facing Jonathan, I was still in a stew over Ernie. What business was it of his where I was going or why? And how was it that he knew Jonathan had changed his name? So, instead of going right up Maple, I elected to walk around the block and come at Jonathan's place from the backside. After all, this was the neighborhood I had grown up in. Walnut was the street right next to Maple, and my folks' house is still there, a little more weathered, but still standing solid. I used to know who lived there, but not any longer. After giving up my car, I kind of lost track of what was happening on this side of the river. I heard the old place had been sold, but I did not know the new people.

I walked by the folks' house real slow like, not wanting to stare but eager to see the place again. Same old two-story Victorian with a porch in the center and big, bay windows on either side. The house was painted white again, just like my parents used to keep it. I was glad to spot a tricycle in the driveway and some toys on the porch. It would've made my folks happy to know there were young ones in the house again. It'd been a long time. Just as I was passing by, a young woman came out onto the porch and shook out a dust mop.

"Hello," she said when she saw me watching her. "Nice day, isn't it?"

"Yes, it is."

I couldn't help noticing how attractive she was, just plain healthy looking. Big-boned, with pink cheeks and some real meat on her. A country girl by the looks of her. Wearing a red peasant's scarf over her hair.

"Are you looking for anyone in particular?" she asked. "We haven't lived here too long, but I do know most of the neighbors."

"Thanks, but I'm actually going around the block to my friend's house. I came this way just to see the old place again. My parents used to live here."

"You must be Mr. Hessel, then?"

"That's right. Frank Hessel."

"You taught my cousin, Johanna Karnes, in the high school. The neighbors told me that you lived across the river. Would you like to come in and see the place, again? It's a mess because of the kids, but you might get a kick out of it."

"Could I have a rain-check? I need to meet my friend, but I would like to see the place, sometime."

"Sure, whenever you like. Nice meeting you Mr. Hessel," she said, nodding. "I'm Sally Rudolph."

"My pleasure, Mrs. Rudolph."

She moved back inside, and I headed up the block to keep my appointment. Except for Ernie, this was turning out to be a pretty good trip. In fact, the more distance I put between myself and the river, the less upset I was with Ernie. Heck, he was just doing his job as he saw it. Ernie Warden, the self-appointed guardian of the river. Charon at the River Styx. Our border guard.

THE CLOSER I GOT TO JONATHAN'S HOUSE, the more familiar it looked. The nicest house on the block. Then I remembered—it was the old Peterson place. Dr. Peterson was our dentist, and his son Alan was a grade behind us in school, until he skipped one and joined us. Talk about *deja vu* all over again—it's an old joke, I know, but I still like it. Kind of like saying hamburger meat or tuna fish. Why say the same thing twice? *Deja vu* and "all over again"—get it?

Those are the kind of jokes I used to tell my classes. Some liked them, some didn't. Anyhow, my classmate, Alan Peterson, had been a scientist even back then. He had his own darkroom, telescope, microscope, and a chemistry set you could build bombs with. Alan got a scholarship to MIT and never looked back. Like so many kids who grew up in the valley, he saw his chance to get out and took it, without so much as a backward glance. My God, I hadn't thought of Alan in years.

Walking up the steps to the house, I felt like I was moving back in time. How long? Twenty years, at least, since I'd been to this house. Same old wrought iron gate into an open air entry, in front of the solid, dark, and heavy front door. It was good being back in the old neighborhood. Maybe even good for the soul, and it all had something to do with Lent and one of my Lenten resolutions, which I've already told you something about. No sense going into that stuff with Sarah again, for fear of jinxing the resolution. Taking a deep breath, I reached out my hand and pushed the bell. Ding dong, it was time to pay the piper. The door opened, and there he stood. Carl had warned me that I would recognize him, but this was ridiculous. Jonathan was exactly the same guy, except for his gray hair.

"Hello, Frank."

"Hi, Jonathan. It's good to see you."

"Come in," he said, opening the door all the way.

We shook hands briefly, like two kids who'd been forced to do it by their parents, all the while looking each other up and down. *Into the lion's den*, I thought.

"Did you know this was the Peterson place?" I asked, making small talk as I looked around.

"Sure, Alan and I were in the grade school Science Club together."

"Yes, that's right. I guess I'd forgotten."

"Science never was your strong suit, Frank," he said with a wry smile.

"You said a mouthful there. Getting out of Mr. Graef's

physics class was my crowning achievement in high school—but you were gone by then, weren't you?"

"Long gone and forgotten."

That's great, Frank—I told myself—*just put your foot in your mouth again. Why try to change at this late date?*

"Where did you go to high school?" I asked.

"Trenton."

"How about college?"

"University of Chicago, then Harvard Law," he said without any apparent pride or interest, though it sure impressed the heck out of me. Harvard!

"Pretty nice," I said. "I just managed to sneak through Worten College. Graduated by the skin of my teeth."

"Oh, I doubt that, Frank. You weren't much in math or science, but you were always at the top of the class in English and humanities."

"True enough, Jonathan. I majored in English at college."

"I still remember a book report you did in fourth or fifth grade. Something about the American buffalo? It wasn't very factual, but it was romantic as all get out," he said, smiling.

"*The American Bison: Friend of the Indian*," I said, laughing out loud while I held up my hands as if to frame the title in the air. "Good grief, I haven't thought of that in centuries."

Jonathan was laughing too. The ice was slowly breaking. The years were melting away. He pointed to a couch in the living room, and I sat down, glad to be off my feet.

"So, what have you been doing all these years, Frank? Did you ever leave the valley?"

"No, I never did. After graduating from Worten, I started teaching at the high school. Did that for forty years. Probably still be doing it, if they'd let me."

"I was a teacher, too."

"No kidding?"

"Law professor. I finally retired last year."

"I heard you were a judge," I said, surprised.

"I was, for two terms," he said. "I practiced law and taught for a while before getting appointed to the bench. But I continued doing a seminar every year."

I whistled softly, duly impressed. Jonathan didn't seem to be impressed with himself at all, but he had always been self-contained like that.

"Why did you come back here?" I asked, jumping right into it again, feet first.

"I came for revenge," he said, with a snort and a jerk of his head.

"Revenge?" I asked, feeling my heart drop into my lap.

"An eye for an eye —"

"Because of what we said?"

"What?" he asked, looking confused for a minute, until he seemed to figure out what I'd meant. "You mean in the yard at school? No, Frank, not because of what you said, though that was all a part of it, in a way."

"I wondered because Carl said you'd seen me in the store, once or twice, but you never said hello or anything —"

He just sat still for a minute, thinking it through, before speaking. "I guess that *was* it, Frank, what all of you said to me that day, though avoiding you wasn't even a conscious decision on my part. I saw you and just turned the other way without really thinking about it." He sighed and shook his head, never taking his eyes from mine.

"I've never forgiven myself," I confessed.

"For what?" he asked, tilting his head as he looked at me. "You never actually said anything that day, did you?"

"No, but I should have stopped it somehow. Those were hateful things they said. I'm sorry."

"They were hateful times, Frank. But thanks for the apology, anyway. If I remember correctly, I wasn't any too kind to you, either. I lumped you in with everyone else. I'm sorry. You deserved better."

The words of forgiveness sounded good—it's what I'd come for, after all—but there was no emotion behind them. Jonathan said the words as a matter of form, as if they did not matter any longer and he couldn't have cared less. Cold and sterile. I felt a shiver run up my arms and across my shoulders; it was that cold.

"You're married, I understand," I said, in a clumsy attempt to change the subject.

"Yes, Miriam left this morning for New York, to visit our son and the grandkids."

"You didn't stay in town just because I was coming over, did you?" I asked, as self-focused as ever.

"Oh, no," he answered, smiling. "Believe it or not, I have some legal work to take care of, and here I thought that I'd retired."

I finally looked around the room, closely, and saw the things that Carl had warned me to expect. On a table in front of the window was a seven-candle menorah, resting next to a colorful prayer shawl.

"Your wife's Jewish?" I asked without thinking. Good grief, what kind of surprise was that? Jonathan was Jewish, too.

"Yes, sabra."

"What?"

"Palestinian—she's from Palestine. We met when I taught at the university in Tel Aviv."

"You're kidding."

"About what?"

"Everything, I guess. Your teaching in Israel, traveling the world. It's all so overwhelming to someone like me who's never made it out of the valley."

"No big deal, really. It's all the same, no matter where you go."

Again he spoke without inflection or any emotion behind his words. Like words from the tomb.

"What did you mean by *revenge*?" I asked.

39

For a long time, we just sat there looking at each other, until he was ready to answer. I know now that he was weighing the serious, adult things I asked about against the strength of a childhood friendship that existed some sixty years in the past. *Could he or should he trust me?* Those were the questions he must have asked himself.

"We *were* pretty good friends, weren't we?" he began. Having resolved that, he almost but not quite smiled before beginning with the story.

TWO HOURS LATER, I WALKED BACK to the river, trying to put it all together. Jonathan had told me a lot, both with words and with the way he delivered those words. He told me things I had forgotten and things I'd never heard before that afternoon. Things that threatened my whole view of the valley.

"Nice visit?" Ernie asked me on the trip back.

"I don't know, Ernie. I don't have it all figured out yet."

"Yep. He's a moody one all right, but people tell me Jews are like that."

When in the world, I wondered, *could Ernie Warden have met Jonathan?* Though I waited for Ernie to continue, he didn't say another word, not until I tried to pay him for the trip.

"No charge this trip, Frank."

His simple act of generosity confused me as much as anything I had heard from Jonathan. On the walk back to my house, I knew that I would have to speak with Carl about it all. Maybe he could help me put things in place.

THE NEXT DAY I PHONED CARL and invited him to lunch. We met at Luigi's. I was determined to ask him about the things Jonathan had suggested about his father's treatment here.

"Carl," I said, right off the bat, "do you remember when Jonathan left the valley?"

"Sure, what about it?"

"Just that he was telling me some stuff I didn't remember—about how his dad had been forced out of business?"

"Yeah, so what?"

"Well, is it true?" I asked.

"More or less."

We just sat there, me waiting for him to continue, and him concentrating on the salad.

"Are you going to tell me about it?" I asked him, finally.

"Why do you want to go dredging up all that old history?"

"Just do, I guess. So, tell me."

"Do you remember when they were talking about putting the rail line through the valley?" he asked.

"I remember it was going to be a big deal, give us a switching yard and a station, all that. My dad was against it, even though it was the Depression and it could mean new jobs."

"Well, my father was all for it, and it was really going to be something. Make us a major stop for the commuter trains."

"What were they going to do about the river?" I asked him, suddenly struck by the physical difficulties.

"Big bridge, I suppose. Guess it would've been right in the middle of the valley."

"Kind of a dumb idea, wasn't it?" I asked. "I mean look at where the railroad actually does run now. Makes a lot more sense to have it over there than running through our valley."

"Nobody was thinking that way back then. Red Brubaker had a cousin on the state planning commission. Supposedly, the route was in the bag, and Himmelberg was going to be a real city. Some big hotel was coming in here. The whole valley was going to be another Catskills. You know—resorts, tourists, and all the like."

"Who was going to put up a hotel in the middle of the Depression?" I asked, calculating that the time period had to be in the middle to late 1930s.

"How am I supposed to know that?" Carl demanded.

"What happened?" I asked.

"The other route got picked."

"No, I mean what happened here in the valley, with Jonathan's father and all that stuff?"

"There was a big scramble for land along the right-of-way. He just got bought out."

"That's not the way Jonathan remembers it. He says that his dad got cheated."

"Bullshit. They made him a dozen different offers on his business, but he wouldn't sell. The whole place wasn't worth a tinker's damn—hell, you remember where he had that shop. Useless, rundown area, but oh, no, he wouldn't sell, so the City Council had to condemn it."

"How do you know all this?" I asked him. "I never heard a word about it."

"My father was on the council. I heard them talking about it in our living room."

"Why didn't you tell me?" I asked.

"It wasn't any of your business," he said, shrugging and looking away.

"You didn't tell me because you knew it was wrong. That's it, isn't it, Carl?"

"No, Frank," he answered, glaring back at me. "It was because you were just like your father, a couple of liberal do-gooders, standing in the way of progress. Hell, I'll bet you still vote Democrat, don't you?"

"Yes, I do, Carl, and I'm proud of it. My father thought FDR was the best president this country ever had. I think so, too."

"See what I mean?" Carl said with a smirk. "Your dad was a Jew-lover, too. That's why the council kept him in the dark until it was too late for him to screw it up."

"Damn it, Carl. You were supposed to be my friend."

"I am your friend, you jackass. All that crap was sixty years ago. Forget it! You got yourself all worked up over something that's dead and buried, just like FDR himself."

"It isn't dead for Jonathan."

"That's his problem."

"Do you know what finally happened to his father, Carl?"

"They said he abandoned the family, just moved off to Philadelphia."

"He went there to work, while the kids finished up the school year," I told him.

"They left the valley, that's all I know."

"That store of his was all he had. He'd saved up for twenty years to buy the place. I'll bet you don't even remember what he was?"

"Jeweler, I think."

"A silversmith, an artisan. Jonathan still has some of his pieces. They're beautiful."

"Yeah, well, it had to be something to do with gold or silver. All those Jews are like that—they corner the market and charge you an arm and a leg."

"Carl, how did you ever get so prejudiced?"

"What the hell are you talking about? I'm not prejudiced. I just know what's right and what's wrong, that all."

"What's wrong is what this valley did to the man. He got about a quarter of what the business was worth. It ruined him, and it ruined his health, too. He got sick and died a year after they left."

"I didn't know that."

"Remember how he always looked so frail? He'd had TB as a kid. Once he lost the business, he lost heart and just faded away."

"Well, I'm sorry to hear that, Frank, but what the hell's it got to do with me? And stop staring at me like that. I didn't kill the man."

"Somebody did. Somebody in this valley."

"Jesus, Frank, let it go. It's ancient history."

FRIDAY, SARAH AND I HAD OUR regular date. By then I was a little calmed down, but not much. We tried the diner on her side of the river this time, just for a change. Normally she drives around to my side, then we walk to the movie theater which is just four blocks from my house, and near Luigi's Restaurant. While we ate our soup and salad, I asked her what she remembered about all the fuss over the railroad, but she didn't really know what I was talking about, being just enough younger than I am to have been a real kid at the time. Heck, I had been too young, myself, to know what was happening, so anyone behind me in age would've missed the whole thing, unless their fathers were directly involved.

"Why are you so pensive, Frank?" Sarah asked. "Is there something about the railroad that's bothering you?"

"The whole thing, really, but mostly that I don't know what happened back then and I should have."

"You can't be responsible for the whole world," she said, giving the back of my hand a warm pat while she smiled at me. I've always liked her smile.

"Oh, it's not that," I answered, knowing that my old habits were coming out, my old teacher ways. "It's just that my class in school missed so much by an eyelash. We saw the Depression, but we didn't really suffer through it, not the way our parents did. Same with the war, we read about it and knew lots of older people who were involved, but we were just high school students. How seriously did we take anything or even understand what was happening in the world?"

"All I know about the railroad is that it runs through the next valley, and I'm glad of it," she said. "They're fun to watch from a distance, but not close up."

"Yes, I suppose you're right," I said, willing to let the matter drop until I had some more information.

About that time, our main courses arrived. I can't remember what Sarah ordered, but I had my usual Friday fish. The diner does a decent job, but nothing like Luigi's seafood pasta. Not quite like what mom used to make, but the bass was pretty good. Every now and then I amuse myself with my choices. Like I said before, Catholics are no longer required to eat fish on Fridays, but I still do. Call me a stick-in-the-mud, if you like, but it does make life simpler, just knowing what you can count on.

As we ate, we chatted, with Sarah doing most of the talking. I have a hard time trying to concentrate on eating and talking at the same time, mostly because I enjoy doing each one so much on its own. Basically, I pretty much like to knock off one task at a time. Not that I have the slightest idea why I'm even mentioning my foibles, other than to prepare you for the rest of this story. You already have a pretty good idea that I can get to be like a dog with a bone. Once I start on something, I do tend to get a little obsessed with the thing until it's resolved.

To tell you the truth, I don't have the slightest idea what Sarah talked about during that dinner because I was so preoccupied with my own thoughts. I'll admit that to you, now, though I'm not real proud to have anyone read it. Mostly I just like to watch her talk. She has a nice way about her—friendly and open, smiling and pleasant. We've been friends for a long time, now.

So why didn't I ever do something more about it? None of your business, and now it's too damned late anyway because of the leukemia. You're trying to put the cart before a dead horse. I'll get around to explaining it all, but in my own time. Forget the rules of storytelling. You're stuck with me, and it's my own story.

"What are you going to do about the railroad?" she asked me with a wry smile, the mention of railroad perking me right up again.

"Why do you ask?" I asked her back.

"Because I know you."

"Uh huh. What's that supposed to mean?"

"Oh, I just wondered if I should plan on our doing anything together for the next six months or so."

Six months, she'd said, *as if we had a real future*. I felt a twinge inside, but I tried to hide it. Another Friday night was slipping past without my talking to her about our breaking up. I just couldn't do it, not yet. Sarah was smiling, so I knew she wasn't upset, just kind of being playful with me.

"I might spend a little time on it," I said, meaning the bridge, as I moved my fork around the plate, "do some research. You know."

"Yes, I do know. Just remember, you still haven't got a street sign."

"Now that's low blow," I said, finally able to smile about it, though I could still get worked up over the thing, if I let myself. "Are you ready to go?" I asked.

"Yes, Frank," she said, grinning at me from behind her napkin.

We have that kind of a comfortable, teasing relationship. It's one of the good things in my life, something I'll really miss.

YOU ALREADY KNOW A LITTLE BIT ABOUT the street sign, namely that I have a slight problem giving directions to my house because of the lack of a sign. There's only two houses on my end of a dead end street. Across the intersection there is a sign and everyone on the Highway Commission—both of them (remember this is a small town)—seem to think that's enough. The whole Commission (both of them) came out and looked at my problem and agreed they would put up a sign, just so long as I paid for it.

"Why don't you see if Ed Shrader will go in on it with you?" Bob Morgan suggested, he being the senior member of the Commission, having been on it ten years longer than his partner, Phil Murcheson, who always concedes to Bob's seniority. Off they drove, knowing full well that Ed would never agree to part with the money for a sign. Shoot, he wouldn't pay for his own mother's surgery, he's that tight with a dollar.

Naturally, I was a little irritated over the matter. You've no idea how much restraint I had exercised already. Remember what Bob said? "See if Ed Shrader will go *in on it with* you." Four—count them, four—prepositions in a row, except that one of them's a pronoun, now that I think of it. My every instinct as an English teacher demanded that I correct the matter, on top of which, by that point, I was ready to blow, anyway, having seen the sign issue all the way through the City Council into the Highway Commission, and right out onto the road in front of my house. Except that's just where the issue ended—with me, standing in front of my house, watching the Commission drive away.

You get the idea, I'm sure. That's why Sarah knew she'd get a rise out of me, just by mentioning the sign. Needless to say, I still haven't got the stupid thing, and if you think I'm going to pay for it all by myself, then you don't know Germans very well.

Chapter Two:
   Second Sunday in Lent

THE REMINISCERE

TO REMINISCE IS TO REMEMBER, to ponder the past, and that's just what I did for the next few days. I had always sworn to myself that I would apologize to Jonathan if I ever got the chance. Well, the chance had just moved back into town, and I'd done it, but it had only opened up a bigger can of worms. Talking with him had left me with even more questions than I'd started with, in the beginning.

People say that's what we old timers do best—reminisce, just sit around and think about the past. Well, this surely was the week for it, its even being sanctioned by the Church and all. On top of everything else, looking at those old high school annuals of mine was a good enough cause for going off on a nostalgia craze.

Father Einsphar's sermon on Sunday morning never did have a thing to do with *The Reminiscere,* nor did I recall that last week's sermon had dealt with the theme for that week, either. I could remember nothing at all about invoking anything. Why was I trying to follow the theme of each week, if our own priest wasn't paying it any attention? Oh well, I'm just being negative, I guess. Father Einsphar is a big improvement over the last priest we had. Good Lord, how long ago was that? Near as I can recall, Father Egan's been gone for twenty years if it's a day. Can you believe that? An Irish priest in a German valley?

I don't think he could believe it, either. Father Egan came here directly from some big city—might have been New York, now that I think of it—anyway, he was full of hot ideas for civic activities and improvements in our life style. He was a young man then, full of life and vitality, but when he came to the valley, he walked right into a buzzsaw of German stoicism. Let me give you an example. Father Egan tried to institute a Bingo Night on Wednesday's. Germans playing bingo? Well, you might think that all Catholics were raised with a bingo card in one hand, but not in this valley. I tried it one of those first Wednesday's, but I was never so bored in my whole life. Me and everyone else who came. Bingo Night was a big flop. I don't think the idea lasted a month.

Once Father Egan experienced his first Oktoberfest, he did seem to hit his stride. The man could surely drink some beer, I'll say that for him. For most of his stay in the valley, we kept a keen eye out for any more of his ideas. No matter what good things he accomplished in his time here, Father Egan will always be remembered for the bingo. The very thought makes me shudder.

I WAS STILL THINKING ABOUT JONATHAN'S father on Monday. Carl and Sarah had both suggested that I not worry about something that happened years ago. Well, I couldn't just let it go. Never have been able to do that. Once I get an idea, I'm like a dog with a bone. I'll gnaw on that thing until I get it resolved. The problem of Jonathan's father and the railroad really stuck with me because it went against everything I believed about our little community. We're all good Christians here in the valley. Everyone I know goes to one or the other of the two churches. We have some friendly rivalry out of it, like the annual softball game, but I believe that anyone who attends the Lutheran church across the river is just as religious as we are who attend the Catholic church over here. What's the difference, really? Aren't we all Christians? Won't we all be saved?

Once I'd finished with that last thought, I had to stop. The line about Salvation had come from a lifetime of being a Catholic, accepting my faith, building my life around it. What did I believe about the Jews? All my training, all my instincts, told me they were damned. Right along with the Buddhists, Mohammedans, and downright pagans. It was an easy belief, one I had accepted right along with being a Democrat and a member of the Teacher's Union. Right was right, wrong was wrong, and that's just the way things went. Here I was, coming near the end of my life, finally questioning some of the stuff I'd always taken for granted. Would God really damn my friend, Jonathan? Damn him for being one of the Chosen People?

Good Lord, I had a headache. All my teaching career, I'd challenged my students to think for themselves, always, but, as it turned out, maybe not about some things. Religious matters you didn't challenge. Right was right. Wrong was wrong. Never the twain shall meet. The phone rang.

"Hello," I said, my mind still out in left field someplace.

"Hello, Frank." It was Jonathan, himself. The same man I'd just said was damned.

"Jonathan—how are you?" Gone to hell is how he was. *Stop it, Frank*, I told myself. *Knock it off.*

"Fine, Frank. Could I get you to do something for me?"

"Sure, what is it?"

"Meet me at the library in about an hour?"

"No problem. Something important?"

"I'll explain it when I see you."

"Okay, I'll be there in an hour."

After I hung up the phone, I just sat there staring at the thing. What was I supposed to do now? I'd never been one for proselytizing. Here in the valley, we didn't have to do much of anything to get people into attendance. The whole social life of our community pretty much centers around the two churches. Once, we had some Jehovah's Witnesses come through the valley. Far as I know, they struck out—a big fat zero for a batting average. No idea where they came from, where they went, or how long they stayed. Everybody bad-mouthed them for a day or so, and then clean forgot about them.

Maybe that's the source of our strength and our weakness both—maybe we're so homogenous in Happy Valley that we don't allow for any diversity at all? What's the difference between a Catholic and a Lutheran, for heaven's sake? They gave up some of the Latin earlier than we did, and their ministers are married. After that? Not much difference from what I can see. We make out like there's some major theological problems there, but not really. Things like the Great Schisms and all that just don't make a whole lot of sense anymore. Easy for me to say, now, but my mind went back to the original question, like a metal filing to a magnet—What about the Jews? Don't we all worship the same God? What did I really believe about them?

Somewhere along the line, I'd actually been taught that *they* had crucified the Lord. Not just the Jews of Christ's lifetime but the Jews walking down the streets today. Who would've put an idea like that into a kid's head? Maybe everybody believed stuff like that before the war, but after the Holocaust, who could voice such a horrible thought?

AN HOUR LATER, ERNIE DROPPED ME OFF on the other side of the river. He seemed to think it was pretty darn funny that I was going to the library after being a teacher for all those years.

"Just can't stay away, is that it, Frank?"

"Something like that, Ernie. Us highbrows are always trying to learn something new."

"Is that a fact," he answered, my highbrow crack going right over his head, so to speak.

"Thought I might check out some Nietzsche," I threw in for a laugh.

"Um huh," Ernie said. "That'll be a dollar."

"Keep the change," I said, handing him a single.

"There ain't none, Frank."

SOMETIMES, THE MAN COULD BE A REAL source of irritation. Maybe it was because I had to depend on him so much these days, now that I don't have a car. By the time I'd walked the three blocks to the library, I was done fussing over Ernie. In fact, I was so relaxed that I was able to see how nice a job the Auxiliary ladies were doing on the landscaping. The bushes were well-trimmed, and the flowers along the path to the entrance were blooming in all the colors of spring. I was glad to have a chance to see it.

In front of the main entrance, on either side of the porch, were the two concrete lions, crouching. Big lions, too. Big enough for a castle. A little pretentious, perhaps, since the whole library itself was only three rooms big, or small, as the case may be. You might want to envision it as being the size of your local branch library. The lions have been there since before I can remember. Every kid in the valley has climbed up on top of them to sit, at one time or another, riding the things like a horse. Someone's good idea from the previous century, I suppose. Thirty or forty years ago, the porch had to be rebuilt. Seems that the weight of the lions was just about to tip the building over. Comical when you think about it, but most people feel just like me, I'm sure—What would a library be without a pair of lions?

I didn't see Jonathan, at first, because he was back among the bookcases, so I visited with the librarian, Mary Fiedler. She'd been at that job for all her working lifetime. Wonder when they're going to make her retire?

"Good to see you, Frank," she whispered, though there wasn't a soul in sight.

"You, too, Mary," I whispered back, looking to see if she had the cameo brooch pinned to her blouse. Yes, it was there, just like every other time I'd checked over the past forty years.

Just as I knew she had a pencil stuck in the bun she pulled her hair into on the back of her head.

"Anything I can help you with?"

"No, thanks. I'm meeting Jonathan Green here."

"He's using the far table. Oh, there he is now, coming out of the stacks."

Jonathan never looked up from the book he was scanning, so I just walked over and joined him.

"Good book?" I said just loud enough to draw a critical stare from Mary. Sometimes I just can't resist temptation.

"Hi, Frank. I didn't see you. Let's step out on the porch," he said, in a professorial undertone. His years of practice in whispering around libraries must've pleased Mary something grand.

ONCE WE WERE OUTSIDE, I watched him light up a cigarette, wondering if he'd ever tried to quit. I did, right after the Surgeon General's report. It wasn't easy, but I managed to quit and stick with it because it seemed like the best thing to do. Yet, here was a brilliant law professor still with the habit.

"Mind if I smoke?" he asked, after the fact.

"No, go ahead."

"I've quit a million times," he said, catching whatever I couldn't hide in my expression.

"The garden's pretty, isn't it?" I said, just making small talk, but really changing the subject.

"Garden?" he answered, looking around as if he'd never even seen it. "Yes, it is nice," he said, matter of factly.

Nice? The roses were magnificent. Whatever Jonathan had in mind kept him from seeing their beauty, unless he were just that way by nature?

"So, why the library?" I asked while he inhaled, and I don't mean the scent of the roses.

"What do you know about the latest bridge project?" he asked.

"Just that a lot of people want to see it back up, again,"

I said. "They believe that it would be a lot more convenient for the businesses on either side of the river."

"Any idea who's spearheading the movement?" he went on, grilling me.

"Most of the current City Council, I would imagine. The last election was a clean sweep in that direction. Lots of arguing in the local paper—that sort of thing."

"Any one individual leader?" he asked.

"Well, I would start with Carl's son, Jim. He likes to play the back seat role, the power behind the throne, so to speak."

"That's pretty much the way I've got it figured, too."

"You could have asked me that on the phone," I said, still curious as to why he had me come over.

"What?" he said, still very much distracted.

"I just said that you could've asked me that on the phone, instead of having me come all the way over here."

"I'm sorry, Frank. All those questions just popped into my head. Actually, there's some other stuff I want you to look at inside. Okay if I finish my cigarette first?"

"Sure, take your time. It's pleasant out here."

"Yes, it is," he answered me, looking around as if he were seeing it for the first time. Either he was very distracted, or he had tremendous powers of concentration. Maybe both.

"How does your wife like the valley?" I asked.

Instead of answering me, immediately, he looked at me again, the same way he'd done in his house the week before. As if he were deciding just how much he should trust me. Probably a habitual thing with lawyers and judges. When he started talking, I thought at first he'd lost my question.

"Have you ever been to Germany, Frank?"

"Ruthie and I went once, just after we were married. Did all of Europe on the economy package in one fun-packed month. Youth hostels and all that. Why do you ask?"

"Did you visit any of the concentration camps? Dachau, for instance?"

"No, people were trying to forget that stuff then. It was later on that they turned some of the camps into memorials and museums."

"They're still trying to forget, Frank. Believe me, they're still trying to pretend it never happened."

Without asking my permission, Jonathan lit up another cigarette, right off the stub of the first one.

"Did you lose people in the Holocaust?" I asked him.

"Yes, of course," he answered, almost matter-of-factly. "Anyone who's Jewish lost people to the ovens."

It was the way he said it that added to the horror. Jonathan was absolutely emotionless. Not as if he didn't care, but as if he couldn't feel.

"My father was the oldest in his family," he continued. "Once he died, there was no one left who could trace our ancestry. We have some names, but they belong to people I never met."

"I'm sorry —" I said, lamely.

"Miriam is a different story," he went on as if he hadn't heard me. "She was born in Palestine, just after the war, when it was still under British rule. Somehow her father got her family into the country even before it was a country. She's the baby of the family, so all her brothers and sisters were born in Europe, but she was born there, in the Promised Land."

I couldn't help but hear the sadness, perhaps even sarcasm, in his voice, coupled with a disappointment when he said Promised Land, like it was anything but flowing with milk and honey.

"Her father saw the writing on the wall through what was happening in Germany and Poland," he continued. No one else in the family would listen to him. They all remained where they were, in Europe, and they all died."

For a long time, Jonathan just stood there looking out over the garden. He held the cigarette but did not smoke it.

"Everyone?" I asked, finally.

"Every single one," he answered.

"Jesus," I said, without thinking.

"I don't think Jesus had anything to do with Hitler, Frank. His inspiration came from another quarter."

JONATHAN NEVER DID ANSWER my question about whether his wife liked Happy Valley, nor did I ask it again. I couldn't help but wonder how she was going to respond to Oktoberfest? How would a Jew born in Palestine handle a festival celebrating Germany? Eventually, Jonathan and I returned to the library where he showed me some records from the war years. He'd been looking up the stuff about his father's business.

Why would such records be in a public library, you ask? Remember this is just a small town. At one point, all civic records were stored in City Hall, a building about the size of your average gas station, and that includes the courtroom which serves double duty by also functioning as the meeting room for the City Council. Eventually, they had records stored in broom closets and under stairwells, with cardboard boxes piled up everywhere. It was either store them in the library or build a new City Hall. The compromise decision was to begin a section in the library for historical documents. Once something got to be a certain age, it was classified as historically relevant, instead of politically so.

Jonathan laid it all out for me from the documents he had on the table. I had a little trouble following some of it, not being familiar with all the legalities he was explaining, but the bottom line goes like this—his father had definitely been cheated out of his business. Other properties of the same size and location sold for double and triple what he received, even during the height (or depth) of the Depression. There was no denying the numbers.

"I'm sorry, Jonathan," I said. "I had no idea something like this could happen."

"It's not even very well disguised. It only took me one afternoon to dig it out."

"What can you do about it?" I asked, in all innocence.

"Do?" he asked. "You mean like a lawsuit?"

"I don't know what I mean, really. How can you right something this old?"

"That's ancient history, Frank, but this isn't," he said, pointing to another stack of material, a combination of books, documents and xeroxed sheets, copies of deeds and such things which he must have gotten from City Hall.

"What's all this stuff?" I asked.

"Somebody is buying up property around the old bridge site, and has been for quite a while."

One by one, he showed me the documents, explaining that the new owners of the properties were operating through blind partnerships going back to holding companies. So far, he hadn't been able to come up with a single real name, just businesses and aliases.

"Sounds like what happened with the railroad, way back when we were kids," I said, drawing on my newly discovered information from Carl.

"Exactly," he answered.

"And you think that something on the same order is happening now?" I asked.

"History repeats itself, Frank. That's one lesson I've learned from being a judge. Nothing ever changes, not really. It just comes around again."

AFTER WE LEFT THE LIBRARY, we headed for Jonathan's house, with my helping him carry some of the materials he'd gathered in doing his research. We passed my folks' street, and, once again, I thought of visiting the old place, actually going inside. It was too late tonight, but Sally Rudolph had given me an open invitation. One of these days, I'd drop in for a visit.

Once we got back to their place, I met Jonathan's wife,

Miriam, for the first time. No telling what kind of subconscious prejudices I'd been carrying around with me for the past two weeks, but she was nothing like the picture I'd formed ahead of time. What had I expected? Carl told me she was a lot younger than Jonathan and very Jewish. Younger suggested someone on the giddy side, enamored of an older man, but that also made me think of the modern term, bimbo. Pardon the bias, but bimbo made me think of blondes, from all the blonde bimbo jokes going around. A very Jewish blonde bimbo didn't fit with any of my prejudices, either. Ultimately, I'd been left with a vague, half-formed picture of a plain, drably dressed, insecure schoolgirl. Then when Jonathan told me about her losing all of her family in the war, I imagined that same sad schoolgirl, but now looking like a political refugee, a lost waif.

Instead, I met a beautiful, sophisticated woman of the world. She was dressed stylishly—if that's the right word—in brightly colored clothes. A burgundy blouse, probably of silk, worn over a simple skirt, with a floral scarf worn as a shawl—she was overdressed by Happy Valley standards, but quite suitable for New York or London, I'm sure. Miriam is younger than Jonathan by twenty years, I would guess, but they sure don't look or act like a father and daughter. They are an obvious couple, moving and talking in harmony with each other.

"Frank, this is my wife, Miriam," he said, then turning back to me added, "and my friend, Frank Hessel."

I mumbled something like "pleased to meet you," and she spoke a greeting, in the same soft accent, Israeli, I supposed, that I had heard on the phone.

"Welcome to our home, Frank," she said. Thank God she hadn't called me Mr. Hessel—that would've made me feel ancient. She shook hands like a man—firm and decisive, just two quick shakes. It was a European style that I'd come across before. Her smile was warm, but guarded. Her hair was long but naturally very curly, so tightly curled that it was almost kinky, with deep red highlights. I thought of the exotic Bathsheba, the biblical woman David saw bathing on the rooftop.

Suddenly, as I watched her walk across the room, I knew that this woman of the world would be just as comfortable in a foxhole, holding an Uzi. In fact, I knew from my reading that she'd probably been there, doing just that. Every Israeli boy and girl has to serve in the military for one or two years after high school.

Miriam made me feel shy, like a small boy who'd just met someone famous. I wanted to dig my toes into the dirt.

WHEN MIRIAM LEFT US TO MAKE COFFEE, Jonathan and I just looked at each other, suddenly reduced to small talk. I had a million questions, but I did not know how to ask any of them. Miriam returned a few minutes later.

"So, you and my husband were children together?" she asked as she poured my coffee.

"Yes," I answered. "A long time ago, right here in the valley."

"What was he like?" she asked, glancing at Jonathan, with an impish look on her face.

"Good grief, Miriam," he said. "Let the man drink his coffee in peace."

I couldn't resist joining in on Miriam's game. It reminded me of a mother pulling out the bearskin photographs of her baby, when the date was sitting right there on the couch.

"No problem, at all, Jonathan," I said. "I've got one or two stories I could tell her."

Jonathan just sat there, looking glum, as he spun his coffee cup on the saucer.

"Tell me about Jonathan as a young boy," she said, smiling at me, but for his benefit.

"Well, let's see," I began. "He was always good in mathematics—one of my own failings. One day, Mr. Seboldt was giving an example on the board. Jonathan raised his hand and politely mentioned that he was doing it wrong."

"Politely?" Miriam asked in a teasing way.

"Absolutely," I continued. "'Mr. Seboldt,' he said, 'the first total is wrong.'"

"What did the teacher do?" she asked.

"Just about took my head off, is what he did," Jonathan joined in, but he was smiling.

"Did Jonathan have that same, serious look back then?" she asked. "There, just like that?"

"Oh, yes. Absolutely. Your husband was the most serious of us all, by far. Even more serious than I was."

We sat around for an hour or so, just talking over the olden times like that. Mostly at Jonathan's expense, but he told a good one or two on me, just to get even. It was a fun evening, and I really liked Miriam. In fact, I really liked the two of them together. They were a good match.

ON WEDNESDAY, CARL AND I DID SOMETHING special for our lunch together, at least I thought it was going to be special when he suggested it. Carl said he was tired of eating in the valley, especially at The Manor, where he was living.

"Let's go eat in Carpenterville. What do you say?" he asked on the phone.

"It's a long drive just for lunch, but if you want to, well, sure," I said. "I haven't been there in years."

Even when I still had a car, I hadn't made the drive in so long that I couldn't remember when, for sure. Maybe all the way back to when my wife, Ruth, was still alive? Most of the memories I had of the place went back many years ago, all the way back to when we were young married couples. Carpenterville had a big dance hall, and they used to bring in some pretty good dance bands, none of the headliners, of course, but good enough for our purposes.

Carl picked me up at eleven in the morning, and off we

headed. He was unusually quiet, especially for him. I don't know if all salesmen are like Carl, but he could keep you in stitches for hours—one story after another. Since he didn't seem interested in talking this morning, I just settled back in the seat and watched the country rolling by.

The valley is beautiful this time of year. The new crops had just started to come up in the fields, and the wildflowers were growing along the sides of the road. Everything was green and fresh. Once again, I was reminded of why I love the valley. Sometimes, in the middle of the winter, it's easy to forget the beauty of springtime. At the north end of the valley, we had to cross the bridge to get to the highway. Even the bridge was beautiful. It had been reinforced with concrete, years before, but the old style and flavor of the original wooden bridges had been maintained. You could even imagine the days when horse drawn carriages passed over them. Not so long ago, really, when you think about it.

Carl turned onto the highway, and after two or three turns in the road, we were through the pass and on our way to Carpenterville.

"Damn, but it's good to get out of the valley," Carl said, breaking his long silence.

I didn't know what to say. I was enjoying the drive, and I sure didn't feel the way he did. "It is good to get out, every now and then," I said, lamely, wondering what had gotten into him.

"How did you stand it for all those years?" he asked.

"I like the valley, Carl—always have. There really isn't anything I have to 'stand' about it."

"God, I feel like I'm being suffocated there, like all the life is being smothered right out of me."

"Give it time, Carl," I said. "You've only been back a few weeks. You'll get used to it."

"I hope not," he said. "If I ever got used to, I'd be just like everyone else—the walking dead."

Carl was just blowing off steam—I knew that so I didn't

take anything he said personally. Good grief, the man's wife had just died the year before, and now he was living in a retirement home. Lots of changes for him to handle. I could remember just how lost and confused I'd been after Ruthie died. Thank heavens, I'd had my teaching to keep me busy.

I don't think he said another word for half-an-hour or more, not until we started seeing signs for Carpenterville.

"Just another ten miles," he said, his spirits seeming to pick up a little at the sight of the mileage sign. "It's all starting to look familiar. Remember when we used to come over here in high school."

"Sure, I remember," I said.

What I remembered mostly was hitchhiking in the backs of trucks, getting all dusty and smokey, just for an afternoon and evening in the "big city," if Carpenterville ever fit that bill. I tried to remember what we'd done that Carl seemed to think was so much fun, but mostly all I could recall is trying to get someone to buy us some beer and cigarettes. At that age, we couldn't get into any of the bars, but the pool hall did let minors use the tables, even if they wouldn't serve us anything but root beer.

Carl was a good pool player, and our group used to back him against the local pool sharks in nearby cities. A couple of times, the pool games led to fights out back, but that was rare because we usually had a good sized group with us, often with some of the football players being along. The local girls would flirt with us in the park, but you could tell it was mostly to make their boyfriends jealous. Carl was the only one of us that had any "luck" with the local girls.

"Do you remember Nadine?" Carl asked, as if he were reading my mind. I glanced at him, watching the casual way he steered with one hand.

"Sure, I remember her."

"She was my first," Carl reminded me.

"I know Carl. You told me all about it a million times."

"I'll never forget that night," he said, "right out there in a haystack. We've got to be getting pretty close, now. It was on this side of town, somewhere."

Carl acted just like he expected to see Nadine herself, any minute now, coming out from behind a pile of hay.

What would he have seen? I remembered a skinny girl with limp hair, and a puppy dog look of adoration on her face when she saw Carl. I told you he was a handsome man. Well, he was the same as a kid. Carl zeroed in on Nadine like she'd given off a scent. Within an hour, he was taking liberties with her that embarrassed me, for her and for myself.

One of the guy's uncles had agreed to pick us up at nine o'clock and run us back to the valley. He'd been at the farmer's market that morning, trying to unload his excess corn. Carl just barely made the trip back, and I mean barely. He came running out of the fields with his shirt hanging out of his pants, and his shoes untied, but with a look of triumph on his face that rivalled any of his touchdowns.

That's pretty much what I remember of our high school days in Carpenterville. Maybe it was those dreams that Carl was chasing.

"Son of a bitch," he said suddenly. "Look at that."

"Is that the dance hall?" I asked, knowing that it was, but still shocked by the sight.

In its heyday, the Roadium Dance Hall had drawn people in from miles and miles around. Now it was just a shell of a building, ready to collapse in a good wind—obviously abandoned for years.

"Damn," Carl said, "I can't believe it. That place used to be the hottest ticket in the county."

Five minutes later, we were in downtown Carpenterville. Carl never said a word, at first, but I could tell how it was hitting him just from the way he looked around.

The place was just about as I remembered it, and that might have been the problem. The pool hall was still there, looking pretty much the same as ever. A little shabbier than I remembered, but it had never pretended to being much in the first place. The hotel was still there, both stories of it, though the name was different. The Vacancy sign was lit, of which I had no doubt there were plenty. Carl continued driving right on through the town. He might have kept on going right into the next county for all I knew, but I saw a Denny's off to the right. At least that was modern.

"Carl," I said, "are we going to stop for lunch."

"What?" he asked. "Oh sure, I guess this is as good as anything."

He pulled into the parking lot, mechanically, but just sat there with the engine running.

"Are you all right?" I asked.

"Just dandy," he said, tough as ever. "It's all gone, Frank. Every damn bit of it. Gone like a leaf in the wind."

It was a quiet lunch, and a long drive home.

FRIDAY NIGHT, SARAH AND I HAD DINNER at Luigi's, and then we walked over to the community theater, both of them being on my side of the river. Sarah drove her car around, but we walked to the restaurant and theater. Don't even ask—yes, I had pretty much decided I would talk with Sarah tonight, about our breaking up. What a night for something like that! Go to a musical, have a good time, then dump your girlfriend. It's just that we had *such* a good time we never seemed to get around to talking seriously.

The truth is that I didn't want to do anything that would hurt Sarah. Sometime during Lent didn't mean right away, did it? It could wait for a little longer. The play was great, and just because I taught English doesn't mean that I have any dramatic talent, none at all, in fact, zippo. I couldn't act my way out of a paper bag, so to speak. Matter of fact, if you ever see me trying to act, you have my permission to put a bag over my head and put me out of my misery. On top of everything else, the play was a musical. I love to sing, but you definitely wouldn't pay a dime to hear it.

"How are you doing on the research?" Sarah asked me over coffee at Luigi's.

"What research is that?"

"Don't play innocent with me, Frank," she said. "I know you too well for that. On the railroad and the bridge—that research."

"Oh, yeah," I answered, lamely.

Eventually, I told her all of it. Everything Jonathan had explained to me. At first Sarah couldn't believe it either, just as I had reacted.

"He's sure, Frank?"

"It seems like it, yes."

"Well, it just makes me sad," Sarah said, as I helped her on with her coat. "Just think that something bad like that could have happened right here in the valley. Or that it could be happening again."

The community theater did a presentation of *Oklahoma*, with Phil Murcheson, lately of the Highway Commission, stomping around the stage in a new pair of cowboy boots. You'll never guess who played the part of Aunt Eller—it was Sally Rudolph, the lady in my folks' old house. They did a pretty good job, considering that the whole cast numbered eight people.

Some of the songs in this musical are so good that you can't keep from tapping your toes.

"O-o-kla-ho-ma, when the wind comes blowing through the trees —"

All I could think of, watching farmers in boots and straw hats stomping through the fields with their pitchforks, was the girl, Nadine, from Carpenterville. Carl and I had driven for over an hour trying to capture her memory, and here she was, the whole time, on the stage of the community theater. Forever young, with a piece of straw stuck in her hair.

AFTER THE PLAY, SARAH AND I walked back to my place. I still thought that this might be the night when I told her about my decision, but Sarah looked so happy as we walked along that I didn't have the heart. She held my hand as we strolled, and she was humming the songs from *Oklahoma*. Sarah can always make me smile. As she chatted away about village gossip and the latest news from her family, I watched her. I've told you that she's pretty, but the word doesn't do her justice. Sarah has beautiful bone structure in her face. She was lovely as a young girl, as a woman, and now as a senior citizen. Sort of like Katherine Hepburn, I suppose. She's aged gracefully, accepting life's changes.

What would I do without her? Not only is she a partner for me socially, but she's a friend. In fact, she's my best friend. With a deep, burning pang in my heart, I tried to imagine my life without her, but it hurt too much.

We came to my street and turned up the hill.

"Would you like to come in for a cup of coffee?" I asked, hoping she would, but afraid at the same time. What if I just blurted it out? Blurted out that I was dying, and I had to turn her loose?

"No thanks, Frank," she said as we reached her car which was parked in my driveway. "I've got to get up early tomorrow and open up the shop." She worked part time at a friend's business.

"Okay," I said, relieved mostly.

"Maybe next time?" she asked, reaching up to give me a kiss on the cheek.

"Sure," I said.

"Are you feeling all right, Frank?" she asked, still up on her tiptoes as she stained to look me in the eyes from the light of the street lamp.

"Yes," I lied. "I'm fine."

"Well, don't get too wrapped up in your research. I know how you can be."

Then she gave my arm a squeeze and got behind the wheel of her car. In a minute, she had started it up, backed out of my driveway, and was making her way down the hill toward the main road. I watched her tail lights all the way to the bottom of the hill and around the corner, until they disappeared behind the trees. In a minute they reappeared on the other side of the grove as she made her way along the river.

When I could no longer see the lights from her car, I looked up at the moon, which was almost full now. Sarah would be able to see it, too, just above the horizon, maybe over the river itself. The thought made me feel connected to her. I watched the moon for a long time, until I started getting cold.

Chapter Three:
    Third Sunday in Lent

THE OCULI

I DON'T HAVE A CLUE ON THIS ONE—the *oculi*—though the word was listed right there in my bible, under the Third Sunday in Lent. It must have something to do with watching or vision, I suppose, otherwise why the ocular base and all? But watch what?—that's the question. Watch and wait, perhaps? Well, there isn't much else to do when you get to be my age. We senior citizens do a lot of watching and waiting: looking out the front windows at the world, waiting for the mail to come, waiting to die. Here we are in Lent, and as usual I am moody. It is a season for thought and prayer, contemplation. Jesus knew he was going to die, even though he was only thirty-three years old. I wonder if it really makes any difference? Being young and knowing you are going to die, or being old and knowing the same thing? Time to get out of this mood, that's for sure.

I couldn't get the story of Jonathan's father out of my mind. How could I have lived in the valley and not seen something like that? Hadn't I always taught a unit on prejudice? On my way through town one morning, I passed by the real estate office, and following an impulse, thought I'd stop in to see Mel Bruer.

"Hi, Mr. Hessel. How're you today?" It was Mel's boy, Hank. Boy? Good grief, Hank is fifty-five if he's a day and pretty much runs the place now, except for his dad's deciding vote. Hank had been one of my students so long ago that I don't care to figure out just when it was.

"Hello, Hank. And it's Frank, remember?"

"Sure, Frank. What can I do for you?"

Hank and Frank—it sounds like a slapstick comedy routine, something straight out of vaudeville, doesn't it?

"I was curious about something, Hank. Do we have any Jews living in Himmelberg?"

"Why do you ask?" he said, suddenly a little guarded, nothing obvious, but something I could sense from his body language, especially when compared to how glad he'd been to see me just a minute before.

"Just that an old friend of mine has moved into town—Jonathan Green."

"Oh, sure," Hank said, looking relieved. "We sold him the old Peterson place. He's a retired judge, you know. Heck, Mr. Hessel—Frank—you don't have to worry about him," he said with a smile.

Worry about him? What was that supposed to mean, I wondered, why would I *worry* about him? "Are there other Jews in the valley?" I asked.

"Some, but not many," he answered me, again forming his words carefully.

"So we don't have any kind of a policy against selling to Jews, anything like that?"

"Mr. Hessel, that would be illegal," he answered me, his face a mask.

"And you and your father would never do anything illegal, would you?"

"What do you mean?"

"Nothing, Hank, nothing at all."

"Look, Mr. Hessel. We didn't have a thing to do with that flack over the Turner farm, not one damn thing, and anybody who says we did is a liar."

I didn't have the slightest idea what he was talking about. Sure, I knew where the old Turner place was located, but I didn't remember any scandal about it. Obviously, there was more to his mentioning of it than I knew because something had sure pushed Hank's buttons. He looked like he was on the verge of apoplexy.

"Take it easy, Hank. I'm not accusing you of anything." Suddenly we were back in the old, familiar roles of teacher and pupil.

"I hope not, sir. Please, don't go judging us by what's gone on in this valley. Like I told you, we sold that place to the Greens. But just ask yourself something—How many Jewish students did you have at the high school?"

"None, that I can think of."

"See? That's what I mean. Don't go blaming us for everything. This valley's been the way it is for a long, long time."

"Are you saying we're all prejudiced?"

"No, sir. I'm not saying that at all. This office abides by all federal guidelines. You *did* say that Judge Green was a friend of yours?"

NONE CAN SEE SO CLEARLY AS THE BLIND. How could I have lived through World War II, seen all the newsreels of the released Jews looking like walking skeletons, and not seen what was happening in my own backyard? It is inconceivable. I'm a decent person, a good Christian—at least that's what I've always thought. Maybe the truth is that I'm just a hypocrite. Maybe this whole damned valley is a sham, and me right along with it. Happy Valley, home of the white and the free. Once I started thinking along these lines, I tried to remember the number of black students I'd had over the years. Some Blacks and Asians did come through the valley, on occasion, mostly working in the restaurants and gas stations, but had any of their families ever bought a home here? Ever been welcomed here?

For the first time in my life, I was taking a good hard look at my community, my home. We are mostly Aryan, to borrow a term from the most feared and hated man in my generation, Adolph Hitler. What Hitler tried to accomplish in Germany had become a reality in Happy Valley. We rid ourselves of any minorities, any flaws in the gene pool. Even as I thought these things, I knew I was overreacting to a new insight, but still—where was I grossly wrong?

Across the street, I saw a sign in the window of a shop that supported the new bridge. It read:

A BRIDGE INTO THE FUTURE
—REUNIFICATION—
A good thing for our Community

THE SIGN REMINDED ME OF SOMETHING I'd heard after the Berlin Wall had been torn down. One of my more cynical friends had remarked, "Here we go again. Look out for World War III." I asked him how he thought that modern Germany could affect the world that much and his answer was, "Where two or three Germans are gathered together, you have the potential for another war. It's our egos, Frank—you ought to know that—the god-dammed German Ego."

Sigmund Freud had built his whole theory around that Ego. I'm oversimplifying the issue, of course, but is it any accident that Freud would have been the one to come up with his insights into the human psyche? Right people, right country? Or was Freud Austrian, like Hitler was supposed to be? Just lately, I'd read that Freud is less "popular" than he used to be—if that term applies in clinical circles—with Carl Jung and his followers coming to the forefront. The gist of the article comes down to this: Freud dealt with diseased psyches, while Jung dealt with healthier versions. This was supposed to be significant, somehow, but that's all I can remember. Freud and Jung, both dealing with the German psyche. Did either one of them live to see Hitler? I wondered. No doubt about whether his Ego was sick or healthy.

I'd been opposed to the bridge because I wanted to keep the valley as it's always been, but maybe I was wrong. Maybe change would be good for us? Maybe we all need it, and the faster the better. Two days ago, I had all the answers. Now, suddenly, I have none.

LATE THE NEXT MORNING, I WOKE UP in my chair, one of the bonuses of getting old—you can fall asleep anywhere and everywhere, especially places you least expect it. Truth is I had been up and down all night long, worrying about this stupid bridge thing, trying to figure out which side was right. All I did was give myself a headache and a sleepless night. Now, as I sat in my chair, more or less awake, I kept hearing a loud voice and some music in the background, so I thought I must've left the TV on in the other room, but when I checked it, the screen was dark, whereas the voice continued.

    I glanced out the window just in time to see a pickup truck going through the intersection with a large trumpet-shaped speaker on the top of the cab. In the back of the truck stood a man with a microphone in one hand as, over and over, above the sound of the music, he hollered out something that sounded like, "Help keep Happy Valley happy. A vote against the bridge is a vote for the community." On either side of the man stood two young women in brightly-colored yellow and orange sun dresses who waved just like they were on a Rose Parade float. With my eyesight the way it is, I can't be absolutely sure, but the blond girl on the side nearest me looked just like Harvey Reasoner's daughter—Jill, I think is her name. *Good Lord*, I found myself wondering, *how could he let her out of the house like that, dressed in something that low-cut, busty as she is?* Then just as suddenly as it appeared, the truck was gone, leaving behind it a couple of curious neighbors and a trail of kids on bikes.

    Just what we need—I thought—a full-blown community battle over this stupid bridge. Why couldn't they just leave well enough alone? Just when I was getting grateful for the returning quiet, my phone rang.

    "Hello," I said.

"Frank? This is Jonathan. Is there a loud-speaker truck going through your neighborhood over there?"

"There sure is. It just went past my house a minute ago."

"That's what I was afraid of—but are you all right? You sound funny."

"I'm fine. The truck woke me up is all."

"Sorry it bothered you, Frank."

"Why are you apologizing? Do you have something to do with it?" I asked.

"In a way, I suppose," he said. "I'm working with the committee opposed to the bridge. We had a meeting last night and a speaker truck was one of the ideas that came up, but I never thought they were going to act on it. The idea was supposed to be tabled till next meeting."

"Well," I said, "it seems like somebody didn't get the message because that truck is here bigger than life, but how did you hear about it?"

"Miriam just came back from the store. She told me people were talking about it in the check-out line, then she thought she could hear the music in the parking lot, coming from all the way across the river."

"I believe it," I said, rubbing my temple. "You'd better get ready for worse than this. Small towns get all worked up over the littlest things."

"It's not a little thing to me," Jonathan said, sounding deadly serious. "They'll put that bridge up over my dead body. Sorry it bothered you, Frank. I've got to go now and see if I can get them to stop the truck. Talk to you later."

The click on the line told me that he was gone without so much as a goodby. Good Lord, the man was a judge, and now he's all worked up over a wooden bridge. "Over my dead body," he'd said.

FOR THE NEXT FEW DAYS, I KEPT MY EYES and ears open to what was happening in the community. If you've ever lived in a small town, you'll understand how these things get blown out of all proportion. While the rest of the world is watching pro football, a small town will turn out for the local high school game—every man, woman and child, as if the course of human development depended on a child's game. Fist fights in the parking lot, before and after the game, students and parents both. Prayers for victory in front of the altar, several altars, on both sides of the game, in both of the towns involved, as if God really gave a fig over who won. Some of the arguments about the game turn into blood feuds within families, so people don't speak for years on end. It's comical when you think about it. Comical or tragic.

It was the same way with the bridge, just as I feared it would be—the same way it'd been with the train when we were kids. I've spent a lot of time since Jonathan's return thinking about our mutual histories. He's happily married, with children apparently doing well, yet here he is, still tortured by the past, enough so that he would return to the valley for the sake of revenge. An eye for an eye was how the Old Testament law went. Jonathan had pictures of his kids on the mantle, or maybe it was his wife who put them there. Do men feel the same way about their children? I've never had the chance to find out. My wife, Ruth, had wanted children, of course, but it was not to be. She'd been pregnant twice, gotten deathly sick, and miscarried both times. Dr. Keller said to forget it, but that was easy to say, hard to do.

Ruthie had cried for weeks, grieving the children she would never have. We talked about adoption, but by then we were both getting into our late thirties, maybe early forties for me, and it just didn't seem fair to the kid, bringing him or her into a family so much older and different than others in the valley. My struggling through college for all those years had thrown us way behind schedule. Back in those days, most people did *not* go on to attend college—that was a simple fact of the world—it was too expensive and there were too few openings. Heck, I knew lots of people who never even finished high school. The Depression did that to my generation. College? It was just a dream to most of us. A few years later, things were to change with the GI Bill, but not for a while.

Anyhow, I was talking about kids and my being too old for them. Most people here in the valley used to get married young and have their families young. It was just the way of the world. You can joke all you want to about shotgun weddings, but I've seen plenty of them that worked out just fine. Today, people are divorcing right and left. Get a little bored in the marriage, get a new partner. No big deal, apparently. Ruthie and I had a good marriage, with or without children. She threw herself into teaching Sunday School and I had my own teaching in the high school. I guess we just looked at those young folks like they were ours. We managed.

Still, I couldn't help but remember those pictures of Jonathan's kids, as well as those pictures belonging to the lady now living in my folks' home—Mrs. Rudolph—the one who played Auntie Emm in *Oklahoma* at the Community Theater. She's a nice enough looking woman, but that wasn't why I kept thinking about her. She just breathes life and health, fecundity. Now that I'm thinking about it, I'll bet she's probably pregnant—something I'm guessing from the way she straightened up holding her back and from the loose smock she was wearing when I visited with her in front of her house. Nothing showing yet, but you can just bet I'm right. The thought pleased yet saddened me, too. New life in the old home would be a good thing, but that new life should have come from me and Ruth. It would have made my folks so happy.

"Oh, Frank," my mother said when I finally told them there would be no children, "I'm so sorry. I've prayed so many times that you'd have children. God's will, I guess, God's will."

"Just biology, mom," I said, offering her a handkerchief for the tears.

"Nothing's that simple, son."

"Well, I'm sorry to disappoint you. I know how much you wanted more grandkids." I thought of how happy my sister's children seemed to make my parents.

"I didn't want them for myself, Frank, but for you. Your dad and I will always have Pru's kids. We love them dearly, but I wanted you to have kids of your own. It's the joy in life. I'm so sorry."

Darn it all. Here I go again, feeling sorry for myself. My sister lives five hundred miles from here. We get together once a year, if we're lucky. I like her kids, but they're scattered all over creation now, with kids of their own. Basically, I'm alone in the world. Plenty of friends, but no family left here in the valley. I worry about dying by myself, alone in the house. Who would ever know? When would they find me? Good grief, what a depressing thought that is. *Pull yourself out of it, Frank*, I told myself, you're just too darn moody. Nobody gives a hoot about your problems, least of all the good folks reading this book.

It isn't easy growing old. Maybe it's easier with a family around, I just don't know.

Why haven't Sarah and I gotten married? The obvious stuff I can tell you—for a long time, she cared for her aged mother, who was a difficult woman at best. I could never have lived with Hannah, that I do realize. It would have been her or me, and I never pushed the issue to the point of learning the truth. I am seventy now, so Sarah must be sixty-two. We've been dating for years—every Friday night we go to the two-for-one early-bird evening movies, usually following dinner at Luigi's, senior citizen discount, of course. How did we ever fall into such a rut? For one thing, there isn't a whole lot else to do in Himmelberg, East or West. A real night out would take at least a forty-five minute drive to someplace else.

I'm getting side-tracked again, or I'm doing it on purpose so I can dodge the bullet. We've talked about getting married, in very general terms, but the truth is that I've never asked her, not formally or officially. My wife died over ten years ago, and

Sarah has been widowed for seven or eight years, after her husband John was killed in a farming accident. She and I started dating a couple of years after his death. Good grief, we've known each other forever, all the way back to when we were kids, though she was eight grades behind me. Eventually, we did get serious enough about each other to sleep together—when we were adults, I mean, and both of us widowed—but not serious enough to get married. Yet we still go to the movies every Friday night. Go figure that one out, if you can. I can't do it. What held us back?

Guilt—that's always a good answer for a Catholic. I'm the one who's Catholic, she's Lutheran, but both of us had the same sense of guilt, still do for that matter. That's why we decided to stop sleeping together. Decided? Like we actually sat down and worked it all out? Not quite that way, not as I recall it.

"Frank," she said, the dim light from the bedroom window illuminating her features, "can we talk a minute?"

Uh oh, I thought, but instead I said, "Sure, Sarah. What's on your mind?"

We had just finished making love, in the earlier days of our going out together. What in the world did I think was on her mind? After my breathing slowed down, I reached out to pull her close, but instead she moved away from me and started to cry. I didn't know what the heck to do.

"What's wrong, Sarah?" I asked.

"Frank, you know how I feel about you ... it's just that this seems wrong, somehow."

"It does?" I asked, knowing full well what she meant but afraid to acknowledge it.

"I can't help it, Frank. I've tried, but I just can't help feeling guilty about this."

"I understand," I said, lying as gracefully as I could under the circumstances. What I wanted to do was reach out and hold her. Maybe that's what I should've done.

"Thanks, Frank," she said. "I was afraid you'd be mad."

"Don't be silly," I offered, ever the gallant.

Sarah rolled back to face me, daubing at her eyes with a kleenex from the end table. This time I did reach out a hand and placed it on her shoulder.

"Maybe if my mother wasn't such a handful," she started out, "maybe things could be different, then?"

"Maybe so," I said with no sense of hope.

We looked at each other for a long time, our eyes locked in an important embrace, maybe the last embrace?

"Can we go back, Frank?"

"Back to what?"

"Like we were before ... you know, just going out together, as friends?"

Oh Lord, I should've known that was coming, but it still surprised me.

"You mean ... not?" I stumbled out. Not ever again to hold her in bed? Ever?

"I guess so?" she said, still with half a question in the words.

"If you think so, sure we can," I said with all the certainty of my faith, not of my convictions.

That was it, the closest we ever came to getting married. Sound stupid? Maybe to someone from your generation, but not to people of our age. You have to understand our sense of values. People in our era stayed in horrible marriages out of a sense of duty, and never entered into relationships that could be wonderful from a sense of guilt. Go figure it.

From that night on, we haven't slept together, not even once. God knows, I've thought about it often enough. We hold hands in the movies, and every now and then I'll get aroused as much as any teenager, but there's nothing to be done.

Even now, knowing what I'm going to tell you, I can't help wondering if maybe it still isn't too late for us? We're senior citizens, but were not dead, yet. John Gunther said I might outlive him. No guarantees, though, no guarantees. While her mother was alive—Hannah was her name, the most hateful old biddy I ever did see—there was no chance for us, but Hannah passed on six or seven months ago. For a few months, Sarah was busy wrapping up all her mother's affairs. After the smoke cleared, she started making some hints to me, like maybe we could get back to the way things were before? In the movies, she gradually started getting more affectionate, just like she used to be. You've got to understand the bind this put me into. I never have told Sarah about the leukemia. Call it German pride or whatever you like, but I haven't told anyone, except for you, and we're strangers! Somehow that makes it safer—your being a stranger.

Why don't I just take her in my arms and propose? Hellfire and brimstone, you can guess why. It's that damn cancer. Excuse me for getting carried away and cursing, but sometimes you just have to vent your feelings. Maybe I should've married Sarah five years ago, but not now, not now. It's just too darned late. Sometimes you can't win for losing—now there's an old adage for you. Does anyone have the slightest idea what that means? Win for losing? Or is it win from losing? Because of losing? Life is one long loss. I just can't face going through any more of them. And I sure don't want to inflict another one on Sarah.

JUST WHEN I GET DOWN IN THE DUMPS, it seems like something nice comes along to pull me out of it. I turned the page in my pocket calendar and saw the notation for my goddaughter's birthday coming up next week. Time to get a card into the mail, but first I just sat around thinking about her, Tracy's her name and her mother, a former student of mine in the high school, is Ruth Ann Gerber, "Rags" for short because of her initials, but I wasn't supposed to know that her friends called her that.

Ruth Ann is the finest student I ever had. It was all I could do to keep myself from teaching the whole hour to her and for her alone. She loved English literature, was quick and insightful in her observations, and wrote some of the best papers I ever received. A student like her only comes along once or twice in a lifetime. Ruth Ann graduated with honors and went on to Worten, my alma mater, where she majored in English. She was married shortly after graduating college and started substitute teaching at the high school. Then she had a baby almost immediately, fast enough that some people were adding up the months, but that's neither here nor there, not by my standards.

Mostly, I was pretty disappointed for her, not about her, and there is a difference. I've always been happy that she stayed in the valley when so many other kids opted to leave here, at a dead run, for the lights of the big city. Once Tracy got into school, Ruth Ann went back to teaching full-time. She's still here at the high school, teaching the classes I used to handle.

No, I don't have any complaints about how she turned out, it's just that I've always wondered if she might not have done better somewhere else. I know, the thought makes me feel like a traitor to the valley. She's happy here, just as happy as I've always been, but still—do you know what I mean? She could have gone on to graduate school, maybe gotten a PhD in English literature, taught college. But that was a dream of mine, not hers. Oh well ...

I had also taught her husband, Robert, a nice kid, not as bright as Ruth Ann, but solid. When they asked me to be their daughter's god-father, I almost choked from pride. Never having had kids of my own, Tracy has always been special to me, in her own right, but also because she's her mother's daughter. Tracy is now an assistant professor of English, in a small college in Texas. She got the opportunity her mother never had, and maybe the same opportunity I never had, either. I've always wondered if it were in me to get a PhD, had things been different when I was young man. No sour grapes, mind you, because I loved teaching high school, but I have wondered, all the same.

Just seeing Tracy's name in my book made me smile. Actually, it made my whole day. I decided to pick out a nice card for her tomorrow and get it into the mail so it'd be there early. What the heck, I might even give her a call. So much for being depressed. So much for crying over spilt milk. So much for missed opportunities. No, I'm not dead, yet, but I've sure been acting like it lately.

SARAH COULDN'T GO TO THE MOVIES on Friday because her church, Our Redeemer, was having some kind of a bazaar on Friday and Saturday—big bake sale, that kind of thing. Sarah is Lutheran. Who knows? If she'd been Catholic, we might have gotten together long ago.

"You're welcome to come, Frank," she told me on the phone, like she had several times before around other events.

"I'll think about it, Sarah," I'd told her, like I usually did, knowing full well that I wouldn't go.

In the past, she's asked me to some of their events, and I've hinted around at her coming over for things in our parish, but we just don't seem to get around to it. Everybody in town knows that we have a standing date on Fridays—you can't keep something like that secret, not in a small town like ours—but starting to attend things together in our churches, well, that always seemed pretty serious, so we just dodged around the doing of it.

Friday night was just about the loneliest evening I've spent in a long while. I tried to watch TV, but found myself thinking so much that I couldn't keep track of what was happening on the show, or else I'd drift off into daydreaming just before they reached the conclusion and solved the crime. Mostly, I was just missing Sarah and the routine we have on Fridays. Call me weak, if you must, but I just couldn't face the idea of telling her that we were through. I simply had to spend another night with her, so I could have something to remember.

ON SATURDAY, I BIT THE BULLET and decided it was time I did something positive instead of sitting around and feeling sorry for myself. I called Sarah.

"Well, hello, Frank," she said. "I was just thinking about you."

"That's why I'm calling. I got to thinking about you, too, and how much I missed you last night."

"Well, thank you, Frank," she said. She paused just long enough that I became pretty certain she was teasing me for getting all romantic on her, but what the heck, let her think what she wanted to. She would understand it all, eventually. Time was flying, so I just went for it.

"I've been thinking about coming over for your Bazaar. What time does it start?"

"That would be very nice, Frank," she said, soft and subdued, but I could tell it made her happy. "I'd love to go with you, so why don't you come here first. I could fix us some dinner. Say around six o'clock."

"Okay, fine. See you then."

Well, you've done it now, Frank, I said to myself, which is another benefit of growing old—you can walk around talking to yourself all day long and no one will ever say a thing about it, except for you, yourself. Maybe I was just nervous. After all, this was a big step, going to the bazaar. I knew it and Sarah knew it, too. She's cooked for me before, but mostly back when her mother was still alive. Believe me, dinners with Hannah sitting across the table were anything but fun. Once I started thinking about it, I came to understand that Sarah's agreeing to cook for me, now, was a big step for her, too.

I SHOWED UP A LITTLE EARLY, carrying some flowers I'd picked up at the corner market—general store, for lack of any better a name. Luke Ebel had been running this place for years, making a living by stocking every useless thing you just have to have every so often. He could pull stuff out of drawers that hadn't been sold retail for twenty years. A good man to know. Luke always wore an apron and a baseball cap, the kind truckers wear with messages on the front, over the bill. The current one must have been a freebie because it advertized Copenhagen chewing tobacco. He wore the caps because of his thinning hair. None of us are getting any younger.

"So, Frank," he said, adding some ferns to the bouquet of carnations he was arranging for me, "you're taking Sarah some flowers tonight, are you?"

"Who said anything about Sarah?" I answered back, trying to see if I could shock him any. It didn't work.

"Now, who else are you going to be seeing in a place this small, Frank? Everyone's got their eye on you two, that's for sure."

"Is that so, Luke?"

"Yep. Just a matter of time, now, we reckon. You been going together long enough. Might just as well make it legal."

That's what I mean about living in a small town. There's no such thing as minding your own business. It's all "our business," every darn bit of it.

ERNIE WASN'T MUCH BETTER ON THE RIDE OVER. In fact, he was just a little bit worse, asking questions, prying into my private business.

"Sarah likes carnations, does she?" he asked.

"She loves them, Ernie."

"That so? First time I can ever recall you taking her any, but of course you might have driven some flowers around to her when you still had the car."

Like it was any of his business at all. In fact, I got to thinking, what business was it of anyone's what kind of flowers I was taking to whatever woman?

"— they always like that, Frank."

"What did you say, Ernie?" I asked, apparently having missed some sterling piece of advice he was giving me.

"I was telling you that women always like a little candy, too. Fay's running a special on rocky road this week," he said, meaning Fay's Candy Shoppe—that's the way she spells it, with the extra P and E on the end, so don't blame me—located just a convenient one block walk from Ernie's water taxi.

"I'll keep it in mind, Ernie," I said, but I was thinking other things to myself, like what business did Ernie Warden have giving me advice about women? Like he was some kind of a romance editor?

"That'll be a dollar, Frank," he said, holding out one hand while steadying the boat with the other.

Instead of paying Ernie for the trip, it felt like I was tipping him for some advice to the lovelorn. You can be sure that I chose not to stop in at Fay's. I wouldn't give Ernie the satisfaction, not on a bet, but I did think about stopping, in spite of myself.

ONCE I GOT ANOTHER LOOK AT SARAH'S front yard, I felt like a fool for bringing her flowers. Sarah is a real gardener, not just some toss-out-the-seeds variety, but one who plans the placement of stuff, so that the colors in one row blend in with what she's planted in the row behind. She's kind of a gardening architect. Now, how come I'd never seen that before?

"Frank, you brought flowers," she said, without missing a beat, too polite to tell me that she could've picked twenty times as nice a bouquet for herself right there in her own front yard. "Thanks for being so sweet," she added, smelling the carnations.

"Guess it was a silly idea," I said, looking around at the other stuff she had in bloom. She didn't say it, so I did. "You could've come up with a lot better right here."

"A lady always appreciates flowers, Frank. Here let me put them in water, then we can sit down to dinner."

She'd set the table real nice with a china pattern I hadn't seen before. When I mentioned it later, she explained.

"It's my grandmother's set. My mother had it boxed up in

the garage. She wouldn't use them while she was alive or ever let me, either. Aren't they nice?"

"Beautiful stuff. Is it Austrian?"

"No, it's German, Bavarian, I guess, from what I can make out on the label underneath."

I turned my coffee cup over and took a look. The cup was empty, just in case you're wondering if I spilled coffee all over Sarah's lace tablecloth. Stuttgart was about all I could make out because it had been printed in a light pink. Stuttgart? How far is that from Dachau? I wondered, thinking of Jonathan. I've forgotten a lot of my German, of course, and the logo had really faded, all except for the name of the city.

"I see what you mean. I can't make out much of it, either," I said. "It is pretty stuff, though."

"My grandmother brought it with her from Germany. It was part of her trousseau. She'd only been married a week when they left for America."

"Have you ever been there, Sarah?" I asked, "Germany, I mean?"

"No, I've always wanted to, but then John died ... well, we just never got around to it."

"You'd like it," I said.

"That's right. You and Ruth went over when you were first married, didn't you?"

"Yes. It was a long time ago."

"Would you like to go back?" she asked.

"I never thought about it," I answered her, truthfully, because the idea had never crossed my mind.

"I would like to go," Sarah said, "if only to meet my cousins face-to-face again."

"You have relatives there?"

"Sure, lots of them. All distant aunts and uncles, third and fourth cousins, however that's figured. Several of them have come over here on vacations, but I've never ... well, you know what I mean."

Sarah went into the kitchen for our coffee, leaving me there to think about what she'd said. For the first time I realized that she'd never gone and would never be able to go, simply because she couldn't afford it. I always knew that Sarah didn't have a lot of money. After John died, she sold their farm and moved into the place she has now, but there couldn't have been a lot of money left over. She's just as alone as I am. Her only child, a son, was killed in Vietnam. I don't even know that she gets social security, John being a self-employed farmer and all. I've never asked her about finances. No surprise there. That's real personal stuff.

I'd always thought that Sarah worked just to keep busy. She has a part-time job in the gift shop near Ernie's dock. Near the candy store, for that matter. She and Rachel Pohr—no kidding, that really is her name, and poor she isn't—have been good friends for a long time, so I just assumed Sarah was helping out in the shop, out of friendship. Maybe Sarah really did need to work, to build up her own social security?

"Would you like some dessert, Frank?" she asked, pouring me a cup of coffee.

"No thanks, Sarah. I'm way too full, now, but the dinner was delicious."

"Thanks, I'm glad you liked it. Maybe we could have a piece of pie when we get back from the bazaar?"

"Sure, that would be great," I said.

I KEPT AN OPEN MIND ON OUR WALK over to Sarah's church, Our Redeemer Lutheran, on Grand Avenue. I figured that I would just see what developed. Mostly I expected to find something real hokey—you know, cardboard booths and crepe paper everywhere, but my first sight of the place was a pleasant surprise. Everything was set up in the parking lot next to the church, meaning that most people who could do so walked over. The booths were made of wood and painted real nice. The costumes were very nice, too, hand sewn and beaded. This was an annual event and the Lutherans went all out. They have a nice church, an old-fashioned frame building, painted white with some beautiful stained glass windows. The altar is made of hand-carved, polished wood. I'd seen the inside of the church several times at funerals.

Sarah was working in a booth that offered hand-crafted items, potholders, towels, and linens, all embroidered—that kind of stuff.

"Frank," she said, "I've got to stay here, but why don't you walk around and look at everything? When you get tired, you can sit in here with me."

"Sure," I said, "see you in a little while."

Well, you wouldn't believe how many old friends I saw as I strolled around, with their making lots of comments like, "You thinking of converting, Frank?" and "What's an Old Catholic like you doing over here? Stuff like that. All well-intentioned. In fact, I saw a whole lot of my Catholic friends from Saint Ignatius, so I figured this was a real community event. Funny that I'd never gone to it before, staying stuck over there on the west side of the river.

AFTER THE BAZAAR, SARAH AND I stood around talking to some old friends until it really started getting late. I told Sarah that I'd better pass on the pie. She kissed me goodby and I headed for the river, where Ernie gave me a lift back to my own side.

"Did you enjoy the bazaar, Frank?"

"I did, Ernie. It was a lot of fun."

"You looked like you were enjoying it," he added.

"I don't remember seeing you there, Ernie."

"I was wearing a pirate costume, in one of the booths across from you and Sarah. You make a nice looking couple."

"Thanks, Ernie. She's a special lady."

"That she is," he said. "That she is."

What do we do now? I wondered. Sarah and I had just

attended an event at her church, just because I was lonely. So what happens next?

I got moody again during the walk up to the house from the river. What right did I have to be tying up Sarah's time?

Chapter Four:
Fourth Sunday in Lent

THE LAETARE

THIS ONE I had to look up. You'd think that after taking Latin in high school and then going through seventy Lenten seasons I would have thought through all this stuff before, but no, not me. I had to make another trip all the way over to the library, which is not only on the other side of the river, in East Himmelberg, as I've already explained, but is another six full blocks off the water. It's just one of those things—we have the good restaurant, they have the library. Anytime, I want to go over there to check out a book, I have to wait for Ernie, that or take the bus all the way around. A forty-five minute bus ride or a one minute boat trip, if Ernie ever showed up, that is. I sat down on the bench and waited.

You can imagine what I was thinking that Monday morning. Matter of fact, you'll have to imagine it because I can't tell you about it. For the most part, all I recall is my head's swirling with random ideas about the bridge, Sarah, leukemia, and my friends, Carl and Jonathan. Round and round like the proverbial hamster in a cage. You know, the one with the wheel, where that hamster runs and runs without ever getting anywhere? That's exactly how I felt and how my head was working.

Maybe it was the colors and excitement of the bazaar, but my mind drifted back to sometime early in our high school days when Carl and I snuck into a carnival that was being held in the next valley over. We rode our bikes for two hours to get there and two hours back.

"Come on, Frank," Carl said, looking back at me. "We've got to keep going or we'll never make it back by dinner."

"I'm coming. Keep your pants on," I said. Carl was the athlete of our group, but I wasn't that bad myself, back then. At least I could ride a bike.

"Here we go," he said as we crested a hill. "We can coast for a while."

I pumped a couple extra times to catch up with him, then we coasted down the hill, side by side, with our arms folded across our chests—showing off, the way boys will do.

"So, what are we going to see?" I asked. Carl had sprung this trip on me. Heck, I hadn't even seen a flyer.

"It's a carnival," he said. "We'll see lots of things. Mostly, I want to see the hootchy-cootchy dancer."

"What's that?" I asked, ever the innocent.

"My uncle says they got this lady that dances and strips right down to the buff," he told me.

"You're kidding me?" I said.

"Honest to God," he said, starting to pump again. "That's why we've got to get a move on."

I watched as Carl pulled ahead of me. What's he going to get me into this time? I asked myself before reaching down for the handlebars. Never a dull minute with Carl around.

THEY WOULDN'T LET US INTO THE TENT, of course. Heck, I think we were only fourteen or fifteen at the time. We did get to see the dancer, though. Little Eva wore a big rhinestone in her belly button, centered between the sequined bra and panties of her outfit, with her arms and legs covered by billows of blue silk. She came out on the barker's platform and did a little bit of a belly dance to stir up the crowd, keeping time with some hand-held cymbals. It worked, especially when she got her hips going a mile a minute. There were lots of whistles and hoots, but she looked bored as all get out.

"Hot stuff, isn't she?" Carl said, giving me a poke in the ribs without taking his eyes off the dancer.

"Yeah, she's great," I said, looking around at the crowd, hoping I wouldn't see anyone I knew, or worse, see someone who knew me and my parents.

Even the passage of fifty years and more can't romanticize my memories. The dancer was called Little Eva, but she wasn't little and she couldn't dance, not very well. Mostly, she just wiggled around the stage, bent over to show her cleavage. Eva wore so much makeup on her eyelids and lashes, that I never could tell what color eyes she had. The whole thing was kind of sad. After Eva went behind the curtain, Carl pushed me into the line for tickets.

"I haven't got enough money, Carl," I told him.

"I got it," he said. "Don't worry about a thing."

Well, I couldn't help worrying, and not just about the money. I checked the crowd again and thought for a second that I saw a neighbor, but it wasn't him. Just the whole idea of going into the tent scared me. It turned out that I had nothing to worry about. We got refused.

"You kids get out of here, but come back in a few years," the oily-haired roustabout said, laughing with the man behind us in the line. "Eva will still be here."

I was actually relieved, but Carl wasn't about to give up that easily.

"Come on," he said, grabbing my arm.

We hid out behind some barrels on the backside of the tent. Carl never made a move until he heard cheers coming from inside the tent as the music started up.

"Here," he said, holding his coat out to me. "Put it over my head so they won't see any light."

Carl lay face down in the dirt until I put the coat over the back of his head, then he squirmed forward until he was under the canvas and partway inside. By that time, the music had gotten really loud and I could hear Eva's little cymbals clanging away. I kept on looking around, just praying that we wouldn't get caught.

All of the sudden, Carl pushed back and jumped to his feet, grabbing for his coat.

"Run," he said. "The guy's coming after us."

We took off like scared rabbits, but half-blinded, Carl tripped over a coil of rope. For a second, he just knelt there, while his eyes adjusted to the light.

"You wouldn't believe what I seen, Frank," he said, then we were off running again toward our bikes, with the greasy-haired guy in hot pursuit. I never saw him, but I could hear him yelling behind us.

I didn't believe what Carl told me, not even after he'd repeated it a hundred times on the ride home. For a week afterwards, I lived in mortal fear that someone had seen us and would tell my parents. Carl just kept telling me about Eva, and what he'd seen her do.

BY THE TIME ERNIE FINALLY MADE HIS sweet time over to my side of the river, I was so lost in these erotic thoughts and old memories that he had to call me twice.

"Frank, you want a ride over or not?"

"Sorry, Ernie," I said, blushing over getting caught like that. "I guess that I was off daydreaming somewhere else." *That's for sure*, I thought. There I was, trapped half-in and half-out of Little Eva's tent.

"Where you headed?" Ernie asked.

"The library."

"You seem to be making a habit of it. I would of thought you'd have enough of those places to last you a lifetime."

"Guess not."

"The bazaar was really nice, Frank," he said quietly.

"Yes, it was."

I kept waiting for Ernie to say something more, to butt in and give me his two cents worth, but he never did. Not a word about my and Sarah's being a nice looking couple, nothing like that at all. For just a second I remembered how much Little Eva's costume had looked like the one Sarah wore the night before to the bazaar, royal blue with silver sequins. I quickly shook off shameful thoughts like that and went back to watching Ernie. *You dirty old man*, I thought—about myself, not about Ernie who still hadn't said anything more. Matter of fact, he was acting pretty moody. After watching Ernie's back for another few seconds while he poled, I just couldn't keep myself from asking.

"The new bridge would put you out of business, wouldn't it, Ernie?"

He just nodded his head, then slowed his poling for a second or two, before turning to face me.

"It's funny, you know?" he said. "I started doing this temporarily, after the mill closed, just to have something to do, but I'd hate to give it up. It's not like I have benefits or anything—retirement or a health package—but I manage."

He just looked at me, sad-like, you know, the way a cocker spaniel can get, then kind of shook himself, turned around and poled me the rest of the way. Good Lord, what did I really know about anything? I'd always looked at Ernie as being one step up from retarded. I mean, what grown man would settle for running a one-boat ferry company? Yet here he was talking about not having retirement benefits and health care, all the time providing a service I depended upon.

"Thanks, Ernie," I said when I got out of his boat and handed him the dollar. "Thanks a lot."

"Sure, Frank. That's what I'm here for."

WHEN I GOT TO THE LIBRARY, I really had to think about what I was doing there, why I'd come in the first place. This time I couldn't blame it on Little Eva's distracting me. Talking to Ernie had thrown me for a loop. I'd really hate to see him shut down his operation. I finally remembered about the Latin

I wanted to translate, but the library wasn't much help at first because I couldn't find a Latin-English dictionary. I guess that Latin really is a dead language, now, when even the church has gone to using English in the mass. The last couple of years of my teaching, our high school dropped Latin as an elective. When I was a student in high school, it had been a requirement. Latin and German, both.

When I finally did locate the right dictionary, the best I could come up with was *laetor, laetari* meaning "to rejoice." The endings threw me for a minute. What conjugation was *-or* and *-ari*, I wondered. All I could remember of my Latin anymore was the standard *amo, amas, amat* or *amo, amare, amavi, amaunt*. "I love, you love, he (she or it) loves." I suppose that could come in handy if you were making out with a Latin-speaking woman, but there haven't been many of them around here lately.

After seventy years, my head is filled with such useless information. Literally tons and tons of it. Iambic pentameter, Spenserian stanzas, heroic couplets—I had taught all that stuff to class after class of high school students. So what? Suddenly, I didn't feel much like rejoicing.

THAT EVENING, THE CITY COUNCIL met to discuss the new bridge. All the past week, people had been stopping me on the street to see if I were going, especially my former students. It looked like a fifty-fifty split to me. People in favor of the bridge said it would unite us again, just like the old days. If you wanted a haircut at Adolph's, all you'd do is walk across the bridge, instead of having to drive all the way around. And there would be more jobs because we'd pick up some of the tourist trade. Those opposed to the bridge said it was too damned expensive—"Have you seen the preliminary estimates?" they asked. We didn't need anything that would bring more people into the valley, jobs or no jobs. They wanted to keep Happy Valley just the way it was.

There was a mob in the council chambers, bigger than anything I could remember. Thank heavens, I'd gotten there early enough to get a seat, but I supposed that one or more of my former students would've gotten up and given me their seat, anyway, out of respect for the elderly and decrepid. It's not so bad getting old, until everyone starts treating you like you're old and decrepit, then it's hell.

"Order in the room, please. Order in the room," the President of the Council hollered out as he banged the gavel, sitting way up high, as if he were the judge. Rick Gerhart was another former student of mine. It made me proud to see him up there as a community leader. Next to the chairman sat Carl's son, James, called Big Jim now. He'd moved back to the valley years ago, while Carl's folks were still alive. Jim had lived with his grandparents for a while and found that he liked it here and stayed. I have to admit he is a good-looking man, tall and handsome, like his dad. Cuts a nice figure in that suit and tie.

The meeting came to order. Old business, then committee reports, and finally on to what everyone was here for—new business.

"The floor is now open for discussion of the proposed bridge."

Back and forth it went, both pro's and con's. Gradually the discussion turned into a debate, then into an argument, then a full-blown tempest in a teapot. Accusations were flying back and forth with such rapidity that I was getting confused by it all. Some of the details that stuck with me were surprising. A four-lane bridge, someone had said. Now why, I asked myself, would we ever need *four* lanes to get from the west side of Himmelberg over to the east side? Something was going on here that was much bigger than met the eye.

Jonathan Greenbaum asked to be recognized, except that he is Jonathan Green now. The audience quieted down when he stepped to the podium. Apparently many people in the room recognized him, not from the old days, but from his work on behalf of the opposition.

"Thank you, Mr. Chairman. Let me repeat what has already been said or implied before. Something is very, very wrong here. Why is the council in such a rush to push through on the bridge? And why will Happy Valley *ever* need a four-lane road across this bridge? Please, either give us an explanation or forget the idea."

I saw lots of heads nodding around the room, but before the chair could recognize another speaker, one of the local hotheads, Cleve Gruber, was on his feet.

"No New York ... lawyer is going to come in here and tell us how to run our valley," he shouted out. Cleve paused just before he said *lawyer*. I think almost said *Jew lawyer*, but he didn't need to because someone in the back said it for him. Even though the slur didn't come over the microphone, I heard it clearly.

Cleve's sentiments were met with a chorus of loud cheers and the banging of the gavel. In spite of my shock, I didn't follow much of what happened after that because I started watching Jonathan. He sat down again, with hardly a glance at Cleve, in spite of what had just been said. There was such control in Jonathan's face that I could think of nothing but the term *poker face*. He showed no emotion at all. His eyes were alert, but they were not on fire with anger. He followed the rest of the debate with interest, but his hands weren't shaking nor did a vein in his forehead stand out from pounding. In fact, I felt a hundred times more upset than Jonathan seemed to be because he wasn't showing anything at all.

Miriam was a different story, altogether, as she sat next to Jonathan. She was smoldering mad. I was struck by a vision of her, dressed in khaki, with a smoking Uzi in her hands as she mowed down Cleve Gruber and all his henchmen.

Before I knew what I was doing, I was on my feet with my hand up, waving to be recognized.

"The chair recognizes Frank Hessel."

What in the world—I asked myself—*are you doing now?* As I walked toward the podium, I recognized several former students watching me, their jaws hanging open in surprise. Well, they couldn't be any more shocked than I was. Politics had never been my thing before this. Surprisingly, the audience got deathly silent when I reached the front of the room. Respect for the aged?

"Thank you, Mr. Chairman," I began. "First, let me give all of you a little homework —"

This was met with a titter of laughter from the audience. Someone in the back called out, "You tell them, teach." It even felt like I was back in the classroom again.

"Sixty years ago," I continued, "we went through something just like this. Before the war, speculators came in here promising to turn this valley into a big-time resort by bringing in a new rail line. We were all going to get rich, or so they said. Well, it never happened ... obviously."

More laughter from the audience.

"Can you get to the point, Mr. Hessel," the chairman asked, his hostility barely held in check by some habitual respect for a former teacher.

"Just this," I suggested. "Instead of jumping into this thing, why don't we do some checking on who owns the land around this bridge site. Who stands to get rich? Who's trying to push this idea through the Council? Finally, what is it really going to do to the valley? Doesn't a four-lane bridge suggest a four-lane highway? Speaking just for myself, I don't want to look out my front window and see a freeway at the bottom of the hill."

As I turned and walked away, several people clapped, but some others booed and hissed. Behind me, I heard Jim Markdoffer start up.

"That's just what I mean! That's an example of the old-fashioned attitudes that are holding us back from our rightful place in this state."

I had my answer, now. I was pretty darned certain that I knew who owned the land around that bridge site. As I sat down, I wondered if Carl would tell me the truth about it, assuming he even knew, of course. Good Lord, maybe he was in on it. The sins of the fathers visited upon the sons and on to their sons. God help us all.

THOSE HATEFUL, ANTISEMITIC words used in the Council Chambers stayed with me for days after that. I thought I knew Cleve Gruber pretty well, not really close, but well enough to think that he wouldn't entertain such thoughts as those he'd almost voiced about Jonathan, but what real experience had I ever had with racial or ethnic prejudice? Long about twenty years ago, during the usual Oktoberfest celebration, we had the only such incident I could remember, one which sparked a lot of community discussion.

In the evenings, the band would play and people would sing along to some of the old standard tunes. The real traditional stuff—the German songs, I mean—always finishing up with *Deutschland, Deutschland, uber alles*. Hell, most of us have been singing that song all our lives, and never thought a thing about it. All dressed up in leiderhosen and suspendered shorts, we really did feel German for a night or two. Mostly it was a way to honor our heritage, remembering the grandparents, or those even further back, who were the first to come across the Atlantic to this country. Singing that song doesn't make us any less American, just less lonely in this huge country.

Right in the middle of the sing-along on *Deutschland, Deutschland*, that one year I'm thinking of, a woman stood up, in shock, obviously, now that I look back on it.

"This is disgusting," she said. "Come on, George, we're leaving."

She wasn't any too quiet about taking her departure, especially since her husband seemed to be enjoying the beer and wanted to stay. I didn't hear too much of their conversation, but I did manage to catch her last comment. So did everyone in the room.

"Fucking, god-dammed Nazis," is what she said, much to everyone's shock.

Heck, everyone knows this isn't a Hitler song, it's one that goes back eons before him. I don't even know if the woman was Jewish or not, but she did take the song as offensive.

You can bet we spent the next few days talking about the incident. It'd come out of left field for most of us—we'd never even considered there was anything offensive in the words. Later that week, my father told me the valley had gone through some similar experiences following World War I, experiences which involved prejudice against Germans, things like delivery drivers from outside the valley making dirty comments and the like, but that stuff was a thing of the past during the next war. I mean no one set up any camps for German Americans the way they did for the Japanese. In fact, several young men from the valley were at the Battle of Bulge, German surnames and all. We have a plaque up in City Hall, honoring the boys who died in the war.

Anyhow, the next week our local paper ran an editorial about the incident, how the lady was just plain overreacting to something she didn't understand. The piece pretty much made everyone feel better, except for a letter to the editor that was printed in the same edition. It was anonymous, in a way, I mean it was signed: A Holocaust Survivor. The letter blasted the valley, Germans in general, and anyone who tried to forget what Hitler had done. I don't know if the same lady wrote the letter, nor did Tom Schrike, the editor of the paper. He said it just arrived in the mail with a Philadelphia post mark. I give Tom credit for printing that letter. He has always been dedicated to the highest principles of journalism.

That letter did get everyone's attention for a while, but it didn't last very long. I did a unit on prejudice in my high school English classes and tried to tie it into the incident at the

Oktoberfest, but that was mostly it. For the next couple of years, I thought about the woman whenever we hit the sing-along portion of our celebrations, but eventually she faded from my memory. Now that Jonathan was back in town, the memory returned, as well. I started to wonder if the woman would have been forgotten so readily had she lived here, in the valley, or if any other Jewish person did. By now, we've all read about modern Germany after the war, where some people just want to forget it all, to put the war behind them, but how others have demanded that Auschwitz and the other camps be kept as museums, as reminders, so that we don't repeat such an atrocity.

All I know for sure is that every October we still sing *Deutschland, Deutschland, uber alles* from the bottom of our hearts. I do feel better knowing that Jonathan is back living here. No telling yet whether his presence will change the festival, or not, but it will be harder to forget, that's for sure, at least for me. I hope that woman is doing well, if she's still alive. I'd just like to assure her that there aren't any Nazis in Happy Valley. Not a one.

EVER SINCE THAT DINNER with Sarah, last week, at her place, followed by the bazaar, I've been thinking about our lives together. Not that we are really "together," except for one night a week, but we could be together, if it hadn't been for Hannah, her mother, and if it weren't for this leukemia I've got now. At one point, after my diagnosis, I was going to sit down with Sarah and tell her about my disease, not to get any pity from it, but just to see if she wanted to continue dating me or not. Well, I never could bring myself to tell her about it, so I chose to do nothing instead. We continued going out on Fridays, just like everything was fine. As time went on, I thought about breaking off with Sarah, so she'd have a chance to meet someone else while she was still young enough. As you already know, I even made a Lenten resolution to do so, but I haven't done it, yet. Mostly, I'm just procrastinating.

Wednesday afternoon, I took a chance and stopped by the doctor's office. I know that's supposed to be golf day for all MD's, but the nearest golf course to Happy Valley is an hour's drive away. John Gunther was in his office, wrapping up some paperwork when I got there.

"Anything wrong, Frank?" he asked, looking concerned. "It's only been a week since you were here."

"No, I'm fine, John. Just a couple of questions."

"Fire away."

"How much time have I got left?" Might as well get down to the meat and potatoes right away, I thought.

"Frank, I've told you before—there's no way to tell. You're in remission. Some people stay like that for years, decades even. You're not getting depressed about it, are you? Or worried?"

"No, nothing like that, honest. I was down for a little while, but I'm doing much better, now. I just needed to know. What about traveling."

"It would be good for you. By all means."

"Could I go to Europe?"

"Sure, why not?"

"I thought maybe not because of all the medicines I have to take."

"Don't worry about that. I'll prescribe enough to get you through the trip. If you get to feeling run down, just see a doctor over there. I could give you some names."

"Can I do anything I want?"

"Sure, within reason. Don't run up and down every hill you see, or try to overdo things, but otherwise you can do things the way you always have."

"What about sex?" I asked.

"Sex?" he repeated, looking surprised. I could see from his reaction just what he was thinking—Is this old coot going to Europe just so he can have lots of sex, Continental style? I will give John credit for the rest of my life. Read that last sentence again—you can sure take it two different ways, both of them true. He could've started laughing, the way I'd leaped into the new subject, but he never did. John treated it very seriously, waiting for me to continue. If he had laughed, I might have walked out and never gotten to what I really wanted to know.

"The two aren't related," I said aloud. *Not yet, anyway*, I thought to myself. "Actually, I've been thinking of asking Sarah Bruene to marry me," I told him. *Good Lord*, I thought, until I said it aloud, I hadn't even admitted it to myself. That was *exactly* what I wanted to do, what I should have done a long time ago.

"Good, Frank," John said, just nodding. "By all means. You have nothing to worry about, I mean nothing more than what is already going on. You can live for a long time in remission. I could even die before you. Travel or marriage won't speed up the cancer or make it kill you faster. Is that what you were worried about?"

"More or less. That pretty much covers it."

"Does Sarah know about the leukemia?"

"No, not yet."

"Would you like me to explain it to her?" John asked.

The idea had never occurred to me. First, that he would do such a thing for me. Second, that I wouldn't tell her myself. The idea had merit, however—because Sarah was bound to have questions. It was only fair that she knew everything she could before making up her mind.

"Thanks, John," I said. "Maybe after I tell her, if she has any questions, well, she and I could come in."

"Just let me know, Frank. I'll be glad to help."

WELL, HERE I AM, making plans for the future when I don't even know if I'm going to have one. In the meanwhile, the whole valley is going nuts over this bridge thing. Speeches every evening, rallies with bands and lots of noise—all the typical things that get the blood rushing to your heart and head, if not down to the balls of your feet, tapping away to the beat of the bass drum. Pretty exciting stuff, except I'd seen way too much of it in the past to get all worked up again. In fact, once I started thinking seriously about Sarah, I was pretty much ready to swing over to the other side of the vote. The bridge would be nice for our getting back and forth on foot. She will keep her car, I'm sure, but a quick walk beats the long drive all the way around. Still, I will have to admit that I've been doing pretty well with Ernie's Ferry Service, lately.

Now I'm going around in circles again when just a minute ago I was patting myself on the back for staying so cool in the midst of the turmoil. Just like a cucumber, cool and collected, when all about me, people are losing their heads. Here I am, calmly planning out a new life for us—me and Sarah—when I haven't even talked to her about my illness or asked her to marry me. *First things first*, I told myself, on the way out the door to do a little shopping for the week. The General Store would be good enough. I didn't need much.

Well, I heard the noise, even before I turned the corner, and sensed the excitement in the air. Standing in the back of a pickup truck was Carl's son, Jim Markdoffer, a big megaphone in his hand, his shirt sleeves rolled up, as he tried to look like one of the working folk. Obviously, this was some pro-bridge rally.

"— to quote from our beloved President Kennedy," he was saying, "Ich bin ein Himmelbergerer!" Everyone cheered, once they put it all together, so he waited, then repeated the words before continuing with the speech, "Ich bin ein Himmelbergerer—eins Himmelberg, one Himmelberg, again." More applause from the twenty or thirty people watching. "That's what the bridge will do for us again—we'll be reunited into the one city we've always been."

Not five minutes before, I'd been ready to vote for the bridge, but now, having witnessed this spectacle, I'll be darned before I'll do so. How dare that pompous jackass use the words of President Kennedy to promote his own political views? Second only to my admiration for FDR is my admiration for JFK. Who knows what he might've gotten done for this country had he lived. I wasn't absolutely certain, but I'd bet money that Jim Markdoffer is a Republican. Look at his father! Carl hates Democrats. Why would his son be any different? Jim never has come out for any single party, though, preferring to straddle the fence. I'll just bet he's really a full-blown Republican, though. He has that look of one. Do you know what I mean?

Kennedy had said, "Today, I am a Berliner," because he was the first American president to set foot on German soil since before the war. It was a great moment, especially great for us in the valley. It restored our faith in ourselves, our being of German descent and all. I loved Kennedy for that speech. Now Jim Markdoffer had stolen Kennedy's words, subverted their meaning just so he could make a few bucks profit on the land he's been buying up around the bridge site. You can just bet on it—he's a Republican, through and through.

BY FRIDAY NIGHT, I'd pretty much calmed down, though the mere mention of the bridge could still get me excited. During the afternoon, as I watched the hands of the clock moving closer and closer to my date with Sarah, I started getting more and more nervous. How would she take it? What would she say? By five o'clock, I was a wreck. I'd looked out my front window a hundred times, trying to spot her car coming around the corner. Where was she?

About ten minutes after five, the phone rang, the very sound just about sending me through the roof.

"Hello," I said.

"Frank, it's Sarah. I'm sorry to be late, but my car wouldn't start. I'm here in the gas station now. It won't be ready until sometime tomorrow. Could you meet me at the ferry? We could walk to the restaurant from there and still be on time for the movies?"

"Sure thing," I said. "I'll head out now."

Well, everything had gone to heck in handcart, or, as it turns out, in Sarah's Dodge sedan. I had planned on talking with her at my house, where we'd have some privacy, but now that was out of the question.

I GOT TO THE RIVER, while Sarah and Ernie were still on their way over. They were laughing and carrying on like they were the best of friends. Until last week, I didn't even know that Sarah knew Ernie. What in the world did the two of them have in common? Well, the church for one thing. If Ernie had been at the bazaar, then he obviously went to her church, too. I couldn't help but feel a little bit jealous, seeing her that happy with another man, even if that man were Ernie.

"Hi, Frank," she said, waving, and then, when they'd touched down, she thanked Ernie and tried to give him a dollar.

"Not this time, Sarah. It's on the house," he said, though she tried to insist. "See you in church on Sunday. Evening, Frank," he said, before heading back to the other side, then stopped himself part-way. "What time do you want me to pick you up?"

"What do you think, Frank?" she asked me.

"Well, the movie's usually over by ten. Maybe ten-fifteen or so?" I said without thinking it through.

"I'll be here," Ernie said, pushing off. "See you then."

Everything was going to pot, now. Not only couldn't we talk before dinner, but now we wouldn't have time to talk after the movies. Talk about your being frustrated—I was it. On top of everything else, I'd just learned for sure that Ernie and Sarah were actually friends. I hadn't even know that much, before.

WHILE WE WALKED TO LUIGI'S, Sarah ran down the problems with the car. It looked like it was the battery, but Lou was going to check out the generator, too. She could pick it up in the morning.

"Why haven't you taken the ferry before?" I asked her.

"I don't know," she answered, "I like Ernie well enough, but a dollar a trip seems a little extravagant."

"You probably spend that much in gas just driving around," I explained, trying to make it sound helpful, though I thought it came out pretty bitter, even condescending.

"Really?" she said. "I didn't know that. Well, if it does then I might start riding with Ernie. No reason not to."

"You know Ernie from your church?"

"Sure," she said. "For years and years. He's a nice guy. I really should support his ferry service, I guess. It sure helps *you* get around."

That was the last thing I needed to hear—how Ernie Warden was doing me any favors. For sure this evening was not going the way I'd planned. Not one single, little bit of it.

HALFWAY THROUGH OUR DINNER, trying to hold up the whole conversation by herself, Sarah asked me something outright.

"What's wrong, Frank?"

"What do you mean?" was my answer, like she couldn't tell I was grumpy as a bear.

"You've hardly said a word all meal long."

"Well, I was hoping we'd get a chance to talk."

"So talk —" she said, encouraging me.

"Not here," I said, "I meant someplace private."

"We could walk back to your house, if you like," she said.

"What about the movies?"

"We can skip the movies one night, Frank. I don't even remember what's playing, for sure."

"Okay," I said. "Let's go back to my place."

I was so eager to get back home with her, that I had the waitress package up our dessert. Sarah just smiled, trying to figure out what I was up to. Heck, I was so nervous on the walk back that I dropped the dessert twice.

ONCE SARAH WAS SITTING on the couch, and comfortable, my mouth went dry. I didn't know what to say because all my rehearsals had been based on a different scenario. She just looked at me, curious for me to begin.

"Sarah," I said, "well ... how've you been?"

"Just fine, Frank. I enjoyed the dinner and our walk back here. I like your house. Pretty good, really."

Now I could tell she was just joking with me, teasing me to see if she could get a reaction. No way was I going to play into her hands like that.

"Good," I said, "that's good."

We just sat there for a minute, looking at each other, me with my tongue sticking to the top of my mouth, Sarah with her head cocked a little to the side looking quizzical, uncertain of what I was driving at.

"Would you like some coffee?" I asked.

"No, thanks," Frank. "You've already asked me that, and I'm still full from dinner."

"Well, Sarah," I said when I finally got started. "We've known each other for a long time now ..."

I kind of let that hang out there for a minute, checking for a reaction. Her smile disappeared for a second, then reappeared, joined with a glow in her eyes and on her cheeks. I don't know any other way to explain it. Like she was glowing from within, somehow. She looked beautiful.

"That's true, Frank," she said, still smiling softly. "We've been friends for a long time, now."

Good Lord, it finally dawned on me that she thought I was going to propose to her. Well, of course, that *is* what I was planning on doing, but not until I talked to her about the other stuff first.

"Wait a minute, Sarah," I jumped in. "I've got to tell you something first."

"First?" she asked, smiling again, coy like.

Oh my, how could I be screwing up this thing so badly? All

I had to do was tell her something first, then ask her something. How difficult is that? First A, then B, but oh, no, I had to jump into B before A, getting her hopes up, only to dash them into the dirt. You jackass, I told myself.

Talk about your everyday idiots! Did you catch that in the previous paragraph? I never did see what I'd written until the revisions. You might as well see me as I am, though, so I'll leave it as is. "Getting her hopes up," is the part I mean, like I was doing her a favor by asking her to marry me, like I was a knight in shining armor come to rescue her from a dull, boring life without me, or like I was some prize package. Blame it on my nerves—after all, it'd been forty-plus years since I'd proposed to someone.

"Sarah, I just have to tell you something."

"Go ahead, Frank," she said, after a pause, when she saw that I wasn't going ahead on my own.

"Do you remember last year, when I was gone for a couple of weeks?"

"When you went to Canada?" she asked.

"Yes, except I didn't go to Canada. I went into a hospital for treatment."

"Treatment?" she said, looking real serious all of the sudden, just as I'd been afraid she would. "What's wrong, Frank?"

"I have leukemia, Sarah," I told her, as I sat there with my hands folded in front of me.

"Oh, no," she said, leaning forward and reaching across the coffee table to take my hands in hers. "How bad is it? I mean what have the doctors told you?"

"It's in remission, now. Has been since last year, for that matter."

"What does it mean for the future?" she asked. "Will you get sick again ... soon?"

"There's no way to tell, really. Dr. Gunther—you know him don't you, John Gunther?—well, he says that I could go on like this for years with no change, or I could get sick again tomorrow," I said as I shrugged, trying to set her at ease, but I could see that I wasn't doing a very good job of it.

"But you're feeling all right now?" she asked.

"Yes, I'm feeling fine—great, in fact. All I have to do is take a series of pills every six weeks, and that's it."

"Thank God," she said, starting to cry a little. "I was afraid you were trying to tell me that you could die tomorrow." She let my hands go while she started searching through her purse for a kleenex.

"Here," I said, jumping up and running into the kitchen for a couple of paper napkins.

"Thanks," she said, wiping her eyes. "I just couldn't face losing you, right on top of losing my mother."

Well, I didn't much like being lumped in the same category with her mother, Hannah—God rest her miserable soul—but I could understand that Sarah had loved her, which meant that she might just love me, if only a little.

"Will you marry me, Sarah?"

Once again, I'd jumped right into it, feet first. No sense giving her time to digest what I'd just told her, or for me to get down on one knee and do it right. Good going, Frank! Tell the woman you're dying then ask her to marry you.

"Oh, Frank, you big jackass," she said, telling me the same thing I'd been telling myself. Then she was crying again, this time for real, so I jumped up and got some more napkins, plus a couple of paper towels, just in case.

"Here, Sarah, use these," I said, holding them out to her.

"Sit down, Frank. Here, next to me," she said, taking the paper goods but just putting them on the coffee table. Well, I did sit down, not knowing if she were going to punch me or kiss me. "Hold me, Frank. Please?" she asked.

Feeling awkward as all get out, I put my arms around her as she cried into my shoulder. It didn't last too long, to my relief. I've never known what to do with a crying woman—it bothers the bejeeber's out of me, always has. She slowed down after a minute or two, then sighed once or twice.

"Are you all right?" I asked.

"Yes, I'm better now," she said, sitting up again, but only after kissing me on the check. That kiss was just what I needed to help set me straight again. At least I knew she wasn't mad at me, or blamed me.

"Would you like some water?" I asked her.

"No, thanks. No water. It's just that I got so scared there for a minute that I was going to lose you, that's all. Stay right here next to me, where I can touch you."

For a long time, we just sat there, with her running her hand over my cheeks and forehead, touching me the way she used to do when we were younger and romantic. For once, I kept my mouth shut, waiting for her.

"Frank, I love you," she said, starting out. "I've loved you for a long time. I would've married you a long time ago, if it had worked out with my mother and all. You know that, don't you?" she asked.

"I think so, I mean I know that I love you and I would've asked you a long time ago, but—"

"You asked me now," she said, putting her fingers on my lips to shut me up, "and I'll never forget it."

I could hear the B-U-T hanging in the air as she said that. Yes, but. If only, but. Earlier, maybe, but ... She was going to turn me down cold. I couldn't stand for that to happen.

"Sarah, John said he could talk to you, to us, about everything, if you had any questions."

"That would be good," she said, nodding. "I'll need to know what to do when you ... if you get sick again."

What was going on here? I thought she was going to turn me down, but now she was talking about being there with me when I got sick. Was it yes or no?

"Sarah—" I started out once more, but again she hushed me up by putting her fingers over my lips.

"I can't give you an answer tonight, Frank. I'm too worked up and confused, but I am going to do something …" she said, looking me in the eyes.

"What?" I asked around her fingers.

"Take you to bed, like I should've been doing all along, like we should've been doing. Oh, Frank, we've wasted so much time—let's not waste another minute. All right?"

WELL, THAT'S ALL YOU NEED to know about that. Sarah and I went to bed and stayed there the whole night. You don't need to hear any of the details, but I will tell you what happened about ten o'clock.

"Oh, Frank—" Sarah exclaimed, sitting bolt upright in bed. "What about Ernie?"

"What about him?"

"He's coming for me in fifteen minutes."

"Oh, God. What do you want to do?" I asked her.

"I want to stay the night, Frank. It would be the first time we ever had a whole night together."

"I want you to stay, too," I said.

"Someone has to tell Ernie," she said, looking my way.

"Who, me?" I asked.

WELL, THAT WASN'T the half of it. I whipped on some clothes and zipped down the street to the ferry stop. All the way down the hill, I kept wondering what I was going to tell Ernie, how I was going to tell him. Ernie was there waiting for me, or rather he was waiting for Sarah, when I got there.

"Ernie—" I started out.

"Yeah, Frank?" he asked, looking pretty smug.

"Well, uh … Sarah isn't going back with you tonight."

"That so, Frank?"

"She's, uh … well, she's —"

"Ease up, Frank," he said, grinning like a Cheshire cat.

"I'm not going to make you squirm. One question, though—What took you so darned long?"

"None of your business, Ernie."

"That's another thing, Frank," he said, not bothered a bit by my telling him off. "I'm one of the few people around here who minds his own business, and keeps his mouth shut. You don't have to worry about me spreading it all over town. You can tell Sarah that, too. It might set her mind at ease."

"Thanks, Ernie," I said.

"No problem. You're both friends of mine. I'm just glad to see you getting together, finally."

Well, I didn't like the way he said *finally*, like he would have moved a lot faster than me, nor was I sure about his calling me a friend, but I did appreciate his promise.

"See you in the morning, Frank. Tell Sarah I'll be here anytime after eight."

"Okay, Ernie. Thanks."

Then he was gone into the night. Without any street lights in the area, it was pretty dark, all except for the junior sized lantern he kept burning on a pole for his night crossings. In the past, I'd barely been civil with Ernie, yet he treated me like a friend. Will wonders never cease?

THE NEXT MORNING I AWOKE slowly and leisurely. It was far later than I usually slept—I could tell that from the light in my bedroom. For just a minute, I had to lie there, trying to figure out what was different. Then I had it. Sarah was curled up around my back, just holding me quietly, like we'd been sleeping together that way forever. Funny, but I could swear I smelled coffee and toast.

"You awake, Frank?" she asked.

"Bright-eyed and bushy-tailed," I answered her.

"You'd better save that for later," she said, punching me in the back. "A good breakfast will give you some energy."

Like I was telling you, old Frank Hessel isn't dead yet, not by a long shot. We got up after a minute or two more of cuddling, then Sarah went off to finish cooking breakfast while I showered. She seemed to be finding everything all right, so I got myself all cleaned up and ready for a shiny new day.

WHEN I SAW THE TABLE, I couldn't help kidding her a little about going overboard on the quantities.

"Who's going to eat all this?" I asked.

"Just you and me," she answered. "I've always eaten a good breakfast, and you can probably use one this morning."

"Lots of times, I just have coffee and toast, sometimes without the toast," I said, putting some jam on my second slice already.

"Well, get used to it, Frank. Things are going to be different from now on."

"Oh, yeah?" I asked, with the piece of toast half in, half out of my mouth. "What's that supposed to mean?" I added, after I swallowed.

"You asked me to marry you last night? Remember?"

"Sure."

"Well, I'm going to hold you to it. There's no backing out now."

"But I thought ... well, what you said last night. I mean I thought you weren't sure."

"You convinced me," she said, wriggling her eyebrows like Groucho Marx. Sarah has a definite earthy quality about her, but you don't need to know any more about her than that.

"You'll marry me?" I asked, still not sure I'd heard right.

"Yes, Frank. I will marry you, and it doesn't have a thing to do with last night, or maybe just a little," she said with a grin. "I just decided that it doesn't matter if we have ten days or ten years—I want to spend them with you. Who knows? I may go before you do. You seem pretty frisky for an old man."

I got up and ran around the table—just to remind her how frisky I could be—and gave her a big hug and a kiss, jam, toast crumbs, and all. Sarah and I spent most of Saturday morning talking and making plans, but mostly just enjoying each other's company.

The way this week started out, I didn't think there would be a whole lot to "rejoice" about, but it sure turned out that way, didn't it?

Chapter Five:
   Fifth Sunday in Lent

THE JUDICA

WHAT IS THE *JUDICA*, YOU ASK? Something to do with judgment or the law, perhaps. The judge is coming, the judge is coming. Who was that? The comedian who played Geraldine? Nipsy Russell, Soupy Sales or ... yes, Flip Wilson, that's who it was. A funny routine for a serious subject. Well, this week's Lenten theme got me to thinking about Jonathan, because of his being a retired judge and law professor. Judge or not, he still has all that unfinished business about his father.

"Revenge—Jonathan told me that was his motivation in returning to Happy Valley. "An eye for an eye, and a tooth for a tooth" is the Old Testament, Hebraic idea of justice. A little too brutal for our modern sensibilities, but there were times throughout history when it sure did make sense. I still couldn't help wondering what Jonathan hoped to accomplish. Even if he should be able to balance matters, like some cosmic scoreboard in the sky, would he feel any better? Would Jonathan's search for justice make his father feel any better? His father who'd been dead and gone these many years? Was there any way for Jonathan to find peace, maybe for himself and his father, at least the memory of his father?

I've had no experience with Schizophrenia—you know, split personalities—not until it started happening to me just lately. Half of me was still thinking about Jonathan, while the other half was thinking about Sarah. Not quite a simple division between past and future because Sarah and I shared a good deal of past memories, too. I also hoped Jonathan would stay here in the valley to be a part of my, our, future. Sad and serious, coupled with happy and giddy—that's the way my mind was working during this period. Sort of like being a teenager in love. Do you remember what those days felt like? Well, believe it or not, it can happen to you as a senior citizen, too. Not that being in love is all bad, anymore than it is for the teenager, but being in love sure comes with ups and downs. Sarah and I never really talked about what we would do next. Were we keeping things a secret for a while, or telling the world?

Where's the justice in all this? My idea of old age had always been settling into a dull routine of pills and doctor's visits. To tell you the truth, the whole idea scared me. That's why I never retired until the legal limit. I didn't want them to drag me out of the classroom, screaming, but I stayed as long as I could. Well, the pills and the doctors all came true, but it hasn't been dull, not lately. Falling in love puts a different cast on everything, like that old country western song—"Rose Colored Glasses."

These were the kinds of thoughts I entertained all morning long, as I looked ahead two weeks to the hope of Easter, but with one foot still stuck in the past. As usual, I went to early mass at St. Ignatius. I knew that Sarah always went to the second service at her church, so there was no point in trying to call until the afternoon.

WHEN SUNDAY AFTERNOON finally arrived, I was so tired of my own company that I decided to give Sarah a call right away, just to see if she wanted to get together for the afternoon. We'd been limited to Friday nights for so many years, that I didn't know what to do now that we were in love, officially in love. I wanted to be with her all the time, but we each still had our separate lives, too. Oh well, we'll figure it out in due time. I picked up the phone and dialed her number.

"Hello," she answered, sweet and pleasant as always. If I could only describe that certain something in her voice ... oh well, you've been there, I'm sure. If not, I hope you get there one of these days—being in love, I mean.

"Hi, it's me," I said.

"I was just thinking about giving you a call," she said. Do you suppose there's a chance that she missed me as much as I missed her?

"If you're not busy," I said, "I was thinking about coming over. Maybe we could take a walk along the river or something?"

"Sounds good to me. How would it be if I make up a picnic lunch to take along with us?"

"I'll be there as soon as Ernie can haul me over."

ON THE WAY DOWN to the ferry, I pulled out my wallet, just to make sure I had a dollar bill for Ernie who was slowly getting rich off me lately. Oh well, what would I do without him? He deserved to be paid for his service.

As I turned down the path to the river, I saw that Ernie was on my side, already, sitting in his boat as if he were waiting for me.

"Right on time, Frank," he said looking at his watch.

"Did we have an appointment?" I asked, trying to remember if I'd arranged yesterday to have him meet me here today. I got into the boat still trying to remember.

"No, I just figured you'd be coming along about now," Ernie told me, pushing off from the shore with his pole.

"You don't even want to know where I'm going?" I asked him, remembering all the times he'd grilled me in the past, the recent past, even.

"I already know where you're going, Frank," he said. "If you've got a lick of sense, that is."

How did Ernie and I suddenly get to be buddies, where he could talk to me like that? When did we get all friendly and intimate? I wondered these things to myself, remembering, of course, that he did have some information I didn't want him blabbing around. No sense in the whole valley getting into our business. I watched Ernie's back as he poled us across the river, and I remembered what he said about keeping his mouth shut. For some reason I believed him. Ernie was an honorable man, someone I could trust. Why hadn't we become friends before now? I'd know him for a long time, but we never seemed to have one single thing in common. Maybe the truth is that I'm a snob. Is that possible?

After Ernie had let me out, I handed him a dollar and said my thank you's.

"Your welcome, Frank," he said.

"Ernie," I just blurted out, "Sarah and I are going to get married." Instantly, I asked myself why I'd said that?

"I'm glad, Frank," he said, holding out his hand for me to shake. "Really glad."

"Thanks, I appreciate it, Ernie."

"Have you told anyone, yet?" he asked.

"No, we're going to make some plans this afternoon," I told him.

"Well, I'll keep it under my hat until you announce it, then," he said, reaching up to tip that fisherman's cap loaded with gold braid.

SARAH AND I HAD A great time on our picnic. We just walked down the river until we found a quiet, open spot where we could watch the water from the blanket.

Now that we were committed, we needed to make some plans—like when would we get married and where? Her church or mine? For Catholics that's a little more of a problem than for Protestants, but that's mostly because of the question about children, in which church they'd be raised and all. Sarah and I were a little beyond that problem, but I could tell she would be disappointed if the wedding wasn't in her church. I could sense it because I'd feel the same way. What were we going to do?

Sarah and I talked about dates. We agreed that the sooner the better, within reason. We had to let our families know first and do some of the basic things. We mentioned our two churches, but by mutual agreement we backed off to give ourselves some time to think it out.

We'd only been in love for two days, and already we'd run right into an obstacle, face first.

What have we been doing for the past ten years, I asked myself, *if we've only been in love for two days?* I just knew you were dying to ask me that very question, so I did it for you. Here comes the answer, just speaking for myself, of course, though I think Sarah would agree. I've loved Sarah for a long time. Shoot, I even told you that we used to sleep together back at the start. I loved her then and have ever since, but I couldn't be "in love" with her because I could see no future in our relationship, not while her mother was alive. It was a matter of duty to family. I understood that, and even went along with it. Had the situation been reversed, we would still have done the same thing. Then after Hannah died, we couldn't have a future because of my illness, at least that's the way I saw our situation.

Love between a man and woman is based on a life shared, a hope for the future, making plans. Sarah and I are doing that now—sharing and planning—all because we're "in love." Last week, before I proposed to her, we loved each other, but the only life we had together was a date every Friday night, the type of thing two old friends could do together. The difference is like night and day.

We walked back to her house, holding hands.

"Do you want to stay the night?" Sarah asked me.

"What about your neighbors?" I asked her back. "Are you sure you want to take a chance on them?"

"I'm taking a chance on you, aren't I?" she said, smiling at me. That's one of the things I like about Sarah—her sense of humor.

THE NEXT MORNING Sarah drove me back to my place. She had some errands on my side of the river anyway. When we turned the corner onto River Road, I thought about ducking down in my seat so Ernie wouldn't see me and know that I'd stayed the night with Sarah, but it dawned on me that Ernie could figure that out for himself since he had brought me over to this side of the river in the first place, though he'd never taken me back. There was no point in trying to fool Ernie, anyway, since he'd already figured it out last Friday night, and I'd told him outright on the boat. Guess we'll just have to hope he can keep his mouth shut like he promised.

We had a nice leisurely drive through the valley, up to the bridge on the north side. We haven't had much rain this spring, not enough to start flooding, but just enough for things to be green and fresh. Funny that I'd just barely noticed before that morning that we were full-blast into spring. Sarah's a good driver, so mostly I relaxed and only twice had to fight off the urge to reach for the steering wheel. Nothing to do with her, it's just me—I've always felt that a man should drive. It's a little late for that now. Not only did I give up my car, but I never bothered renewing my driver's license. Like I was going to pass the vision test, anyway.

When Sarah turned onto my street, I started worrying about my neighbors and what they'd think seeing me come home early in the morning, chauffeured by a lady. I even thought of having Sarah drop me off on the corner and letting me walk from there, but I decided that was a pretty stupid way for a grown man to be behaving. We'll just let my neighbors chew on their suspicions for a while, for all I care. All except for Ed Shrader, of course. I really didn't want him starting in on me about this thing with Sarah. Oh well, if he sees me, he sees me. Maybe he'll choke on a piece of bacon over it.

Sarah pulled up into my driveway and leaned over like she was expecting a kiss, right there by Ed's window. Oh well, what's a man supposed to do? Sarah finds me irresistible, and that's the way it goes.

"Thanks for the lift, Sarah," I said, smooching her. "And the picnic and everything."

"My pleasure," Frank she said, mussing my hair. I could just see Ed going nuts over that. "Guess I won't be seeing you for a few days. I wish that I didn't have to go now." She was talking about the trip she'd planned to visit her sister.

"You'll have a nice visit," I said. "Say hello to Fran for me, and it's okay if you want to tell her about us, you know?"

"She's my only sister, so I'll want her to come in for the wedding anyway." Sarah kissed me again. "I'll miss you."

"Me, too."

I got out of the car and waved goodby to her as she backed out of my driveway and headed down toward the river. When I turned toward my front door, I would swear I saw Ed Shrader's curtains swing closed—Mr. Nosy himself, keeping track of my every move.

THAT AFTERNOON, I STOPPED BY the cemetery. I'd been thinking about Jonathan's father's being buried who-knows-where and thought I might check out an idea or two. The cemetery's only a six-block walk from my house, up around the hill. Pretty convenient, don't you think? That's just my morbid sense of humor acting up. When I got there, I didn't see anyone around outside, so I walked into the offices. Ron Ludeke had been the valley's mortician for years, with his facilities located right here at the cemetery. He and his family had been in this business for four generations, but he was mostly retired now.

Behind the huge, polished mahogany desk was his youngest boy, Mitchell, who waved at me, pointing to the phone in his hand to indicate he'd be with me in a minute. You would have to see Mitch to understand the effect he had on people. Even as a teenager, he'd been so darned good looking, you'd think he was a movie star. Medium height with a natural tan glow to his skin. His hair always seemed just freshly trimmed, even as a little tyke. Gentle brown eyes. Most people couldn't understand why he'd stayed in the valley, especially why he'd been content to stay in the family business of selling grave sites and working on stiffs.

"Hello, Mr. Hessel," he said, soon as he'd hung up the phone. "What can I do for you?" Almost instantly the phone rang again.

"Go ahead, Mitch. I'm not in any hurry."

"Thanks, I'll make it quick," he promised.

Somehow I'd never bothered to correct Mitch's calling me Mr. Hessel. Just about every one of my former students called me Frank after a while. If they didn't do it on their own, then by the time they were thirty or so, I insisted. But the only time I ever saw Mitchell was at church and funerals, so I let the formality stand. Besides which, he would be doing the honors on my mortal remains one of these days. It was hard to be chummy with him on that basis.

I walked around the waiting room looking at the stuff on the walls. Mitch's father, grandfather and great-grandfather's pictures were hanging there. That's the way things are here in the valley—lots of tradition. I'd never known his great-grandfather, but I'd seen the picture many times. All the furniture in the room was muted, both in color and in the polish used on the dark woods. Quiet and padded, comfortable. In harmony with the name of the business: The Ludeke Family Funeral Parlor. How else to furnish a parlor but in muted tones and with overstuffed, comfortable furniture? Just like the parlor at home. Standing there looking around, I wondered how many of my friends had passed through this room—upright or horizontal?

"Sorry, Mr. Hessel," Mitch said from behind me. "The

phone just won't stop ringing today." The carpet's so darned plush, I hadn't heard his walking over.

"Business must be good," I answered in a feeble attempt at a joke as I turned to face him. Ever notice how jokes always go flat in a mortuary? Horizontal?

"What can I do for you?" he asked.

"Mitch, do we have a Jewish section in the cemetery?"

"Yes sir, a small one, but it's got a very nice view of the valley. Do you need a plot?"

It tickled me the way Mitch said that, the way he reacted or rather didn't react—nary a ripple. He'd known me all his life, gone to the same church even, and accepted my question about a Jewish plot as if it were the most natural thing in the world. His father had taught him well. Max himself was the model of discretion and composure, no matter what was going on around him or who was dying.

"Not for myself," I said, hoping to catch some glimmer of a reaction, maybe relief? Nope, not a single twitch. "Maybe for a friend."

"Yes, sir."

"Do you know anything about Jewish burial law?" I asked.

"Just the rudiments. We haven't handled a Jewish service since I've been here, but I believe that my father has."

"Can they rebury a body, Mitch?"

"You mean move the remains from one cemetery to another?"

"I guess so," I answered.

"It might depend on whether the deceased was Orthodox or not. I seem to recall that the departed has to be interred before sunset of the same day, so I don't know if they would allow for moving the body to another site."

"Well, I guess it might not matter anyway. All depends on if the body can even be located. There seems to be some question about finding the departed."

"Yes, sir. I could check on Jewish law for you, if you'd

like, but I would need to know the particular beliefs of the deceased."

"How about this—could a person buy a plot and erect a headstone, without there being an actual body in the grave?"

"Yes, of course, we've had several such internments, for example when the body has been lost at sea or destroyed in a plane crash, or in war, where no physical remains can be located."

"That may be an idea. Let me think on it for a few days."

"Certainly, Mr. Hessel. We'll be glad to help in any way that we can."

"Thanks, Mitch. See you later."

"Goodby, sir."

See you later—did I actually say that? Much later, I hope. Though I like Mitch well enough, conversations with morticians are not among my favorite things, filled as they are with euphemisms, like the Dearly Departed and the Recently Deceased for the dead. Whew! Was I ever glad to get out of there. No man alive can stay in a place like that for very long. Good grief! Did you see what I just wrote? Of course no man alive, no living man, would want to stay there—the whole point of the place was getting rid of the dead. With dignity and honor, to be sure, but just get rid of them, and do it quickly.

CARL AND I HAD LUNCH on Tuesday. We seem to have settled on that day because he can't stand the lunch they serve him in the Lutheran retirement home then.

"Any other day, it's halfway decent," he told me, "but macaroni and cheese, with tomato soup?"

"Sounds okay to me," I said, looking over the menu at the diner. *How many times in a row was I going to have their meatloaf? I asked myself.*

"Well, I've always been a meat and potatoes man, myself," Carl told me.

"Me, too," I told him, my choice having been decided.

"So, why don't you come over to the home for lunch tomorrow?" he asked. One of my table mates knows you. He's been asking me to invite you."

"Oh yeah, who's that?" I asked, wishing that he would stop calling it the "home," like it was for the feeble-minded.

"Lyle Beecher—says he used to teach with you at the high school?"

"Sure," I said, "I know Lyle. I just didn't know he was living over there."

Once Carl started talking about the retirement home, he just kept on talking about it. He didn't seem to like much of anything there, the food's being about the best of the worst, so to speak. From the way he talked, I thought I'd be walking into a concentration camp.

THE NEXT DAY, I headed out for Ernie's ferry in the middle of a soft rain. Nothing much to it, really not worth the mentioning. As I walked down the bank toward the river, I got to wondering what was wrong with Ernie's boat. It took me a minute to realize that the rope was down. The boat was on my side, but Ernie was sitting there on the small dock, coiling his rope round and round in circles, inspecting it as he went.

"What are you up to, Ernie?" I asked.

"Oh hi, Frank," he said. "I'm just inspecting the rope. Didn't figure that I'd have much traffic today, with the rain. I'll be ready for you in just a minute, that is if you're willing to free wheel it."

"Sure, it'll be like white-water rafting," I said, making a little joke. The river was running so slow this year that it hardly made a current.

"Now there's an idea," he said, smiling. "I could take people from one end of the valley to the other. Ernie's Guided Boat Tours, I could call it."

"Might as well think big, I suppose."

"Well, that might pay for a new rope, anyway."

Ernie tied the rope to the tree, just like usual, then put the coiled up remainder in the skiff. He held the boat still until I got in and sat down.

"The rope looks okay to me," I said, inspecting the coils as they lay at my feet.

"It'll last for a while, but I should've bought the one Milt Hitchcock suggested. Thought I'd get away with the cheaper grade."

Ernie poled us over, then jumped out of the boat first and tied it to the larger dock on his side of the river. He gave me a hand out, and then started to pull the rope toward the tree to which it was usually anchored.

"I'll just leave my dollar here, Ernie," I said, indicating a place on the post.

"Thanks, Frank," he said. "I clean forgot about it."

I folded the bill a couple of times the long way and stuck it between two planks where he'd be sure to see the thing. Once or twice, I'd resented paying Ernie, figuring that he was getting rich with his ferry service, but if he couldn't even afford to buy decent rope, maybe I should pay closer attention.

I HADN'T BEEN IN the Our Redeemer Retirement Home for several years. The last time was to visit one of our parishioners who decided to retire over there rather than leave the valley. A Catholic in a Lutheran home was cause for humor, but nothing malicious. After all, it was the only facility like it in the whole valley. As I walked up the front steps, I wondered to myself why it wasn't called The Happy Valley Retirement Home, so people from both sides would be welcomed. The Lutherans didn't turn anyone away on the basis of their religion, but I know that some of my Catholic friends chose alternative care, rather than move in with a bunch of Lutherans.

Carl was waiting for me in the lobby where we'd agreed to meet because his room was tough to find.

"You're late," he said in greeting me.

"Ernie was doing something with his ferry. It took a couple of extra minutes."

"Do you want the tour, or have you been here before?"

"Let's eat first, then you can show me your room. I've seen the rest of the place, though they've repainted the inside."

"Yeah, it's okay, I suppose," he said, sounding like it was of no interest to him at all.

I saw Lyle as soon as we got into the dining room. He was sitting up in a wheelchair, waving at me. He'd been the boys' physical education teacher when I was at the school. He retired several years ahead of me. He was a real athlete, but now look at him. I waved back, trying not to show what I was thinking.

We sat down and shook hands all the way around, as Lyle introduced me to a couple of people at the table that Carl didn't seem to know.

"Good to see you, Lyle."

"You, too, Frank. A friendly face in a storm."

"The salad is up here at the salad bar," Carl said, pointing behind us. "Help yourself whenever you're ready." He walked off with his plate.

"The nurse usually fixes me a plate," Lyle said, shrugging to indicate his lack of mobility.

"What do you like, Lyle?" I asked him. "I can handle that much."

"Beets and potato salad—a big scoop of each."

"You got it," I said, taking both our plates to the line.

The food looked real good, at least the salad fixings were fresh and crisp, with plenty of it. So far, I couldn't see anything to complain about, though Carl always did.

LYLE AND I HAD a nice visit, with several of the table mates joining in. The only glum person at the table was Carl, who got up right after dessert.

"I'll see you out in the lobby, Frank," he said, then turned and walked away.

"Don't worry about him too much, Frank," Lyle told me, once Carl was out of earshot. "It's takes some people longer to settle in than others. Shoot, we've got a million activities here to keep a person occupied. Carl's still young enough to enjoy all of them, if he'd just put his mind to it."

When Lyle's nurse came to push his chair, I shook hands with my friend, wished him well, and promised to come over and see him for a good visit.

On the way out to the lobby, I got to looking over some of the artwork on the walls. It was nice, very nice. In fact, the whole place was pleasant, nothing like what Carl had described to me. It was a lot cleaner and friendlier than the last time I'd visited.

Several small groups of residents had gathered in the lobby area for checkers, cards and just plain gab fests. Carl was standing by the door, all alone, just staring off into space.

"Shall we go see your room, Carl?" I said, coming up behind him.

"Yeah, why not?" he answered me, with about as much enthusiasm as a frog could muster up for a swim in hot water.

We had a nice visit, but I could sure tell that Carl was pretty depressed. Who could blame him, though, with all that had happened to him lately? Being with Carl made me feel grateful for all my blessings.

FRIDAY, SARAH GOT BACK from her sister's, so we decided to have dinner on her side of the river that night. As Sarah and I were leaving the diner, we walked out a little behind another couple who had also eaten there. I'd noticed the man and woman because they seemed to be tourists—at least I didn't know them—but that was just about all I really thought of it. They seemed to be your average, every day couple. Before we'd walked very far, I heard a whistle and a yoo-hoo behind us, and turned to find Susie Kholman waving. She had been our waitress, dressed in her green and white checked uniform. I walked back, but soon realized it wasn't me she was trying to call, but the other couple who continued to stroll down the sidewalk away from us, oblivious to Susie's hollering.

"Oh, shoot," she said, stopping in the middle of the sidewalk and looking back toward the diner.

"What's wrong, Susie?" I asked her.

"That couple up ahead—they left a package by their table, but I can't go after them. I'm alone with a dozen customers. Mr. Hessel, could you try to catch them for me, and tell them about the package?"

"Sure, no problem," I told her, looking ahead at the couple. They were quite a ways off, now, but moving along slowly, just doing some window shopping.

Sarah and I started after the other two. We were headed that direction anyway. Just about the time we got within a shop or two of them, they took off at a brisker pace. We picked up our own pace, but it didn't seem like we were gaining an inch on them.

"Excuse me," I hollered after them, but they just kept on walking. "Come on, Sarah, let's pick up some speed."

"I can't in these shoes, Frank. You go ahead."

Well, I darn near had to run after that couple. By the time I got within a single shop of them, we'd already passed our turnoff, Sarah's and mine, and I was just about out of breath. I sort of gave up at that point and let out a whistle, the loud kind between two fingers, and even doing that took me a couple of tries because I had to catch my breath first. They finally stopped and turned, looking at me curiously.

"You forgot your package in the restaurant," I said from about five feet away, almost gasping.

"Excuse?" the man said.

"I said that you forgot a package in the restaurant."

The man's wife whispered something to him, but he just shrugged and walked closer to me.

"Please," he said, "could you speak slower? I cannot understand."

"Oh sure," I said, finally realizing from his accent that they were foreign tourists.

"You left a package ... in the restaurant," I said very slowly, but the man continued to stare, obviously not able to follow my words.

His wife said something to him that sounded like German. "Deutschelanders?" I asked.

"Ja, ja," he said. "We are German. Sprechen Sie Deutsch?"

"Ja," I said, but then, in a flash of amnesia, every single word I ever knew of German flew right out the window. For a minute, I stood there trying to remember the word for package, but without any luck. Nor could I remember the German word for restaurant. When I finally gave up and pantomimed the square shape of a package in the air and pointed behind us, the man looked even more perplexed and frustrated. Just about that time, Sarah caught up with us.

"Packet zie stuben der food place," she said, figuring out real quick that I wasn't getting anywhere with the problem. That's not really what she said, of course, but you get the idea.

"Ach, das Paket!" the man exclaimed, slapping his forehead, happy to have figured it out. "Danke ... Danke schön," he said, shaking my hand, first, then Sarah's, all the while smiling at us both. He gave a short bow with his head, thanked us again, then he and his wife rushed back up the street to retrieve their package.

"Good grief," I told Sarah, "I couldn't think of a single word of German, and I used to speak it with my grandmother."

"That was a long time ago, Frank. You have to use it to retain it."

"You still remember it," I said to her.

"I still work on it with my cousins in Germany. I try to write them in German and they answer in English—it's good practice for both sides."

"Not a single word —" I said. "I couldn't even think of *paket*, for God's sake. How simple is that?"

"Don't worry about it, Frank," Sarah said, taking my arm.

BUT OF COURSE, I DID worry about it, off and on, for the next week, at least, if not longer. Here I was, living in this German valley, and I couldn't remember a single word of the language when it came down to crunch time. My own father had grown up in this valley actually speaking nothing but German. In fact, he hadn't learned English until he started school. If you think I'm kidding, think again—that's the way things were back then. Everybody here grew up speaking German. I wasn't raised bilingual, but I used to be able to rattle it off pretty well with my grandparents. As Sarah reminded me, though, that was many years ago.

As the days passed, I really wanted to talk with that tourist from Germany. I had a million questions for him. What side of the wall did they live on? What did he do for a living? Was there really a movement afoot that would bring back Hitler's ideas? A Fourth Reich? Was he Catholic or Lutheran, maybe atheist? He could have been a Jew. If so, how were they treated now? I never got a chance to ask any of these questions because I couldn't speak the language that my family had spoken for a jillion years. Frank J. Hessel, the first of the German Hessels who couldn't have spoken to his own ancestors. This isn't sour grapes, though, not really. I am proud to be an American, proud of everything we've accomplished here as a new nation. I have no patriotic sense about being German, none at all. My "German" sense goes to family, heritage, and tradition within a religion. Both sides of me are important—the German and the American—but I was on the verge of losing a whole piece of me, if it weren't lost already.

At one point, I got to thinking about running right down to the adult school to sign up for a course in German. At least I assume they still held such a class, but I never did make a phone call about it. Instead, I got to thinking about Sarah and her cousins in Germany. Why couldn't Sarah and I go over there for a visit, maybe on our honeymoon? The more I got to thinking about it, the better I liked the idea. The money for the trip was just sitting there in the bank, drawing interest. What were savings for, if not something like this? Who was I going to leave it to? The rainy day society? I had a nice retirement and good medical coverage. I could afford this trip. In fact, how could I not afford it? Who knows, I might even pick up a little more German, a refresher course.

You can worry yourself silly over what Sarah and I did for the rest of that Friday night. Mum's the word.

SATURDAY, THE OPPOSITION staged a parade, if you can believe it, except that the opposition in this case were the ones in favor of the bridge, not those opposed to it. Kind of runs your head in circles, doesn't it? It was real obvious which side has the money. This pro-bridge parade included the high school marching band and a real-life float. How they got the "public" high school to agree is beyond me. Maybe on some bogus grounds of the bridge's being safer for the students, instead of their having to commute to the ends of the valley. I wouldn't have gone out of my way to see the parade, but I just happened to be down by the river, anyway, so I decided to watch. It took place across the water, but everyone on our side could see and hear it just fine.

Our being split by the river did make it look as if the Lutherans were all for the bridge, so, by default, the Catholics must be against it. Well, appearances are deceptive. There are plenty of people over here who want the bridge and plenty over there who don't. The vote is scheduled for the Thursday after Easter. I just want the darn thing over with, so I can get a good night's sleep. I still haven't figured out which way would be the best for the valley. I'll probably vote against the bridge, but I may not be certain of that until the last minute.

When the float went past, I was standing there next to my neighbor, Ed Shrader—you remember him, the one who won't go *in on it with* me, meaning the street sign—and we were just tapping our feet to the band music when he turns to me and says, "Only an idiot would vote against the bridge."

Well, this is one idiot who won't take something like that lying down, not after that sign business.

"I'm voting against it, Ed," I told him, loud enough so I was sure he heard me, him being a little deaf.

He turned to look at me, all the tapping and finger snapping gone right out of him. "That figures," he says, then turns and walks away, leaving me standing there.

I should have felt like I'd scored a point against him, but instead I felt like I'd lost one. Don't get worried over it, though, because I'll get him back, soon enough. Ed used to teach math at the high school, and we've been neighbors for a long time, now. I guess we've been needling each other like this for nearly half a century. Neither one of us stays ahead for too long.

When I looked back across the river, the float was just about to turn the corner and head up Main Street. Even considering how bad my eyes are now, I would still swear that the blond girl on the other side of the float was Harvey Reasoner's daughter, Jill, again, but that didn't make one lick of sense. The last time I'd seen her was on the back of the pickup truck, campaigning for the opposition. She's the busty one I mentioned earlier. Well, if that was Jill, I would be sure to hear about it because she was wearing a bikini this time. A girl with a chest like hers should be in a one-piece. I couldn't see her from the front to tell for sure, but it certainly did look like Harvey's daughter. Oh well, maybe next week she could march with our side, again. Makes just as much sense as anything else around Happy Valley these days.

Chapter Six:
 Sixth Sunday in Lent

THE PALMARUM

PALM SUNDAY, the day of Christ's joyous entrance into Jerusalem. The palm fronds waving in the air as people shouted and cheered. A last moment of happiness for the disciples before the events of the week to follow, the unbelievable happenings of Holy Week, leading up to His death on the cross. In spite of the celebratory atmosphere of Palm Sunday, it is a day for reflection and preparation, the saddest yet most meaningful time of the year in the church calendar. This Lent, my joy level has been going up and down like a yo-yo.

Even sitting there in church, while I tried to meditate and keep my mind on religious matters, I couldn't help but remember the parade the day before. A perfect capper to the thing would've been handing out palm fronds for the crowd to wave—that would've proved God wanted the bridge across the river. As you've probably gathered by now, I do get a little cynical at times.

After the benediction, I decided to sit for a while and think. Since I was on the aisle, as I usually am, several friends stopped by to say hello or shake hands. Soon enough, the front of the church was empty except for the altar boy straightening up for the next mass in an hour. I would have half-an-hour of peace before people started drifting in. I started watching the young man go about his duties, thinking back many years ago when I did the same things, right here in the same church. There's a lot to be said for tradition. It knits a community into a cohesive whole. But a lot can be said for change, too, new blood, the excitement of new dreams. Old codgers like me get real wise in our advanced years. You should remember that and listen up when I tell you something.

"How are you this morning, Frank?"

"Good, Father, and yourself?" I answered, not having heard him walk up behind me. Father Einsphar had been here, in the valley, for going on thirty years. He was a good man, the only person, other than Sarah and my doctor, who knew about my illness because he was my confessor.

"I'm well, Frank. How's your health?"

"Better than I deserve—all my counts are normal."

"Good, Frank. You're in my prayers."

"Thanks, Father."

He laid a reassuring hand on my shoulder as he passed over to the side door, and then I was alone in the sanctuary. Alone with my thoughts and prayers, except that there was one more person left to leave the church.

Birdie Stern just had to stop by, though I wished she could on moving out the side door, the same door the priest had just used.

"Morning, Frank," she whispered, all spiritual like. "Did you see Jill Reasoner on the float yesterday? That cheap little hussy should be ashamed of herself, dressed like that and during Lent, no less."

Birdie laid one of her claws on my arm, just to make sure I got her message, then she hobbled out the door, clucking away to herself.

Well, that just about shot my spiritual mood for the day, so I started to leave after another minute or two. Some days you can't win for losing, even on the special days.

AS I PAUSED IN THE AISLE to genuflect, I looked to the altar and had a flash of inspiration. So far, Sarah and I hadn't really been able to talk about where we wanted to get married because it was something so important to each of us. Actually, I'd been avoiding it for fear of having to give up something. Isn't it the woman's family who gets to choose in wedding matters? Well, why couldn't we split it up? We each had a church and a minister that we liked. Couldn't they both be there? If we got married here in my church, we could have the reception in Sarah's church hall. Father Einsphar and Reverend Wagner could both officiate at the service. Sometimes, I amaze myself at the depth and creativity of my own mind.

Taking off like a shot, I hoped to catch my priest before he went into the rectory. Well, I needn't have worried any. Old Birdie Stern had cornered him for me.

"— now, Birdie," he was saying, "I'm sure that Jill didn't mean to offend you or anyone else. Fashions have changed. All the kids today wear bathing suits like hers."

"I still think you might want to say a word to her father, Father. After all, modesty should be prized."

I couldn't help but smile over her repetition of "father, Father" in her address to the priest as he and I stood together, watching Birdie hobble off across the yard. She never realized that she'd repeated the term. Modesty was Birdie's prize, that's for sure—she was wearing a floor length black dress, under a black hat with a half veil. No one dressed for church like that any more, though many of the women used to do so.

"Lord preserve us from an angry woman, Frank."

"Amen, father Father," I said.

"You should learn to be more frank, Frank," he said. That's what I like about Father Einsphar—he enjoys a good joke. "Did you come out here looking for me?" he asked, still smiling.

"Would you agree to a mixed marriage?" I asked.

I'd caught him off guard with that one because he jerked a little. I hoped he didn't think I meant me and Birdie Stern, but he didn't.

"You and Sarah would hardly be a mixed marriage, Frank," he said, grinning at me.

Is there anyone in this entire valley who doesn't know about me and Sarah? I could see the humor in my question, though. Today, a marriage between a Catholic and a Lutheran wouldn't raise an eyebrow. A mixed marriage would involve different races, or maybe a radical difference in religions, like between a Buddhist and a Presbyterian.

"I see what you mean, Father. I was thinking more about having both churches involved?"

"What did you have in mind, Frank? It goes without saying that I would be happy to take part in your wedding. So would Bill Wagner, I'm sure."

"That's what I was thinking, Father. Could both of you do the service?"

"I see," he said, nodding. "A good idea, Frank. That's a very good idea. Sure, why not?"

We talked for a while longer, but I already had my answer, at least part of the answer. It could be done. Now I just had to ask Sarah.

WHILE I WAS WAITING for Ernie to ferry me over, I thought about the problems involved with a wedding that spanned both sides of the river.

Logistically, the whole thing would be a nightmare. Having the wedding in one church and the reception in the other would give Ernie a whole new set of blisters, from ferrying people back and forth. Well, we would be keeping the wedding small, anyway, not to save Ernie any effort, but just so the thing didn't turn into a circus.

"Have you and Sarah set a date, yet?" he asked me, right off the bat, as if he were our wedding consultant.

"Not yet, Ernie, but soon."

"Good, Frank, that's good. It'll be nice getting everyone together again, from both sides."

"It might wear you out a little," I offered.

"Nothing I can't handle. This is one wedding I'm really looking forward to."

Uh oh, I thought, who's going to tell Ernie that we want a small wedding which might not include him? But I should've seen the handwriting on the wall.

WHEN I MENTIONED our keeping the wedding down to a reasonable number of guests, Sarah had other ideas.

"How in the world do you think we could keep it small?" Sarah asked me. "Both of us have lived here all our lives. If we don't invite everyone, there's bound to be hard feelings."

"Everyone?" I said, with a shudder inside. "Maybe we could go to Las Vegas, instead."

One look from Sarah put an end to that idea.

"Which church?" she asked, phrasing the question carefully while looking right at me.

"That's another idea I wanted to run by you," I said. "Father Einsphar said he would be happy to do a joint service, you know, with both ministers there?"

"What a wonderful idea," she said, looking relieved. I could tell that Sarah had been worried about the same things that had been running through my mind. "In which church, though?" she asked, again.

"I guess we need to work that out," I said, equally careful. "We could have the wedding in one church and the reception in the other. What do you think?"

"That would be a perfect solution, Frank," she said, coming alive with the idea, which made me feel proud of myself for having invented it. "Absolutely perfect."

Sarah walked over to the window, obviously thinking, trying to reach a decision. I just kept my mouth shut, something I've just learned to do lately, it seems. My plan was to leave it up to her because wedding matters should be the woman's choice, at least that's what I've always believed.

"How's this, Frank?" she started out slowly, then built up some steam as she went along. "We could have the service in your church, then come over to the hall in my church for the reception. The Auxiliary will handle all the cooking—we've done it lots of times."

While Sarah continued talking, I just stood there, flushed with gratitude. She may have sensed it, already, I don't know, but being married in my church is very important to me. Maybe I'm just an old-fashioned Catholic, but it's really, really important. A Lutheran wedding would be just as binding, and just as solemn, but it wouldn't be in the Church. I don't expect you to understand this. I'm just glad that Sarah did.

"—what do you think?" she asked, interrupting my silent prayer of thanks.

"I think I'm the luckiest man in the world," I said.

"Did you hear a word I said?" she asked, smiling at me, while she shook her head, not in judgment but in fun.

"Sure, I did," I said, not exactly lying because I really had heard a lot of it—disjoint ideas about what dishes to serve, what beverages, what time of day and what day of the week. All that we could work out. The big hurdles were passed.

"I'll bet you didn't hear half of what I told you," she said, walking over to my side. She gave me a kiss on the cheek, just so I'd know she wasn't mad or anything.

"Thanks for the church, Sarah," I said, putting my arm around her shoulders. I could tell she knew just what I meant from her reaction, and that she had made the decision knowing how important it was to me.

"It's a good compromise, Frank," she said.

LATER THAT AFTERNOON, we walked down to her church in order to meet with Reverend Wagner. Sarah had called him to run some of our ideas past him. Like Father Einsphar, he was delighted for us and more than willing to share the honors at the wedding.

"Have you two met?" Sarah asked after we'd been ushered into his office.

"Oh, sure," I said, shaking the minister's hand. "Reverend Wagner did the prayer at graduation several times before I retired."

"Sit down, sit down, please," the minister said, indicating two leather covered chairs in front of his desk. The man was obviously a scholar because the walls were covered with filled bookcases. The single decoration on the walls, other than a couple of photographs, was a simple golden cross.

We talked for a while, mostly chatting, then he got down to the business of pastoral counseling. I had seen it coming, but I was curious to see how the Lutherans did it.

"The good news," he opened with, "is that you are both believers, but strangely enough, that can be the bad news, too, in a way, especially when individual faith is as important as it obviously is to each of you. Have you thought about which church you'll attend?"

Sarah and I just looked at each other. Obviously she hadn't considered the problem any more than I had. Getting past the wedding ceremony was enough of a hurdle for one day.

"No," she admitted, "I hadn't thought about it."

"Neither have I," I said, looking into her eyes.

In my heart of hearts, I knew that I wanted to reach our decisions and our practices together. Once we were married, I didn't want to attend separate churches. That idea turned me off completely.

"When do you attend mass, Frank?" the pastor asked.

"Early, on Sundays," I answered him, "then I usually go a couple times during the week."

"As you know, we only have the two services a week, both on Sunday morning—" he said, leaving the answer to us.

"We'll manage, pastor," I said, looking back to Sarah. "I don't think it'll hurt me any to attend a Lutheran service."

"Thanks, Frank," Sarah said, taking my arm even as we sat there in front of her minister.

Sometimes a compromise can be an act of love. Maybe it always is, if it's done with the good of the other person in mind. So far, we were having a pretty good day.

ONCE WE LEFT Reverend Wagner's office, Sarah offered to drive me home, but I said no, that I'd just take the ferry. She did insist on walking down to the dock with me, and gave me a big smooch, right there in front of Ernie.

"Well, Ernie," I said to him, after we'd pushed off into the river. "You'd better start working out at the YMCA because the wedding's going to be on my side, and the reception on yours. You'll be ferrying people back and forth like crazy."

"Glad to oblige you, Frank," he said, then started chuckling to himself.

"What's wrong?" I asked.

"I won't even be able to charge for the trips," he said.

"Why not?"

"Heck, it'll be a community event, Frank. I just couldn't ask for money."

Since when did Sarah and I become a "community event"? I wondered, but the more I thought about it, the more I could see his point. We did have lots of good friends, here in the valley, on both sides of the river. I made a mental note to myself about seeing that Ernie got an anonymous gratuity for his service.

AS I WALKED UP THE HILL toward my place, I missed Sarah with a pang, just knowing that I was going home alone. That would change soon enough, but not too soon to suit me. Once inside my place, I flopped in the chair and thought through everything that had happened today. I realized that this was all going to work out, every bit of it, God willing.

Sarah had not asked me back to her place after our

counseling session with Reverend Wagner, nor had I tried to ask her. That may seem silly to you, but it's just the way things are with our generation. The day that Sarah and I are married, you can count on one thing—she won't let me see her until she comes down the aisle. Tradition is important. After spending this much of Palm Sunday with priests and ministers, we just couldn't have spent the night together. I know I couldn't have done it, and I believe that Sarah felt the same way. It's not like we're sorry for anything we've done in the past, it's just that we can afford to wait a little while now that the wedding is a reality. We've got the rest of our lives together to catch up on lost time.

I dozed off in my chair for a while—I could tell it from the changes in light and shadow in the room. I dreamt of Sarah, and woke with her face before my eyes, and her name on my lips.

One week before Easter, and my whole life was changing, being reborn, you might say.

CARL AND I HAD LUNCH on Monday, this week. I never did get a chance to tell him about me and Sarah because I noticed right off that he was agitated as all get out. When I asked him what the news was on the bridge project, he darn near exploded at me.

"How do you think it's going? No thanks to you and every other old codger in this valley."

"Do you have money in the thing, Carl?" I asked, cutting straight through to all my suspicions.

"Who, me? Why would you think that?"

"I'm pretty sure that your son, Jim, does, at least judging by his reaction the other night."

"Couldn't say, one way or another."

"Couldn't or wouldn't?" I asked him, point blank.

He just sat there staring back at me, then he dropped his gaze to the coffee cup in front of him. "My son wouldn't tell me, even if he did," he said softly.

I didn't know how to answer something like that, so for a change I just kept my mouth shut.

"Jim and I don't get along too well, Frank. Never have, really."

I'd had some glimmers of this all along, but I thought it was mostly a thing of the past, like back when Jim had been a hot-headed teenager, spending summers here with his grandparents.

"I'm sorry to hear that, Carl."

"I lied to you, earlier," he continued softly, confidentially, "when I said that he asked me to move in with them. He never did. The best he was willing to do was have me in the Lutheran home, but only if I stayed out of his hair. That's just the way he put it, Frank," he said looking back up from his cup. "If I stayed out of his hair. Don't that beat all?"

"I don't know what to say, Carl."

"Nothing you can say, really. It's all my own damn fault."

Don't you say a word, I told myself. Just let him tell it at his own pace. If ever a man looked like he needed to talk, it was Carl.

"Frank," he said, finally, after another long pause, "you know how I never came back to the valley for all those years?"

"Uh huh."

"I was ashamed to come back, simple as that. I didn't want to face any of the old crowd, especially you."

"Why, Carl?"

"Because I was lying, Frank, lying about how well I was doing. It was all a front. Hell, I never even graduated from college. It would've taken me another year to make up for lost credits, so I just quit school and took a job on the strength of my sports. For a while, it was okay. Karen and I were married and settling down, but then everything I tried turned to shit. All that moving around had nothing to do with my getting any promotions. I kept getting fired, and every get-rich scheme I tried went belly up. I'm broke, Frank. Flat broke except for

Social Security. The money from our house went to pay off my debts, the part I didn't drink up, that is."

"Why didn't you tell me, Carl?" I asked, suddenly conscious of the check which he'd slid to his side of the table, earlier, making his usual show of treating me to lunch. He couldn't afford lunches like this, yet more often than not he paid, playing the big shot, I supposed.

"Too much pride, too damned ashamed," he said, shrugging. "Mostly, I was ashamed because of Karen."

"How's that?"

"You know—not being able to do better by her, provide for her. She never complained, Frank, not even once, but I never lived up to any of those things I promised her. I'm just a damned fake, Frank, a walking counterfeit bill."

A tear trickled down his cheek, seemingly unnoticed by my old friend. It was the first time I'd ever seen him cry. Even as kids, he'd never cried, not once, not even when we got the tar kicked out of us in neighborhood fights. In contrast, I'd always cried too easily and seen it as a weakness, fighting all my life not to let it happen, mostly succeeding. Now I threw all that crap out the window and ended up crying with him, not like a couple of old women, sobbing away, but dignified, like a couple of old gentlemen crying over all those wasted years.

"It's okay, Carl," I said, reaching out my hand and putting it on top of one of his. "If you live as long as we have, you make mistakes."

"My whole fucking life's been a mistake," he said, shaking his head.

"Not all of it, Carl. Karen was no mistake. What you had with her was real."

"Yeah," he said, nodding in response. "Yeah, that's true."

As he said the words, and I held his hand there in Luigi's, I came to understand that even his marriage had been a lie. Suddenly, I understood Carl and Karen and me—all of us together. Son of a bitch, what a waste it had been. What a damned, pitiful waste.

When Carl left for the bathroom, to blow his nose and wash his face, I reached out and took the check, for the first time being really grateful for my teacher's pension. Until that moment, I'd always thought of it as being too small. Never in my wildest dreams had I guessed that Carl could be broke. Getting old is hell, if you could only know it. While the waitress was getting my change, I sat there looking out the window, seeing Karen's face and understanding many things for the first time.

THAT EVENING, I SAT IN my front room thinking about the last time I'd kissed Karen. Good Lord, it had to be forty years ago and longer. How is it that the human mind can hang onto a memory like that, vivid as if it were yesterday, and just this morning it had taken me an hour to find my darn glasses? It had never made any sense before, our kissing like that, not until now. She'd come back for a visit to her folks, bringing the kids with her, when little Jimmy was only about five and Stephie was maybe three or so. Carl had not come with them, being "too busy on a business deal." Some *deal*, judging by what Carl had told me at lunch, but she'd never made out that anything was wrong, not so much as a word, yet I still knew something was up.

I ran into Karen and her mom at the grocery store. The kids were with them, mostly pretty well-behaved as I recall, unlike a lot of them you see nowadays. Karen was a good mother to those kids. We visited for a little while, then Karen's mother invited me over for dinner. Just so you understand, this was before Ruthie and I were married or even seriously dating. Karen gave her mother a funny look, now that I think about it, but when I asked Karen if it'd be okay, she'd said sure.

After dinner, Karen's mother told us to take a walk, that she'd clean the table and keep an eye on the kids.

"I'm sorry about my mother, Frank," Karen said, once we were outside.

"Sorry for what?" I asked, truly bewildered.

"For trying to throw us together like that."

"You and me?"

Karen looked at me and started to laugh, again adding to my total confusion.

"You really don't know, do you?" she asked.

"Know what?"

"Dear, dear Frank," she began, putting her hand inside the crook of my elbow as we walked down the block. "My mother's always loved you. She gave me holy hell for running off with Carl and not marrying you."

We walked in silence for a while, as I tried to absorb what she'd told me.

"Carl and I have been having problems," she said. "He's drinking a lot and running around with other women."

"Other women?" I asked, utterly floored by the possibility. How could any man need more than this woman, the one who was walking at my side? "Are you sure?"

"Oh, yes. Very sure."

"Do you want me to talk to him? Would that help?" I asked.

We had stopped under a huge oak tree. Karen turned and faced me as she leaned her shoulder into the oak.

"What would you say to him, Frank?" she asked, not looking like she expected an answer. "No, Frank. You're the last person he'd listen to about this."

Only now can I understand why she said that. It never occurred to me then that Carl could be jealous of me, of the relationship between Karen and me, innocent as it was. You have to try to understand the way things were back then, half a century ago. Karen was a married woman with two kids, while I was just a beginning teacher with so little sexual experience, you'd think I was lying if I told you about it.

What the heck, I've embarrassed myself enough already, so why not tell you? The whole grand total of my experience amounted to a couple of furtive encounters in college, hurried and in the dark, which left me so guilt-ridden that I confessed them first chance I got. I didn't know diddley-squat about male-female relationships, yet here was the woman I still loved, married to one of my best friends, telling me that he was being unfaithful to her. I was floored.

"Karen, I don't know what to say," I told her, looking into her eyes.

"Oh, Frank. It's not your problem."

She reached up to give me a kiss on the cheek, but I moved a little without planning it, so that the corners of our mouths accidentally touched. Karen backed off an inch or two, and we just looked into each other's eyes. I can still feel her breath on my chin. It was the breath of a full-grown woman, not that of the girl I'd dated in high school. It was perfumed and rich, fecund and heated. She kissed me then with a passion that overwhelmed me. I didn't have enough experience to respond, not fully, not the way I could have or should have. Karen realized it first and backed off.

"I'm sorry, Frank," she said. "I never should've done that. Never."

She turned and walked away, leaving me standing under the oak, bewildered and baffled. *Could I really have been that young and naive?* Slowly, I walked back to my place and dreamt about things that I also had to confess. In a couple of days, she was gone, back to Carl with the kids. Karen's father had died when we were in high school. Her mother was still a young woman when I had kissed her daughter, young by my standards today, in any respect. I understand now that she was trying to throw us together that night, in hopes that it would help get Karen out of a failing marriage.

A year later, Karen's mother got breast cancer and died, all in just a few months. I went to the funeral and stood next to

Karen and Carl. After that, there was nothing left to bring them back to the valley, not with Carl's always arguing with his own folks, so it was years before I saw either of them again, at that one class reunion they attended, our twentieth.

Good Lord, I'm seventy years old and that kiss is the single, most vivid memory of my lifetime. Why is that?

CARL AND KAREN DID RETURN for our twentieth class reunion, like I've already told you. Ruthie and I were married by then, of course, and we were all in our late thirties, except for Ruthie, and sharing a table in the high school gym. When I danced with Karen, I couldn't help but remember that last kiss we'd had. Heck, people still have plenty of juices flowing at thirty-eight. If you're not that old yet, then wait and see, if you don't believe me. In spite of everything that I believe about marriage, I still found myself getting excited by Karen's physical presence, as she was pressed up against me during a slow dance. Guess you never forget your first love, no matter how much time passes.

"Remember the last time we danced, Frank," she asked me, so soft that I almost didn't hear her.

"Senior prom?"

"That's right. In this very gym."

Neither of us said anything for a while as we moved around the floor. I was caught in two different times and worlds, then and now, there and here, except the space was the same, we were just different people, in different times. Sort of, anyway. Just like I'd done twenty years ago, I found myself trying to lead her away from my growing erection, except it didn't work any better in the present-past than it had in the past-past. Karen wasn't helping matters any by drifting into me. Then I realized she was giggling, almost laughing aloud. She was doing it on purpose, enjoying the heck out of herself.

"Some things never change, Frank," she said, stopping me

in the middle of the floor and pressing up against my body, letting me know that she knew. "We were so innocent then, weren't we? We didn't have the slightest idea of what we were doing, not the slightest."

I could do nothing but nod, hoping that she wouldn't leave me standing there, exposed. The music changed to a fast song.

"Good," she said, taking my hand and moving away into the steps of the New Yorker. She smiled into my eyes. "That should help the little problem you're having."

It did, and the moment passed. I never asked her about her marriage that night. It just never seemed the right thing to do. Each of us had moved off into different lives. Now where in the world was I in this story? Oh yes, back in Happy Valley.

THE NEXT DAY, Tuesday, I phoned Jonathan to see if he were going to be home. I just couldn't stop thinking about his father's being buried in a city he didn't even like, maybe even buried in a pauper's field. It just didn't seem right to me. Why not bring him home to the valley? It's where I want to be buried, and since Jonathan's moved back, I assume it's where he wants to be, too. Sometimes I wonder why I can't just leave things alone. Was I still trying to atone for the things I had said to Jonathan, way back then? Or was I trying to atone for the whole valley, and what we'd done to his father?

"Hello," he answered.

If I live to be a hundred, and that doesn't seem very likely, I will never get over how his voice is exactly the same as it was back then, when we were kids.

"Hi, Jonathan. It's Frank."

"How are you today?"

"Just fine, thanks. I was wondering if you were going to be home this afternoon. I'd like to stop by for a minute or two."

"Sure," he said. "I'm planning on staying home, catching up on some reading."

"Good. I'll be there as soon as I can get Ernie to haul me over."

"See you then."

"Goodby."

ALL THE WAY DOWN to the river, I kept asking myself what I thought I was going to tell Jonathan or ask him. It felt right to be doing this, but I'd done things in the past that felt right but turned out so very wrong. All the good intentions ... oh, how does that saying go? The road to hell is paved with good intentions—yes, that's it. What that has to do with anything is anybody's guess.

Ernie was on my side of the river for a change, so I didn't have to sit around waiting for him.

"Good afternoon, Frank."

"Hi, Ernie. How are you doing?"

"Fair to middling, I guess."

Soon as I got in his boat and sat down, he started poling me over to the other side, without even questioning me about where I was going.

"You feeling all right, Ernie?" I asked him.

"Hum? Oh sure, I'm all right. Just a little concerned about all the politics going on."

"How do you think the vote will go?" I asked.

"Pretty close right now, I'd guess."

"Well, I'm opposed to the bridge, if that helps you any."

"Thanks, Frank. I already knew that because I was at the meeting when you spoke up."

"Well, keep up the faith, Ernie," I said, stepping out on the other side of the river. I handed him my dollar and he took it, but he did so automatically, without even looking at it.

"You know, Frank, my grandfather ran the ferry here even before the original bridge was put up. It's a family tradition."

"Guess I don't remember that, Ernie."

I looked back when I reached the road and saw him just sitting there in his boat, staring off down the river.

INSTEAD OF GOING RIGHT OVER to Jonathan's house, I turned up toward my folks' old place, as if I were drawn to it by all this talk of family and tradition. Heck, I was so early that I might even see if Mrs.—now what was her name again? Shoot, that's one of the worst things about getting old. I can remember the names of students from forty years ago, but I lose the names of my own neighbors. Sally something, I think. Randolph or Rudolph?

She was just getting out of her car as I walked up to the house. The back seat was full of groceries.

"Can I give you a hand with these?" I offered.

"Sure, I'd appreciate it, Mr. Hessel. That way you could take a look at the house, too. You picked a good day for it. Tomorrow the kids will be running all over when their Easter break starts."

We carried the bags in through the kitchen door on the backside of the house. They'd remodeled the kitchen completely, everything new and sparkling. It was almost like I'd never been in this room before, except for the walls' being in the same places, of course.

"We made some changes," she said.

"Yes, it's nice."

One more trip to the car, and we were done with the shopping bags.

"Well," she asked, "should I give you a tour, or would you just like to roam around while I put this stuff away?"

"You wouldn't mind—?" I started to ask.

"Not at all. Just go ahead. It was your house long before it was ours."

"Thanks, maybe I will."

Walking through the dining room and into the front room was another experience, altogether. The furniture was different, of course, but the fireplace and staircase were just the same as I remembered them. I could almost see my mother bending over the hearth, stirring the embers. Talk about your ghosts of the past.

I thought about going upstairs but felt that would be an imposition, poking through other people's bedrooms, so I just sat down on the sofa facing the fireplace and let my mind run. Over there in the corner, where they have a wing chair, my mother used to put the Christmas tree. The stockings were hung from the mantle, and the nativity scene she put on a table in front of the window, just where the new people have a table now. For just a second, I thought I could smell my father's pipe. Maybe Sally's husband was a smoker?

"Do you take anything in your coffee, Mr. Hessel."

She had come into the front room carrying two cups on a tray with a creamer and sugar.

"Oh, I didn't want you going to any trouble, and please, call me Frank."

"No problem, Frank. It's not fresh, but I made it just before I went shopping."

"Thanks. That's fine, and black is how I take it."

"Lots of memories?" she asked, sitting down next to me on the sofa.

"You've got no idea. I didn't even hear you walk into the room, and then when you did, I thought you were my mother come back from the grave."

I FINALLY HAD TO drag myself out of that house. Sally is one nice lady. I could've stayed there all afternoon just chatting away, but I couldn't keep Jonathan waiting any longer. I'd been right before, too. She is pregnant, again. They're hoping for a girl this time, to go with the two boys. Sally showed me all their pictures—a nice looking family. She said to stop by anytime, maybe for dinner one night. I thanked her and left, happy to have made a new friend.

It was Thomas Wolfe who said, "You can't go home again," at least I think it was him. Could of been Virginia Wolf for all I can remember anymore. Wolfe or Woolf was it? There was a time that such differences really mattered to me. He or she was right, whether it's Wolf or Coyote. You can't go back. Visiting the old place just stirred up stuff in me that might just as easily have been left to rest. I don't know if I can go back again, but I'm glad I went this once.

By the time I reached Jonathan's house, I was a little less spooked, but I was still feeling the effects of my visit to the past.

"Are you all right, Frank?" Jonathan asked, once I'd sat down in the front room.

"Sure, I just went through my folks' place. It kind of shook me up a little, I guess."

"I know the feeling. Coming back to the valley has been like that since the day we got here, maybe not as dramatic, but similar, I'm sure."

"Why did you come back, Jonathan? I mean really, truly why. You told me *revenge*, but that's not enough of a reason."

"Maybe not, really. I was looking for home, I guess. This valley was where I grew up, where I spent my childhood. The year after we left, I had my bar mitzvah in Philadelphia, in my uncle's synagogue. After that I was a man." He shrugged without saying anything more.

"Are you happy you came back?" I asked.

"I don't know how to answer that, Frank. I've reconciled myself to not being happy, not the way most people seem to understand it. My life has been productive, efficient, rewarding, but happy? I just don't know."

For a while, we just sat there, looking at each other and at the walls.

"Do you know where your father's buried?" I blurted out.

"Why in the world do you want to know that?" he answered, obviously shocked by the question.

"I visited the cemetery up by my house the other day and asked some questions."

"Questions about what?" he asked.

"They have a Jewish section there," I answered. "I haven't seen it, yet, but Mitch Ludeke said it has a nice view of the valley."

"Are you suggesting I bury my father here?" he asked, looking shocked.

Guess I'd gone and done it again, putting my stupid foot in my mouth without thinking it through. Darn it all, but it *still* seemed like a good idea!

"Well, why not, Jonathan? Maybe I'm just being nostalgic, but you told me he was buried in a strange city, where he had no ties. Why not bury him here, instead?"

"Good God, Frank. He's been dead for sixty years—why now? Especially after how he was treated here?"

"Why not now?" I said, shrugging my shoulders. "He must have liked the valley to move all of you here. Seems like a good place to end up. I don't see it as revenge, really, just setting things right at last."

Jonathan just sat there staring at me. I couldn't even tell if he were angry, hurt, surprised or what. Holy cow, I'd gone and done it again, sticking my nose in where it didn't belong.

"Why are you doing this, Frank?"

"Guess I just can't help butting in. I'm sorry, Jonathan, I never should've suggested it. Shoot, I don't even know Jewish law about such things, whether it could even be done."

Darn it, I was so stirred up by it all—by my visit to the folks' place and then by this thing with Jonathan—that I stood up and headed for the door. *Why was I such a jackass?*

"Sit down, Frank," he said, his voice stopping me in mid-stride. "Please, stay."

I heard a longing in his voice that touched my heart all the way back to that ten-year-old version of myself that still bounced around inside me. This was the old Jonathan who could laugh and cry and feel. I went back to the couch and sat down facing him.

"Why are you doing this, Frank?" he asked me again.

"Because you're my friend."

Sweet Jesus, this whole day just whelmed up on me, all of a sudden. There I sat with tears running down my cheeks, like some foolish, meddling old lady.

"Thank you, Frank," he said, softly.

We just sat there, me crying, him watching me crying, and not one damn bit of it making any sense at all. Then Jonathan did one of the strangest things I've ever seen. He walked over to the couch, reached down and stood me up. He took my face in his hands and kissed me on both cheeks, then hugged me with such force that I thought we'd both burst. I was crying, and he was crying, just as Miriam walked into the room. I could hardly see her through my own tears, but I could make out enough to see that she stood there, frozen, her mouth open in astonishment. Then she was crying, too.

EARLY THE NEXT DAY, the Wednesday of Holy Week, Jonathan phoned to see if I wanted to go with him to the cemetery.

"Sure," I told him. "I'd be happy to go with you."

"Good. I'll drive around and pick you up, say ten o'clock, if that's all right?"

"Great. See you then."

Well, I thought, maybe I'm not such an old fool after all. Maybe there could be some real good come out of this bunch of crap.

Jonathan's car is a new Mercedes. He must keep it inside his garage because I hadn't seen it before.

"This is a beauty," I said, letting my hand slide across the leather seats. "I finally had to give up driving when my eyes got so bad. I miss it."

"She's smooth. Sure you don't want to give it a try?" he asked, obviously teasing me, given what I'd just told him.

"You'd be sorry, believe me."

"I'm not sure I can find the cemetery anymore. Is it still out Woodly Road?"

"Yes, straight up to the top."

For a while we drove in silence, just enjoying the scenery. Jonathan was the first to speak, satisfying my curiosity about the trip.

"I talked to a rabbi last night, about what you suggested."

"So, it's not totally off the wall, then?" I asked.

"It's unusual enough that he had to think about it for a while. As you already know, almost all Jews follow the dictum of burying their dead before sunset of the same day—it's not just the Orthodox. That does create problems with reburial."

"That's what I was afraid of."

"Under Jewish law, the headstone is not put on the grave until the one year anniversary of the person's death. We did the best we could when my father died," he said, the pain in his voice apparent, "but it was the middle of the Depression. We were very poor and living with my mother's sister and her family. The synagogue in Trenton had to pay for everything. There wasn't much they could do, either. To my knowledge, there may never have been a stone at all."

I thought about telling him how tough things had gotten in the valley, during those same years, but realized I should just keep my council. At least I'd had food on the table, a place to live, and a father and mother.

"My friend—the rabbi—suggested that I could set up a memorial in my synagogue, a plaque would be the most usual thing. When I told him that we were just in the process of organizing a synagogue, he perked right up—" Jonathan turned to me with a smile.

"He was interested?" I asked.

"Yes, he's our age, maybe a little younger, and his

congregation is retiring him, against his protests, apparently. He'll come out next month to check out our situation, even help us locate the synagogue."

"That would be great," I said.

"When I told him about your idea for the cemetery here, he had to think about it, and he even left the phone for a minute to check Judaic Law. As 'off the wall' as your idea might be, he said it would be spiritually proper."

"So, you're going to do it?" I asked.

"I want to see the plot first, but maybe so."

When we got to the offices at the cemetery, I introduced Jonathan to Mitch Ludeke who went with us to the old Jewish section, high on the hill. The view was magnificent, but we had to walk quite a ways to get there from the road.

"I'm sorry," Mitch told us, "but this section has not been in use for a long time. The stones and lawns are cared for, of course, but I'm afraid the road has gone to ruin."

In order to reach the Jewish section, we had to walk through the area in which my parents are buried. I was overdue for a visit, anyway, and I wanted to spend longer than we had time for today, though I did step aside just to take a quick glance at their graves. When I moved back to follow Jonathan and Mitch, I almost tripped over the graves of Carl's parents. Of course, they would be in this area, too, because the sections were developed and sold about the same time, to people of the same ages. What stopped me in my tracks was seeing Karen's grave, right there next to Carl's parents.

I guess that I knew she was here, someplace, but I'd never thought of looking for her grave. I hadn't been able to attend her funeral because I was in the hospital at the time, being treated for my leukemia. In fact, I didn't even know that she had died until I got back home. By then Carl had come and gone, so I hadn't even gotten to see him, either.

Here she lay, in the same section with my parents, my wife, Ruthie, her own parents, and Carl's parents. Sweet Jesus, what a chill ran through me then. Easter was just a few days away, and here they were, all gathered together in a group, waiting for the resurrection.

"Frank, do you want us to wait for you?" asked Jonathan, his voice coming from a distance.

"Go ahead," I answered. "I'll be along in a minute." I moved to the next row and looked down at Ruthie's grave.

BY THE TIME I REACHED THEM, Mitch was pointing out possible sites, suggesting a family sequence of plots for Jonathan and Miriam, too, if they'd be interested in that. Mitch told Jonathan that they could get right to work on the stone because their mason was free right now and could use the job. I walked around the immediate area reading the other stones and dates. They were old, very old. The last Jew to be buried here had died before I'd was born. Rachel Rosen, 1870 to 1912. She'd only been forty-two years old. I wondered what stories she could tell about the valley way back then.

Chapter Seven:
   The Thursday of Holy Week

THE PASSOVER

FRANK HESSEL will be attending his first Passover meal today, if you can believe that. Let me tell you how it happened. First of all, I was surprised to learn that Passover was not always on the Thursday of the Christian Holy Week, as it must have been during the year of Christ's death and resurrection. Wasn't that right? Lets, see—the Last Supper on Thursday, Judas leaves, Jesus goes to the Garden of Gethsemane where he is betrayed and taken before Pilate. Friday, He is crucified, dies and is buried before sunset, then spends all day Saturday in the tomb, before it is discovered that He is gone on Sunday morning. I knew that Easter itself was determined by the full moon, somehow, and since the Jewish calendar was also lunar-based, I'd always assumed the two days would stay the same, at least in relationship to each other. Jonathan explained the difference in my living room, over a cup of coffee, after we'd come back from the cemetery.

"Passover is the fourteenth day of Nisan. It can fall on any day of the week."

"Nissan, like the car?" I asked, not realizing how stupid that would be until I'd said it.

"Not quite," he said with a smile, "I haven't run into too many Japanese Jews."

"I guess not," I answered, feeling a little embarrassed.

"Passover is actually tomorrow, and this year it does fall on your traditional Thursday. It's always close to your Easter, but it can vary by a few days. Would you like to join us for Seder?"

"Me?"

"Why not? It's not against your religion is it? Like a sin or a heresy?"

"No, of course not," I answered, trying to sound more certain than I felt inside. *Maybe it was a heresy?*

"Good. Come about five o'clock."

I WOKE UP EARLY ON PASSOVER—it still sounds strange for me, a lifelong Catholic, to be writing something like that, even though it's just about the most biblical of all the Holy Days, counting from the very start of Genesis, anyway. Better make that Exodus, when the Passover was actually instituted. Call me superstitious, or whatever you like, but I walked down to Saint Ignatius for the early mass, maybe to build up points for myself against the Jewish ceremonies to come later in the day. Who knows what I was thinking? My mind was a whirl.

As I sat in my regular pew, waiting for the mass to begin, I thought about what it means to be German, from the viewpoint of religion, anyway. If you were born German when I was a child, you were most likely one of three possibilities—Catholic, Lutheran or Jewish. That was before the Second World War, of course, both here in the United States, and even in Germany itself. For many years after the war, you could be born in Germany—in East Germany, anyway—and inherit atheism as your religion, or lack of religion, I guess. How many Jews are born in Germany these days? I found myself wondering. Did they return after the war? Were there any Jews left who thought of themselves as German?

Questions like this are enough to drive you crazy. In my own church instruction many years ago, I learned about Germany's replacing Rome after the fall of the Eternal City to the Huns. This was the medieval Catholic church, of course. We also studied the apostasy of Martin Lutheran, himself a

Catholic priest before he renounced the Church. At one time, then, Germany housed the seat of Catholicism as well as the seeds of the Protestant Reformation, beginning with Luther and Melanchthon. No matter which side of German Christianity you were on, each side had people and events worthy of mention. From what I've read, the medieval church needed some reforming, so it's hard to quarrel with much of what Luther urged. The usual Catholic opinion was that he should have worked his reforms from within the church instead of breaking away from her.

I could go on and on like this for pages, all to do with German theology and philosophy. Kant was German, so was Marx, though hardly a Christian. Deep thinkers both, who helped shape the world. When did anti-Semitism come into this picture? Was it always there, from the very beginnings of the early church? But the earliest members of the church were all Jewish, so how did Christianity get to be an exclusively gentile religion? When did the early church turn against its Jewish roots? Was antisemitism rife from one end of Europe to the other? Throughout all of Western Civilization? What I'm asking is this—Could the Holocaust have happened anywhere in Europe, or only in Germany? Was Hitler an aberration or was he the natural outgrowth of a sick culture?

Sweet Mother of God, I've lived here in Happy Valley, a German valley, through and through, and all my life ignored such questions. It couldn't happen here, it didn't happen here, what happened in Germany was all Hitler's fault—these were things I believed to be true. They *had* to be true, else none of my own faith made any sense. How could German Catholicism have turned its back on the German Jews? How could German Lutheranism have done the same? In God's name, who *is* to blame? Adolph Hitler did not act alone. Is Hitler the world's scapegoat, and Germany's scapegoat? Or was he indeed the voice of Germany, the active arm of her hate?

I closed my eyes and prayed. Even as the bells began to

ring, signaling the call to worship, I thought of my friend, Jonathan Green, the only Jew I've ever known. I prayed for him and for his people, asking God's forgiveness for my denial and for the Denial of the Church. I crossed myself in the name of Christ, the Ultimate Jew, the Son of God, the same God worshiped by Jews world wide, Jews in Jerusalem, even one Jew in Happy Valley, Jonathan's wife, Miriam. Somewhere along the line, Jonathan seems to have lost his faith. Who in the world could blame him?

As the mass proceeded, I watched the priest's every move, every familiar ritual step. The genuflecting before the bread and the wine, the body and blood of the Lord. The sacrament was begun on this day, this very day, the day of the Jewish Passover.

The bells and the smoke from the censor were particularly moving to me this morning. The Sacrament of Communion was begun on this day by a roomful of Jews. One Jew left early in order to betray his Master. Judas Iscariot. Was he the model and forerunner of Adolph Hitler? Who else could contemplate such crimes against man and God?

WHEN I GOT BACK HOME from mass, I phoned Sarah, just to hear her voice. The phone rang and rang. Normally, I would have hung up after five or six rings, but I let it go on and on. Just when I was going to give up, she answered.

"Hello," she said, a little out of breath.

"Good morning, Sarah. I hope I'm not disturbing you?"

"No, Frank, of course not. I was out in the garden. That's why it took me so long to answer."

"Sorry that I made you run."

"Don't be silly. I'm glad you called."

"Sarah, can I come over for lunch?"

"Sure ... is there something wrong, Frank?"

"I'm just in a weird mood, I guess. All to do with this being Passover and all."

Sarah knew that I was going to the Greens for Seder. In fact, she wished she could go with me, and even offered to change her plans at her own church, except it would have left them in a bind, apparently. She was involved in some kind of church dinner preparations. We had already agreed that I would go by myself, and she would get to meet them later, as soon as we could arrange it, maybe next week, sometime.

"You're sure you're feeling all right?" she asked.

"Yeah, sure. Just moody, I suppose. How about if I come over in an hour or so?"

"Fine, Frank. See you then."

WHEN I GOT TO THE FERRY, Ernie was in the middle of the river, halfway through a trip to my side. He was hauling Carl over, a first time for that, so far as I knew. They didn't see me at first, so I just watched as they came closer. I wondered if Ernie knew who Carl was? I mean if he knew that Carl's son, Jim, was trying to put his ferry service out of business?

Being inside Ernie's ferry was a whole different thing than watching it in operation from outside of it. I'd always thought of Ernie as being our Charon, the ferryman for the River Styx in Greek mythology. Seen from a distance, he really did remind me of an illustration I'd seen once for Dante's Inferno, where the ferryman stood in the same pose as Ernie. The major difference is that Ernie's silly Greek fisherman's cap added a touch of surrealism to the whole picture.

Here it was Passover and Ernie was helping people "pass over" from one side of the river to the other. Good grief, I sure was being moody and melodramatic.

"Frank," Carl hollered out when he saw me. "I was just on my way to your place."

"Well, I'm on my way to your side of the river. Want to ride back with me?" I asked him.

"Sure, I just need to talk with you for a minute," Carl said.

Carl moved over so there was room on the seat for the two

of us. I'd seen Ernie haul couples together, but I wasn't sure about two grown men.

"Is it okay, Ernie?" I asked before getting in.

"No problem, Frank."

That was the only thing Ernie said on the whole trip, so I took his silence to mean that he did know about Carl's being Jim Markdoffer's father. It dawned on me that it had to be pretty tough, providing a service to your opposition.

"Thanks, Ernie," I said, handing him the payment. He just nodded. When Carl and I started walking up the bank together, it was obvious to me that he had something important on his mind, but I just had to know about the ferry, first of all. "Why didn't you drive over, Carl?"

"I didn't want to miss you. I tried phoning a couple of times, but your line was busy so I knew you were there. This was the only way I could be sure of catching you."

Carl never did seem to catch the irony of his using the ferry for speed's sake, when his family seemed to be doing everything they could to put the ferry out of business.

"What's on your mind, Carl?" I asked him.

"Have you seen that bastard, Jonathan Green, lately?" he asked, without so much as a howdy-do.

Well, I can tell you one thing—with an introduction like that, I wasn't about to tell him I was going to see Jonathan that very night and spend Passover with him to boot.

"Yes, I saw him just the other day," I told Carl.

"Do you think that you could get him to lay off my son for a while?"

"What do you mean?" I asked.

"He's got injunctions out against Jim that are freezing up any further work on the bridge idea. It will cost their committee a ton of money fighting him in court. Green's acting like he's on a mission or something."

"Like I told you, Carl," I said. "I think it all goes back to his father and how he was cheated out of his business."

"Do you really believe that, Frank?"

"He's got proof of it."

"You're kidding me? Proof from sixty years ago?"

"Sure, it's all public record."

"Well, I'll be damned," Carl said. "What's he planning on doing with it? Suing the dead? Or is he going to take vengeance on the whole valley?"

"I don't know, Carl."

We stood there on top of the bank while Carl kicked some rocks down toward the water. I noticed that Ernie was moving around his boat, but keeping an eye on us at the same time.

"Damn it," Carl said vehemently, but then seemed to calm down a little. "Well, how about some lunch anyway, now that you're over here."

"I'm on my way to Sarah's for lunch."

"Sarah's? Oh, your lady-friend's?"

"That's right. Maybe we can do it next week sometime?" I suggested.

"Sure, some other time. I'll see you later, Frank."

I watched Carl as he headed off toward the diner by himself, but then he slowed down and changed directions, moving back up the street toward the Lutheran retirement home, looking lonely and lost.

I FOUND SARAH WORKING in her garden when I walked up the block to her place. She took one look at me and sat me down on a bench in the shade, right there in her garden, without so much as a hello kiss or anything. She asked me what was the matter, so I told her, everything, all my wacky thoughts about Germans and the Holocaust, my fears about this valley, and those of us living in it, and then running into Carl, looking so lonely. Sarah and I had already planned on a simple Easter dinner together, just the two of us. I asked her if I could invite Carl over, too. She said yes. After I wound down a little, Sarah reached up and kissed me on the cheek.

"That's one of the reasons I love you, Frank. You really care about people."

"But there's so much that I've missed, that I never even knew was happening, or pretended not to know."

"None of us is perfect, Frank. You can't carry the guilt of the world on your shoulders."

Her phrasing jolted me because Father Einsphar had used a similar phrase in describing Christ's experience in the Garden of Gethsemane, the guilt of the whole world bearing down on His shoulders, manifested in His sweating blood.

"What did you say? About the guilt?" I asked her.

"Just that you can't carry it all," she repeated.

We talked for a long time after that, just sitting there among all her flowers. It was a warm and pleasant day. Sarah made some lemonade and brought it out for us to enjoy in the sunshine. She didn't have the same kind of reaction as I did to the Holocaust, but she'd thought about it, too, wondering how Germans could do such a thing.

"I really believe it was the devil's work, Frank. That Hitler was the devil's tool."

"Carl told me that Lutherans don't believe in the devil."

"You mean with a pitchfork and a tail?" she asked, laughing for a minute. "Maybe not quite that graphic, but I do believe in the presence of evil here in this world. During World War II, I think that evil almost won the world."

"I know what you mean," I said. "If we hadn't finally gotten into the war, all of Europe could be Nazi now—what a thought that is!"

"But we did get into it, and that changed the balance, the balance of good and evil."

"Is it that simple —?" I asked, but I had no other words.

"It's just something I believe, Frank. Germans succumbed to Hitler's evil, ignoring the Holocaust while it was going on around them in a blind, patriotic support of their country's policies, wrong as they were. American Germans or German

Americans, however you want to say it—we finally got into the war, on the side of good. Our people killed each other, German against German, and good won out. I hope we never have to experience anything like it again."

That was the longest speech I'd ever heard Sarah make, and every word of it made sense to me. She simplified all the random, crazy thoughts that had been flying around in my head, simplified them down to Good versus Evil. It was the oldest battle since the beginning of time—the battle of good and evil in the world, in every community and society, and in every human heart.

"It's no wonder I love you, Sarah," I said, leaning over to give her a kiss on the lips. "You're a good woman."

"I think were both pretty lucky, Frank."

We sat there kissing and hugging on the bench in her garden, not exactly getting carried away like a couple of teenagers, but close enough.

"Sarah," I asked her, "could we —?"

"In the morning, Frank? Before noon, even?" she answered, smiling at me. "Well, why not?"

You don't need to know any more about that morning and afternoon, other than what I've told you already. I really am one lucky man. Sarah took me to her breast and healed me that day, healed me of a soul sickness. She was right. I didn't need to bear the guilt of the world. God had already done that for me, for us. My task was to love my neighbor.

I SHOWED UP AT THE GREEN'S, ready for anything, but I was still holding a piece of my immortal soul in check. Unconsciously, I caught myself saying an Our Father and a Hail Mary as I moved up the walkway to their house. The door was opened by Miriam, even before I could push the bell.

"Welcome to our home, Frank."

"Thanks, Miriam. I brought some wine for you—it's Manischewitz."

"Thank you, Frank," she said, smiling as if at some private joke.

"Is it all right?" I asked.

"Perfectly kosher."

"Good, good."

"Please sit. Jonathan will be out in a minute. I have him cutting the vegetables."

That exhausted my entire store of knowledge about Jewish customs. I had actually gone to the store looking for Mogen David wine, the only name I could remember, but found myself attracted to the Star of David on the Manischewitz label right next to the other brand. Not until I'd picked up the square bottle and was holding it in my hand, did I even consider the likelihood of a Himmelberg store's carrying a kosher wine. Were there actually some other Jews living in the valley?

"Welcome to our home, Frank," Jonathan said, as he entered the room.

The greeting must be some form of Passover ritual, I reasoned. I liked it, just as I always liked the familiar rituals of the Catholic Church.

"Thanks for having me," I said, shaking the hand he offered. Without thinking first, I asked him the question that was on my mind, "Jonathan, are there other Jews living in the valley?"

"Not many, Frank, but a surprising number. Enough in fact that they were already looking for a rabbi. My friend should work out perfectly. I don't think the valley has ever had a synagogue, do you?"

"Not to my knowledge, at least none that I can remember. There may have been one years ago, though I'm not sure." Nor could I even think of anyone I could ask.

"There was none when we moved here," Jonathan said.

"What did your family do? About services, I mean."

"Nothing. My father never attended synagogue, that I can

remember. My mother would have gone, but she didn't argue the matter."

"What do you mean?"

"My mother was the religious one. She had real community ties and never wanted to move here. The whole thing was my father's idea."

"I didn't know that."

"We didn't talk about such things outside of the family."

"Why did your father pick a place like the valley to live?"

"He didn't really want to be Jewish, at least that's my guess. Once he got out of the big city, he didn't have to be conscious of his heritage."

"But didn't he wear a yarmulke in his shop?"

"Yes, he did. My father was a bundle of contradictions."

"Shall we begin?" Miriam asked from the doorway leading to the dining room.

As we filed in for dinner, I was left with several more questions, but I had part of the answer now. Time would give me the rest.

I WATCHED IN AWE as Miriam completed the Seder rituals. She was dressed conservatively in a long woolen gown, old-fashioned even by valley standards. On her head she wore a scarf. I knew from Catholic ritual that it was to cover her hair, a woman's vanity. Our religions and rituals came from the same source, the Old Testament, emphasis on *old*. Some of these rituals were almost timeless. As I watched Miriam continue, I wondered if she minded her role as a woman in the Jewish faith. Jonathan had told me that she'd served two years in the Israeli military, bearing arms, something American women were only beginning to do. But how could Miriam feel like a second class citizen, when in many ways she was the focus of the ceremony?

"Halicome Yahwatee" is the best I can do in paraphrasing her words. The Hebrew was soft and lilting in her woman's voice but still guttural and full of aspirations compared to English.

After lighting the Seder candle, she wafted the smoke toward her face, reciting more Hebrew words that I didn't try to memorize because I was too caught up in the mysticism of the moment. Even I, the gentile guest, could sense the solemnity of the moment.

Soon it was the man's turn, apparently. From some of the things Jonathan had told me, I assumed he had lost his faith along the way, but he had no hesitation in handling his part of the ritual.

"Baruch Adonai," he intoned, going on for a little longer in Hebrew before switching into English. For my sake? I wondered. He was a powerful presence in that room. It made me guess that he would be a dynamic lecturer and a formidable judge. He thanked me for joining their family and asked God to bless the meal.

"Amen," I said.

Miriam turned to me, looked into my eyes and smiled, relieving me of the fear that I had pulled yet another blunder. I don't think I've ever felt so totally welcomed into a home.

THE FOOD WAS DELICIOUS, simply cooked but subtly spiced. A Paschal lamb served with beets and German potato pancakes. If this was Jewish food, I was more than happy. Maybe I had expected matzo balls and gefilte fish, names that were just about the limit of my expertise in Jewish cuisine. One "dish" she served consisted of parsley and salt, to remind Jews of the bitter tears they'd shed in captivity. The bread was unleavened to remind them of the speed they needed on the road out of Egypt. All these things Miriam explained to me, patiently, as if to a child, but not condescendingly, with pleasure instead, and a light in her eyes. After the meal, Miriam chased us into the living room while she cleaned up. Jonathan and I picked up the conversation where we'd left off.

"I still don't understand why your father would move you here, where you'd be the only Jews in the community."

"We weren't the *only* Jews, just the last."

"What do you mean?" I asked. "I don't remember any other Jewish families here."

"They were all gone by the time we got into middle school. We alone remained."

"You're kidding me?"

"No, Frank. It's the God's truth. All the other families were driven out, and then so was my father."

"You mean they were driven out because they were Jewish?" I said, stumbling over the thought, one I still had great difficulty associating with Happy Valley.

"Yes."

"I can't believe that, Jonathan."

And I couldn't, I swear to you that I could not believe it. Even as I sit here writing this story, it seems impossible. I am of an age where I can remember World War II, having been in the theaters to see the footage of Hitler's speeches in the news reels. I saw the pictures of the Jewish prisoners released from the concentration camps. I heard tapes of the interviews. As I talked with Jonathan, all those memories were newly refreshed in my mind. Such things could not have happened here in Happy Valley, they just couldn't.

Jonathan did not answer me. Instead we sat looking at each other. The coffee was untouched in our cups.

"You're a good man, Frank," he said softly. "I've always known that, but are you really that innocent, that naive?"

"Maybe I am, Jonathan. Tell me what happened. Please."

He explained what being Jewish in America had been like for his family in the years before the war, the years when Hitler was purging and purifying Germany. In many ways America did the same, those sympathetic to Hitler's views anyway. Synagogues were bombed and spray-painted. The Orthodox and Hasidic Jews caught the brunt of it because they physically stood out from the crowd, but anyone recognized as a Jew was a potential target.

"Why didn't they fight back?" I asked. "You know, like what the Jewish Defense League urged when Israel sought statehood?"

"That wasn't the JDL you're thinking about, Frank. More likely one of the activist fringe groups. Most American Jews of that time had a history of European ghettoes and pogroms behind them, a history which did not encourage standing up and complaining. My parents were born in this country but raised in a Jewish section of New York. They were born into fear and cultivated it in me."

"I was aware that country clubs and places like that were closed to Jews," I said, "but I never knew there was active prejudice. Like that wasn't active enough, I guess."

"The private clubs and housing were the most obvious," he answered me, "but antisemitism was woven into the whole fabric of this country, perhaps not as insidiously as in European nations, but we all came from those same attitudes."

"Surely *you* haven't experienced—" I started to say but realized how stupid the thought was. Of course he'd experienced prejudice, even as a judge, some of it from our friends, as a child. All his life, he'd faced prejudice. "What did you do?" I asked him after a pause.

"I took the standard route available, one of the routes, anyway, that of the Jewish over-achiever. I was an outstanding student—scholarships, law school, then a judgeship for a while, and finally a professor of law. None of it ever mattered, not completely. When the bottom line was reached, I was still the Jew, trying to fit into a white society."

"You don't think of yourself as white?" I asked him in surprise. Jonathan was as German as I, and white, for many generations. That much I did know.

"That's Miriam's influence, I guess," he said with a smile. "She used to remind me that we are Semitic, mid-Eastern and

Arabic, but certainly not white, not Aryan. That was Hitler's word—Aryan—his term for the pure."

"Guess I'd never thought of it that way," I confessed. "I just thought of you as German."

"Take my suggestion and don't get Miriam going on the subject." Again he smiled, openly, loosely, just as he used to smile when we were kids. "She was an art minor in college—a strange choice for a Jew in Israel, believe me. She's got a real thing about medieval art's portraying Christ as a bearded, blue-eyed Italian aristocrat."

I thought of my favorite picture of Christ, the one they used to hand out in Sunday School, and probably still do. Of course it was ridiculous to believe He'd looked like that, but I couldn't see him as an Arab, either. I did remember that someone had once painted an Angry Christ, in which He was depicted as olive-skinned with dark, flashing eyes and a scraggly beard. The picture had actually made me feel uncomfortable.

"Strange things ... stereotypes," I said, musing even as I spoke.

"Strange indeed," Miriam remarked, as she set a fresh coffee cup in front of me. I hadn't heard her enter the room. "Who would have thought we'd have you here, such an old friend of Jonathan's from the valley, as a guest for our Seder?"

AFTER SERVING THE COFFEE, Miriam returned to the kitchen to finish her cleaning up and leaving us to continue our former conversation.

"Did you never hear any of this before?" Jonathan asked, after we'd talked some more about what he could remember of the valley back then.

"None of it. Sure, I heard people say antisemitic things, as you know. I'm not proud of the things we said, to you especially, but I never knew anything about the rest of it. Are you absolutely sure?"

"Yes, Frank, I am. How could you not have known?"

"Good grief, Jonathan, I was only ten years old."

"So was I."

That difference stood like a gulf between us, the difference between a ten-year-old Catholic boy and a ten-year-old Jewish boy, each of them living in the same valley.

"Why didn't you tell me?" I asked.

"Why didn't you know?" he responded.

Again we fell into a silence, each trying to fathom the events of over half-a-century in the past. But just in saying that, I may be speaking out of turn for Jonathan. He may already have fathomed those events. On the other hand, I'd only begun to see them. *How much of this*—I wondered—*was still going on?*

Miriam walked back into the room, smiling, with more coffee, but she quickly stopped dead in her tracks.

"None of this, now!" she said. "Passover is a solemn event, but it's not a funeral. Look at the two of you. This might as well be a grave site."

We tried our best, but poor Miriam had to carry the bulk of the conversation from then on. Unfortunately, I was the guest, so I became the target of her questions. At least it kept me from thinking too much.

"Jonathan's not told me if you have children?"

"No, we never did."

"You're a widower?"

"Yes, my wife died—ten years ago, now."

"And you never remarried?" she asked, the surprise apparent in her voice.

"No, I couldn't." I struggled to explain the unexplainable. "Her dying stretched over three long years. It took the heart out of me." Was it that simple, really? Should I tell them the whole story about Sarah and me?

"I'm sorry, Frank. It is not good for a man to be alone."

Her phrasing struck me as curious, even so beyond the fact

that English was her second language. "Would it be any different for a woman being alone?" I asked.

"I don't know," she answered. "It just seems a woman is better able to handle solitude."

She looked at Jonathan as she said those words, words formed aloud for the first time, if I was right. He looked back, equally curious about her response.

"Well," I said, trying to bridge the silence that my question caused, "at the time, it just seemed easier to remain single. Actually, I don't believe I even thought about it much."

Both of them looked at me then, in such a way that I started to wonder if something really was wrong with me? Like maybe something was woefully lacking in my makeup? Male hormones, perhaps. How *could* I have stayed alone so long, for all these years? Settling for the movies on Friday?

Shoot, I couldn't let them continue looking at me like that. So far, Sarah and I hadn't told anyone about our plans, but we had to start sometime.

"Actually," I said, "Sarah Bruene and I are talking about getting married. Soon."

"That's wonderful, Frank," Miriam said. "You should have brought her tonight, then. We really must meet her."

"She couldn't, or I would have," I explained. "Her church had some kind of an affair tonight."

"I hope we get to meet her soon," Miriam said.

"You will," I told her and Jonathan. "I promise."

THEY WANTED TO KNOW all the details, of course, and kept me pretty busy by pumping for more information. When it got close to nine o'clock, I tried to say my goodbyes. I'd told Ernie I would meet him at the river about that time, but Jonathan wouldn't let me go until he'd given me something.

"I want you to have this, Frank. It's one of my father's pieces." He handed me an engraved silver cup, like a miniature of the cup used in communion.

"Oh, Jonathan. It's beautiful, but I couldn't take it. This is something that should go to your children."

"I've already given them several pieces. This one is for you."

"I don't know what to say."

"You are one of the few people in the valley who remember my father. We want you to have it, in his honor."

Miriam wrapped the cup in a cloth for me, and put it in a box.

"Thank you," I said. "Thank you, very much."

ALL THE WAY DOWN to the water, I thought through the evening. I was glad I had gone, if only for the Seder experience. I was a teacher, after all. New experiences were supposed to be my thing—learning and education. I was deeply touched by Jonathan's gift, and it had been good getting to know Miriam better, but all things considered, I was still going home alone. What had happened to me along the way, that I would end up like this? Thank God, that was changing. Soon Sarah and I would be an acknowledged couple.

Ernie was there waiting for me, looking ruffled as ever, dressed like a poor man's admiral, as he stood next to his ten-foot skiff.

"Evening, Frank."

"Hi, Ernie." I watched as he went about his preparations. What did I really know about the man? "Have you ever been married, Ernie?" I asked.

"Sure, Frank. Over thirty years, now."

"No kidding."

"That's right. I thought you knew?"

"Guess we never talked about it."

"I'm married to Ephie Bachman. She was in one of your classes at the high school. Long time ago, now."

"Sure, she used to go to my church, too."

"She's Lutheran now. We go to Our Redeemer, over here on

our side of the river, but you know that, from it being Sarah's church, too."

"Say hello to Ephie for me, will you, Ernie?"

"Glad to, Frank."

I WAS HALFWAY HOME before I realized that I'd forgotten to give Ernie his dollar and he had never asked for it. *What, I asked myself, was going on here?* Everything in my world was turning upside down. Even the simple things. Had I really lived here all my life and never seen what was going on right in front of me?

When I got home, I put Jonathan's silver cup on the mantle above the fireplace, among my precious photographs and other valuable memories. I sat down to think. It was Passover, and I got to wondering just how much of my life had passed right over my head?

The imagery of "passing over" was not lost on me in another way. I had just crossed over the river in Ernie's boat. I had always liked to think of him as Charon, ferrying souls from one side to the other, where the River Styx separated this world from the next, the temporal from the eternal, this life from the afterlife. But you could also see our river as something that separated us as a people, into East Himmelberg and West Himmelberg, not unlike the Berlin Wall that separated Germany into two nations during the many years of the Cold War.

I can still remember John Kennedy's "Ich ein Berliner" speech. It made me proud to be an American and a German-American. Kennedy was a Democrat, of course, but it took a Republican, Ronald Reagan, to finally say, "Mr. Gorbachev, take down this wall!" Both of them were prophets in a way because they realized just how small our modern world really is. We need to learn how to live together. Wasn't it also time for us in Happy Valley to end this East-West bickering? I was absolutely opposed to a four-lane bridge because that would mean a four lane highway on both sides of the valley and all the congestion and traffic it would bring, but a two-lane bridge with pedestrian walks on both sides would reunite us as a city. If the bridge meant that change must follow, so be it.

Chapter Eight:
   The Countdown to Easter

GOOD FRIDAY

I ALWAYS LOOK FORWARD to the Tre Ore Services on Good Friday, when all of Christendom grows silent and pensive during the three hours of Christ's suffering on the cross. This year I went with Sarah to her church, a daring new adventure in my spiritual journey. We talked it over the night before, after I'd gotten home from Jonathan's. I phoned Sarah and suggested that it was time for us to start telling people. In fact, I'd already told a couple, the Greens. That's when she invited me over for their services. It was a chance to hear from some of the lay speakers in the Our Redeemer Lutheran Church. Had I known who those speakers were going to be, one of them anyway, I might not have gone.

Carl's son, Jim, looked all prim and proper up there in his suit and tie, but I couldn't much enjoy his appearance for what I was thinking about him. Hypocrite, thief, con-man, liar, and cheat—and those were just some of the nicer things I called him in my mind. As far as I was concerned, Jim's idea for the bridge was based on greed and profit, not any altruistic love for the city. I had no idea how much real estate he had already bought up in anticipation of the shopping centers and malls that his freeway and four-lane bridge would need. Here I was in a church and having some very un-Christian thoughts, so I tried to put it to rest, at least for a while, until Easter was past.

Each of the seven lay speakers were to talk on one of the seven Words of Christ from the Cross. Jim was one of the earlier speakers, and his topic was (appropriately enough) based on the episode involving the two thieves, one crucified on either side of the Lord. Now, how's that for a little irony? A thief! Even before Jim began his talk, I ran the Biblical story through my mind. The one thief ridiculed Christ, but the second one believed in Him. Christ promised that man, "This day shall thou be with me in Paradise." He'd been forgiven, but who was there to forgive Jim Markdoffer? Not me, that's for sure.

On the other side of the aisle and closer to the front, Carl was sitting with Jim's wife, Joanne, both of them looking proud as punch. I wondered what that was all about. Wasn't this the son who'd barely allowed Carl into the valley? Had they reconciled, or was it all for show?

IN SPITE OF MY CYNICISM and suspicions, I found myself getting all caught up in Jim's talk. It was the first time I'd really heard him do any sort of public speaking. Though he'd been active in local politics for a long time, he was usually the man behind the scenes. Everyone knew him, but they didn't know much about him. At least none of the people I knew really knew him—if that makes any sense. Maybe it was different here in his own church, the Lutheran church. I wondered if he was the hypocrite or if I was? Hadn't I already judged him and found him wanting without really knowing him? Hadn't I already condemned him?

Jim didn't so much preach on that part of the Passion Story as he rewrote it from a different angle. He put himself into the role of the repentant thief, and gave us the story that way.

"Shut up," he hollered to the other thief. "This man's done nothing to you. Leave him alone."

"Tell me," the repentant thief said to the Lord, "are you really what they say?"

"What is it that men say I am?" Christ answered.

"Some say you are the Son of God. Others say you're just another false prophet."

"What do *you* believe?" Christ asked him.

"The thief turned his head as far he could, against the pain of the ropes that bound him to the cross, trying to see into the face of our Lord. For a moment, Jesus struggled against His own physical pain, His pain being that of the nails through his palms and ankles, and that of the Crown of Thorns. Slowly, Christ lifted and turned His face toward the thief.

"What do you think he saw in that face?" Jim Markdoffer asked us, the congregation. "What did the thief see in the face of our Lord?

"Use your own imaginations. Did he see a light, perhaps a halo around Christ's head? Did a light reach from Jesus's eyes all the way into the heart of the thief? Did the man just look into that face and see God? Or did he look into those eyes and see an innocent Man sent from God? Whatever he saw made him believe.

"'Remember me when you come into your kingdom, Lord,' the man asked, a simple profession of faith.

"'This day, shalt thou be with me in Paradise,' was Christ's answer.

"This very day, Christ promised the man, each of them knowing they would die before the sun set. This very day.

"We are gathered here to celebrate this day in history. We grieve Christ's death, but we celebrate what His dying means for the world, what it meant for that thief on the cross."

Jim sat down then, and we all sang a hymn.

I DIDN'T HEAR MUCH of the next speaker's talk because I was still thinking about Jim's sermon, his homily, or whatever Lutherans call them. He was sincere, which made me more confused than ever. I had good reason to mistrust the man, from what Carl had told me about their relationship, and from what I already suspected about his involvement in the bridge project. But Carl had been sitting right there, up front, listening to his son, proud as punch. What was the truth? Would I ever know?

And what made me think there was a single Truth, a shining, singular essence?

Here I go, getting philosophical again, but I just can't seem to help it. Maybe it's that time of year, again—the Lenten season. Human nature can turn a man into a thief, but that same man can recognize the presence of God. Go figure it. I've seen it every way possible—good, bad, indifferent. Every time I think I've got it nailed down tight, something shifts, or the light changes, and I've lost it, lost the Truth.

SARAH AND I LEFT after one more speaker. You didn't have to stay for the whole three hours. People drifted in and out all the time, obviously coming to hear someone they knew or just dropping in for a few minutes to honor the occasion. One of Sarah's girlfriends was the final speaker that we heard. I didn't think much about it until Sarah told me it was the first year that a woman had been allowed to take part. I knew that women were making similar demands in my own Church, some nuns even asking to be made priests. Lots of changes going on everywhere in the world.

Around three o'clock, I was still at Sarah's place when a sudden spring thunder storm moved in. One minute, the air was warm but heavy, and the next there was so much electricity in the atmosphere that I shocked myself just walking across the carpet. The light in the room changed, at that moment, as if someone had pulled down the shades.

"Here we go," I told Sarah after looking out her window. The sky had grown black and angry almost in an instant. Even as I watched, I saw lighting on the horizon, followed a few seconds later by thunder.

"I hope it doesn't ruin our Easter plans," she said, walking into the doorway between the living room and her kitchen. She stood there for a minute, drying her hands on the apron she wore. "What's wrong?" she asked, when she saw that I was watching her.

"Nothing at all," I said. "I'm just looking at the most beautiful woman in the world."

Just then a bolt of lightning flashed behind Sarah, illuminating her in an eerie, incandescent glow. The second flash and the crack of thunder which followed it were very close together. As the rains began, Sarah was again lit from behind, the light coming through the kitchen window. The vertical and horizontal molding in that window formed a cross over her shoulder. I was almost hypnotized by the picture Sarah made—she and the cross and the light.

"I love you," came a voice, soft and melodious from out of the thunder and lighting.

"Forgive me for being such a fool?" I asked. "For waiting so long?"

"All that's in the past, Frank. Now, we have nothing but the future."

Sarah walked into my arms, we kissed, and then we stood in her front room, in the bay window, listening to the thunder and watching for the lighting. The storm was intense but brief. At one moment, the sky was split asunder by the ferocity of the elements, then the sun lit up the sky even though the rain continued to fall for a few minutes longer. In another minute, the only trace of the storm's passing was the steady dripping of the water from the rooftop.

MUCH TOO SOON, I had to leave for the ferry. Sarah had already planned to have an early dinner with a friend, someone from her Ladies Auxiliary. She was going to drive around later and pick me up for some visits she wanted to make, but I needed to be home for a phone call. I had promised my sister, Pru, that I would be home in the late afternoon to wish her whole family a Happy Easter. When I called yesterday, she was there by herself. We had a nice enough visit, but our tradition is that each of us gets to talk with the other, first, then I get to say hello to all the rest of her family. I was planning on telling her about our wedding plans, but as I walked down Sarah's street, I started having second doubts. Pru had always been good friends with my first wife, Ruthie. Suddenly, I wondered how it would sit with my sister that I was going to marry again.

Ernie was in a surprisingly good state of mind. I mean the man had been pretty moody lately, what with his livelihood being threatened by the possibility of a new bridge.

"So how are you this fine day, Frank?" he greeted me.

"Pretty good, Ernie. What's gotten into you?"

"I've always loved the rain, Frank. Ever since I was a little kid. Lots of people don't like it, I know, but it just makes me happy."

"Even if it costs you some business?" I asked.

"Shoot, Frank, business will take care of itself."

Today, the man was utterly irrepressible. Ernie whistled and did a little dance all the way across the river as he poled me to the other side. I couldn't help but smile watching him.

"You're a card, Ernie," I told him as I got out of his boat.

"No reason not to be happy, Frank. That's why they call it Good Friday."

His words stayed with me all the way up the hill and into my own front room. Why had I always seen Good Friday as a time of mourning, when it was called "good?" It was a good day, not just for Ernie, but for me, and for everyone.

MY SISTER CALLED ME before I had the chance to call them. I'd just sat down on my couch to look out my front window at the beauty of God's world. The shadows were starting to lengthen now that the afternoon was slipping away.

"Hello," I said picking up the phone on the first ring.

"It's me, Frank," Pru said. "Happy Easter."

"Happy Easter to you, too."

"Let me get the kids—" she started to say.

"Wait a minute, Pru," I said. "I've got something to tell you first." Why wait? I asked myself.

"What's that, big brother?"

"Do you remember Sarah Bruene?" I asked.

"Sure, she was right ahead of me in school."

"Well, she and I've been seeing a lot of each other." I just let that statement hang out there for her to ponder.

"A lot, like serious?" she asked.

"Yes, we're thinking about getting married."

"That makes me cry, Frank. I'm so happy for you."

"That's good," I said. "It's a relief."

"Relief?" she said, sniffling. "Were you worried about what I'd think?"

"Sort of, you know—you and Ruth were always so close."

"I loved Ruthie like a sister, Frank. I'll never forget her, but she's been gone a long while now. It's time you found someone, long overdue, in fact. You and Sarah are perfect for each other. I remember when her husband was killed. You'll be good for her, too. When's the wedding?"

"Well, we were hoping for a quiet ceremony —"

"Right, brother. You can forget that," she said, interrupting my feeble efforts. "The whole valley will be there, including me and mine. God, I hope you don't faint. You almost did when you married Ruth. Remember?"

That's all I needed to start thinking about, now. After forty years of teaching, I'd finally gotten used to talking in front of groups of people, but each new school year, my heart would pound in fear. What would the new classes be like? Would there be troublemakers? Or good students? It was always the same, no matter how many classes I met. The one good thing about my school was that Mildred Klein, who taught social studies, was always worse than I was. She would throw up every year on opening day. I don't know that her getting sick helped me any, other than making me feel less foolish, but I was always grateful for Mildred.

Everybody at my first wedding had kidded me about being weak in the knees. I laughed off the first two or three jokes, but after a couple more said the same thing, I figured that I must have looked like a wreck. Thank God, I settled down before my vows and managed to repeat the minster's words without any problem.

"Thanks for reminding me, Pru," I told my sister.

"You'll be fine, Frank—here, let me get Mike and the kids to say hello to you."

Pru's husband, Mike, congratulated me, even asked if I was going to have a bachelor's party. I can just see that now—a roomful of old geezers staring at a stripper. The kids got on the line and we all wished each other a Happy Easter.

SARAH PULLED HER CAR into my driveway just around sunset. Though it was Friday, she came over not so much for our regular date, because she could have just taken the ferry for that, but she had some church work to do. She was going to visit a couple of shut-in's from her church who lived on my side of the river.

"Would you like to go with me?" she'd asked after we'd had an early lunch at her place, before the Tre Ore services.

"I don't know," I said, "what's involved?"

"Nothing much. We just visit, let them talk about their families, their lives, say a prayer together—that kind of thing. Most of them are lonely, that's all."

"Sure, I guess."

If that sounds less than enthusiastic, it was. How would you like to do something like that for part of your Friday night? The only reason I said yes was because I wanted to be with Sarah, to spend time with her and support her activities. I never even considered the possibility that I would know any of these shut-in's, though I should've realized that was possible, considering how small our valley really is.

The first place was way up a hill. Even before we got to the house, I could see why the person was shut in—an older person would really find it tough going up and down the steep approach to the place. But when we got to the top, I could just as readily see why someone would choose to live up here and want to keep on doing it, no matter what. The house was angled so that the front view was a panorama of the valley, as it showed the meandering of the river until it disappeared through the south pass. Bad as my eyes are, the view was breathtaking. We arrived just as the sun was setting behind the house.

"This is beautiful," I told Sarah. For a minute, we stood there, holding hands, just looking at the valley in the changing light. "I don't think I've been up here since I was a kid."

"Do you know whose house this is?" she asked me.

"No," I said, looking at the place, "though I think I've been inside before, sometime. It's just that I can't remember when or with whom."

Sarah led me up to the front door. She knocked loudly on the door before pushing it open.

"Maude? It's me, Sarah, and a friend."

"Come in," I heard a firm, dignified voice respond.

Maude? I thought to myself, *now how many Maudes have I ever known*? Then it came to me—Maude Joesting, it had to be her. She was the widow of Ken Joesting, the last of the family that founded or help found the valley. Maude had to be ninety-five if she were a day. My God, I'll bet she was born at the turn of the century.

Sure enough, it was she. I recognized Maude from back when she was more active. She's a dignified, stately woman. Even her being confined to a chair in her own front room hadn't destroyed that part of her. Maude was dressed for a visit, everything from earrings and brooch to polished shoes. All she lacked was gloves and a hat, and she could've gone to the opera.

"Do you remember Frank Hessel, Maude, from the high school?" Sarah asked her, pushing me forward.

"Of course, I do," the old lady said, holding out her hand for me to take. "How are you, Frank?"

"Just fine, Mrs. Joesting. It's good to see you again."

"It's just Maude, Frank. We're too old to stand on formalities, don't you think?"

"Yes, ma'am," I answered her, "Maude, I mean," though I wasn't too sure I liked being included in her generation, one of the "too old" people.

"Sit down, sit down," she said, indicating a velvet upholstered couch that faced the window.

"Your view is absolutely beautiful," I said, sitting alongside Sarah. And I meant it. The whole valley was laid out before us. The view remained beautiful even as the sky darkened, because one-by-one the lights of the city started coming on. I don't think I could remember seeing a night view from a nicer angle. Still and all, I was trying to remember the last time I'd been here. Too much of the house and its furnishings were familiar.

"Do you remember the last time you were here, Frank?" Mrs. Joesting asked as if she were reading my mind.

"That's what I was trying to recall—Maude. I know I've been here, but it must be a long time ago."

"Right after the war, for William's funeral."

"Of course," I said, as it all came rushing back.

William Joesting, Bill we all called him. Four years ahead of me in school. He'd been killed in a plane over Germany while on a bombing mission. In a B-29, if I remembered correctly. Rumor had it that he was buried, here, but with nothing of him in the casket because the plane had just exploded in air. There were plenty of eyewitnesses in other planes, but no bodies to recover.

Fifty years ago it had made the headlines of the local paper, Bill being the only one from the valley to have died on or over German soil, just before the final land push toward Berlin. He was the last soldier from the valley to die in the war.

"You knew my son?" she asked.

"Sure, Bill was four years ahead of me in school, but I always knew who he was. Shoot, everyone knew him."

Chin up, eyes clear, staring out the window—this dignified old woman nodded in agreement.

What a loss, I thought to myself. Bill had been the last of the Joestings. His father and mother both survived him, but now only Maude remained. The last member of one of the oldest, founding families. When she started talking, it was like listening to living history.

"My goal, Frank, is to make it to the next century. Sarah knows all about that. She thinks I'll do it, but we'll just have to see. If I should live so long, I'd be over a hundred years old and have lived in three different centuries."

"Did you know Rachel Rosen?" I asked, the name coming back to me from the gravestone in the cemetery.

"Yes, I knew the Rosens well. Their daughter, Naomi, was my age. We played together until they moved away. Mrs. Rosen, Rachel, died and the husband took them to be with the rest of the family, somewhere in the midwest, I think. Chicago it might've been. That was before the First War. How could you possibly have known them?" she asked.

"I didn't," I answered her. "I just saw the headstone in the cemetery this week. The name stayed with me. Were there many Jews in the valley, then?"

"Well, let me think a minute. There were the Rosens, the Weisses, the Goldsteins, and then the Greenbaums, later on. Yes, there were quite a few at one time. Sarah, could you bring me the scrapbook from the shelf there, the one on the very far end?"

In that book, Maude actually found pictures of Jonathan's parents, and one of him as a boy, taken in the 1930's.

"Mrs. Joesting," I asked her, "could I bring a friend of mine to see you? Would you be willing to speak with him and show him your pictures?"

"Of course, Frank. Anytime."

I COULD'VE STAYED THERE for another hour, but Maude Joesting was getting tired. Even I could see that, so we left after wishing her a Happy Easter. Sarah said a simple prayer with her, and off we went to the next visitation. I had a million questions for Maude Joesting, but Sarah explained that it took her an hour to get ready for a visitor—and only then with the help of her long-term housekeeper, who was almost as old as Maude, herself—but that she could only visit for so long before getting very tired. We'd already been there for half an hour and that was the limit Sarah would stay. You've already guessed what I was thinking—about taking my friend, Jonathan, over to see Maude Joesting. She would be happy to talk with him, and the trip might do Jonathan some real good.

"I thought we had another stop?" I said to Sarah, when I saw that she was pulling into my street, Bucher Lane.

"We do. It's your neighbor."

"You're going to see Ed Shrader?" I asked, astonished. I never even knew that cranky old bastard went to church. He must sneak out after I leave for mass.

"We're going to see him, Frank. You and me, together."

"Oh, no, Sarah," I said. "There is a limit. I draw the line at Ed—that's going too far."

"Just come with me, Frank. I might need your protection if he's as bad as you say."

I had already heard that Ed recently broken his arm in a fall, but I sure wasn't planning on visiting him, even if he did live right next door to me. Oh well, I thought, if Sarah needs me along with her, I might as well go. Sarah rang the bell, and we heard a voice from inside.

"Come on in, it's open."

"Hello, Ed, it's Sarah and Frank come to visit."

"Frank who?" he asked before he'd seen me, as gracious a host as he'd always been. "Oh, it's you," he said.

"Hi, Ed," I said greeting him in all Christian charity. "Sorry to see you laid up."

"Uh huh," he said. "Did you convert or what?"

"No, I'm just keeping Sarah company."

"That's good," he said. "I can't see you as a Lutheran."

"What's that supposed to mean —" I said, rising to the bait.

"Knock it off, you two," Sarah said with a smile, but she was serious. I could see it, and so could Ed. "How's the arm, Ed?" she asked him.

"It's getting better, slow but sure. The doctor said there's nothing I can do for it but to take it easy, get as much rest as I can."

"Hurts, does it?" I asked, less out of Christian charity, this time, than wanting to needle him.

"So bad that I wouldn't even wish it on you, Frank."

"Anything we can do for you, Ed?" Sarah asked, interrupting us before we could get started again.

"No, thanks, Sarah," he answered her. "I've got plenty of food in the house. It's a struggle but I can get in and out of the kitchen now."

"Tell you what," Sarah said. "I'll send over a couple of casseroles with Frank. You can just reheat them, or have Frank do it for you."

I looked at the woman like she'd lost her mind. When I glanced over at Ed, I saw he was looking at her the same way, as if he'd sooner starve than have me fix him a meal. Ed looked at me, and I tried to glance away, the whole thing striking me as ironic, if not downright funny.

"What's so danged funny?" he asked, looking right at me.

"I was just thinking about my fixing you some dinner, Ed. Nice picture, don't you think?"

"Yeah, it's downright hysterical."

The more I thought about it, the funnier it got. During all the rest of our visit, I got to looking forward to bringing Ed a casserole and heating it up for him. It would be the perfect way to get one up on that old coot. I could hardly wait.

We didn't stay too long after that, just enough time for Sarah to say another quick prayer over Ed. I didn't even close my eyes, but Ed did. Son of a gun, I guess there was some hope for him, after all.

"See you later, Ed," I promised him on the way out, hardly able to stand the wait until I could fix him a tray.

"You, too, Frank," he said. "Maybe I can return the favor sometime, but just sprain something, will you? I wouldn't wish a broken bone on anyone, even you."

"Bye, Ed," Sarah said, pushing me out the door before I could answer him back.

"Bye, Sarah," he said. "Thanks for coming."

"Honestly, you two," she said to me on the porch after she'd closed the door. "You're just like a couple of kids."

"How soon can you have those casseroles ready?" I asked her, hardly able to wait.

SINCE WE HAD BEGUN the day at Sarah's church, Our Redeemer, we ended it with the Midnight Mass at St. Ignatius. In many ways it's my favorite service of the year. Instead of the modern folk mass, this one used all the old ritual, the Latin liturgy with the choir and the parishioners singing back and forth. I remember from the morning service that I had not been certain of when to stand and when to sit or kneel, so I made sure that I cued Sarah ahead of time.

One of my former students had written in his weekly journal about his confusion when he visiting a Catholic church with a friend. "They went up and down like yo-yo's," he wrote. I've never forgotten the imagery. He made it very funny with his standing up when everyone else sat down, and sitting down when everyone else jumped to their feet. Sarah and I stood and sat and kneeled together, as if we had been doing it all out lives.

Afterwards, several friends came up to say hello, far more than normal, but that was because they all wanted to greet Sarah. I tried to ignore their silly grins, but I found myself smiling right along with them. Because of her part-time job at the gift shop, Sarah already knew most of them anyway. Those she didn't know, I introduced. Then we walked the three blocks back to my house. It was a chilly, clear night, with thousands of stars looking down on us. We held hands all the way home.

Chapter Nine:
   Holy Saturday

HOLY SATURDAY

ON SATURDAY OF HOLY WEEK, usually called Holy Saturday, I woke up next to Sarah Bruene, the love of my life. I had a moment's guilt when I thought of Ruth, my first wife, because this had been our bedroom, but I knew she would understand. Ruth always liked Sarah, and Sarah liked her. Those were just some of the many thoughts I had that morning as I watched Sarah at rest. As I've already told you, she is a handsome woman. Asleep, there was an innocence about her that could soften the hardest heart.

Perhaps I should have felt guilty about sleeping with a woman before we were married, but I'm a little too old and too much in love to waste time on thoughts like that. We'll be married soon enough. We've already wasted too much time.

Around 6:00 am, I slid out of bed and went to the kitchen. Coffee, toast, bacon and eggs would have to do. I'm not a great chef, but I'm a pretty good cook, with just the basics. I knew that Sarah did not get up as early as I did, so I read the paper first, cooked the food and at 7:00 went in to wake her for our first breakfast alone together. It was a good way to start our new life.

LATER, I RODE ACROSS the river to have lunch with Sarah. She left right after breakfast to do some errands on her side of the river. Her car had sat there in my driveway all night long.

Oh well, I thought, soon enough we'll be married and it won't matter a fig what people think, even people like Ed Shrader.

Ernie poled slower than usual, as if he had a lot on his mind. It was a complete contrast to how happy he'd been the day before. Ernie darn near came to a complete stop in the middle of the river. What the heck? I wasn't in a hurry.

Downstream from us, I noticed a young man walk out of the woods toward the river. He had skin the color of the Angry Christ, in marked contrast to the white swim trunks he wore. The man stepped out onto Robert's Rock, just as we used to do as kids, in preparation for diving into the river at its deepest point within the town limits. Generations of kids had been doing the same thing on that selfsame spot. Don't ask me who Robert is—of Robert's Rock—because I don't have a clue.

The young man, probably still a teenager, put one foot into the water but quickly pulled it out again. Though the day was pleasant enough, it was still April and the water had to be freezing cold this time of year. He placed the wet foot on top of his other one, probably to warm it. In order to keep his balance, he put both arms out straight, away from his body. I almost gasped because he looked just like a living Crucifix—without the cross, of course, but the pose was the same. The sunlight reflected off the water, bathing his skin with an eerie golden glow.

"Jesus," I heard Ernie say.

"Amen," I whispered in response, then realized that he'd phrased it in the Spanish—Hay-Seuss. Ernie then went on to say something else that I didn't understand.

"What'd you say, Ernie?" I asked, my eyes still riveted on the young man, even though he had now dropped the pose.

"Mexicans is what I said," Ernie explained. "Don't know how they can use Jesus's name like that, even if they do pronounce it different."

"He's Mexican?" I asked.

"Um huh. Je-sus Morales. Works over at the diner. You didn't think he was the real thing, did you?"

"Who me?" I answered, laughing in defense.

"I did, too, for just a second," Ernie said, ignoring my feeble denial. "My heart darned near quit on me. Day before Easter and all."

ON THE WAY to Sarah's I stopped in at the only travel agency in town. It's not even that, really. The place is an insurance office, but George Zhender and his wife make arrangements for trips through a firm in Madison. They carry all the brochures and stuff right there in the office. Millie Zhender was standing behind the counter when I walked in.

"Good morning, Frank," she said. "I haven't seen you in a good long while. What can I do for you?"

"Hi, Millie. I was wondering if you have any packaged trips to Germany?"

"Sure do, right over here. For how long? A week, two weeks?"

"Let's start with two weeks, and see how much that's going to cost."

"For just yourself?" she asks.

"No, figure it for two people."

"Oh good, so you and Sarah are thinking about going over?" she asked.

Was there anyone in this entire valley who didn't know about me and Sarah? One single, solitary soul?

"I'm thinking about taking her, but please, Millie, don't say anything. It would be a surprise. She doesn't know about it yet."

"Sure thing, Frank. I just love secrets. This wouldn't be a honeymoon trip, would it?" she asked, then added, when she saw my expression, "Sorry, Frank, not another word." She actually pantomimed zipping her lips with a finger.

Millie got busy, then, pulling out pamphlets from the racks

in front of her and a couple from the cabinets underneath, smiling and humming to herself the whole time. She can be an irritating woman at times.

"Thanks, Millie," I said, when she plunked the first batch in front of me.

"Oh, I'm not done yet, Frank," she said. "You've got a lot of reading ahead of you."

"Isn't there a single package, already put together?" I asked her, already overwhelmed by the stack she'd given me.

"There's a million different packages. You just have to tell me what you want to see."

"Well, Sarah's got some cousins over there that she wants to visit."

"Where do they live?" she asked.

"I don't have the slightest idea," I told her.

"Well, that would be a good place to start," she said, smiling at me again, in that irritating way. "Anything that you wanted to see in particular."

"I'd like to see East Germany—East Berlin, anyway—at least to walk into it, and see where the wall used to be."

"Sure, any of the Berlin tours do that."

"Have you and George been to Germany?" I asked.

"Lots of times. For several years, we guided a tour through Germany. Two weeks every summer."

"Have you seen any of the concentration camps?" I asked.

"Two in Germany, Dachau for one, but Auschwitz or Oswiecim in Poland is the one that they've preserved the best."

"Why did you go?"

"Probably for the same reason you're asking about them," she said, looking at me closely. "I had to see them for myself before I could believe something like that could really happen. You know, how could civilized people do that? Germans, no less. How could our people do that?"

"Yeah," I answered her. "I know what you mean."

"Tell you what, Frank. If you're really planning on

surprising Sarah, why don't you take these two and put them in a card for her? Then the two of you could come in together and decide on an itinerary."

"Thanks, Millie," I said. "That's a good idea. I'll do it. See you later on."

"Sure, Frank, and mum's the word," she said, zipping her lips with her finger once more.

Millie was smiling again as I turned to walk out of the store. She is just about the smilingest woman I've ever met.

I HAD ALREADY PICKED UP an Easter card for Sarah, which I had with me, so I sat down outside the drugstore to figure out a message to write inside. "Happy Easter, I love you, let's go to Germany on our honeymoon"—that was just about what I wrote, nothing too fancy. For all the English teaching I did, I've never been any good at poetry, especially love poetry.

This would just have to do, I thought, as I put the two brochures inside the card. I'd already sealed the envelop and written Sarah's name on the outside before I realized that I hadn't looked at the brochures myself, other than the covers. Oh well, I would be at her house in a little while. We could do it, together.

For just a minute, I sat on the bench, right there in East Himmelberg, looking around. I've lived on the west side for so long, that I actually saw some changes for the first time. A couple of new businesses were struggling to get started. One a new beauty shop and manicurist. The other a New Age bookstore. I didn't know what "new age" meant for sure, until I walked past it on the way to Sarah's. In the window, was a crystal ball draped in cloth, and lots of quartz pendants hanging around. I gave it about one month before they went broke, but what did I know anymore about what people read? Several of the books were of the self-help variety. You know the kind—How to find a man and get pregnant, all in one hour, and How to make a million dollars in your spare time. Who knows? Maybe the Easterners are into this kind of stuff?

I continued on to Sarah's place, saying hello or nodding to several people along the way. We were all one people anyway, so what could the bridge hurt? For one thing, it might bring in more occult bookstores.

Sarah thanked me for the card, and said that she would open it the next day, which made sense, because that would be Easter Sunday, but I wanted her to see the brochures right away.

"Why don't you open it now, Sarah?" I said to her, getting antsy to see her reaction.

"Honestly, Frank. You're just like a little kid, sometimes. I should make you wait until tomorrow."

"No, you shouldn't. This is special."

"Special?" she asked, looking intrigued. "Well, okay, but only this once."

Even before she opened the card itself, one of the brochures fell out of it onto her lap. It was blue, with a simple title across the top in white, capital letters—GERMANY. For a minute, Sarah just sat there looking at the brochure.

"Like it?" I asked.

"Are you serious?" she asked. "Really?"

"Open it up. I thought we could go for a honeymoon."

"Oh, Frank. That would be so wonderful," she said, reaching out and giving me a kiss on the cheek. "Are you sure about this?"

"Sure of what? Marrying you or taking the trip?" I said, teasing her a little.

Well, we spent the rest of the afternoon making plans, trying to figure out a wedding date, and what places we would like to visit. Stuff like that, with a little spooning thrown in, along the way. It serves you right, if you have to look that one up in the dictionary—spooning, I mean.

I left about 5:30 or so, not wanting to set Sarah's neighbors to talking. It was already bad enough with everyone else looking into our business. Besides which, Sarah had some kind of a meeting of her women's auxiliary. She was coming over in the morning for Easter services with me, so I'd see her soon enough.

"Let me get the casseroles for Ed," she said, remembering them just before I got out the door.

"Anything I need to know about them?"

"Nothing special. Just heat them up at three-fifty. They're ready to eat."

I gave Sarah a passionate kiss and said goodby. Let the neighbors stew on that one for a while.

ERNIE THOUGHT IT WAS funny as all get out that I would be taking food to Ed Shrader. Without my telling him, he knew it would be a perfect comeback in our ongoing feud.

"That's a good one, Frank," he told me. "It'll take Ed a couple of years to get even with you."

"Just what I'm hoping, Ernie. What do you think? Should I serve him on paper plates or my best china?"

"The china would be a good touch, but pretty risky—he might up and throw it at you."

"Yeah," I said, thinking to myself that the paper plates would have to do.

THAT IS JUST WHAT I DID—heated up a tuna noodle casserole for my neighbor, Ed Shrader. Believe it or not, we didn't come to blows or anything of the sort. In fact, we enjoyed just about the most decent conversation we've had together since we both retired from teaching. Don't hold your breath any. It was just a conversation, nothing more. What the heck. Maybe it's just the Easter season or something, but he's not such a bad duck, after all, and this feeding him casseroles really puts me one up on him—that's for sure.

Before I left, after feeding the man, I got to wondering if he would be needing anything on Easter. A week ago, it never would've crossed my mind, but now, well, what was I supposed to do?

"Say, Ed," I asked as I washed up the glasses we'd used. "Do you have someone coming over for Easter?"

"Yeah, my son and his family are coming over to take me out. We've got reservations at Luigi's."

"That's good," I said.

"You're not starting to worry about me, are you Frank?" he asked, with a smirk on his face.

"Fat chance," I answered.

"You know something, Frank?" he said. "You'll make someone a good wife one of these days. If you need an apron, they're in that middle drawer."

I was very tempted to tell the man about Sarah, and our getting married, but I thought I'd save that for next week sometime, maybe when he had his mouth full of one of Sarah's casseroles.

The truth is I didn't want to argue with Ed anymore, not today. I was feeling much too good for that. Besides which, I really was glad he had a dinner planned—not for myself, so I wouldn't have to fix him a plate—but just that no one should be alone on Easter, not even Ed Shrader.

Chapter Ten:
Easter Sunday

THE FEAST OF THE RESURRECTION

AS I HAD FOR NEARLY every year of my life, I went to the sunrise Easter mass at St. Ignatius. The only times I can recall missing were two of the years in college when I stayed on campus over the holiday break to study and maybe two other times when I was just too sick to attend, one being last year while I was in the hospital having my leukemia diagnosed. This Easter, Sarah sat beside me for the first time ever. As I held her hand, I couldn't help wondering how we would resolve our commitments to different churches. Somehow, we would work it out. I met her at the river after making arrangements with Ernie to bring her over early. He normally didn't start up his ferry until eight o'clock, but he said that he was happy to oblige but only on one condition.

"You got to promise not to convert her, Frank. We need Sarah in the choir." As it turns out, Ernie has also been singing in the Lutheran choir for years—something else I didn't know.

"We'll work it out, Ernie. It's all the same God, no matter what."

"Reckon that's true, Frank. Think you'll ever get Jonathan Green to attend mass with you," he said, with a twinkle in his eye.

"He just might, if he had a good reason ... but wait, did you know they are going to start up a synagogue?"

"No kidding. Say, what side of the river do you suppose it'll be on?"

"I have no idea."

"Well, I guess it wouldn't really matter," he said. "Who knows? I might end up with a little extra business out of it. Friday nights and Saturdays, I guess it'd be. Who would have thought that I'd be ferrying Jews back-and-forth to their synagogue?"

Ernie had gotten so lost in his thoughts, that he stopped poling for a minute. Once again, we hung there, in the middle of the river, his cable holding us still against the gentle current. This time there was no strange vision. Instead of the usual thirty-six-second ride, we just sat there talking, like the old friends we should have been all along. Between the two of us, we'd seen a lot of changes in the valley, that's for sure. A man could never have too many friends, even if some of them are Lutherans.

SARAH WENT HOME right after the mass to start the turkey cooking plus who knows how many side dishes. Then she had to get ready for her own service at Our Redeemer, where she would sing in the choir. I was going to catch Ernie's last shuttle before he had to shut down so he could get up to the same church. When I got to Sarah's house, the front door was open, like she always left it when I was coming over. Believe it or not, most folks in Happy Valley do still leave their front doors unlocked, most of the time, anyway. It really is a nice place to live. Not only was the door unlocked, but it was standing wide open, and that was a little unusual. I poked my head in and called out to her.

"Sarah? It's Frank. Are you in there?"

No response. I put one foot inside and looked around. The house seemed empty.

"Sarah," I called again.

"Who are you seeking?" said a deep voice from behind me, totally unexpected.

I almost fell over because I hadn't heard any footsteps but

also because of the words. When I turned, Sarah was standing behind me, holding a basket full of flowers from her garden. Easter lilies and some early tulips. She had a big grin on her face, from the joke she'd pulled. I never even knew she could make her voice sound that deep.

"You scared me to death," I said, helping her with the basket.

"Who'd you think I was, silly?" she asked, still smiling, knowing full well whose words she'd imitated.

Well, you can guess what was going through my mind, after having seen Je-sus on the rock yesterday. Like I warned you earlier, I do get a little weird during the Lenten season, Easter morning especially.

AS THE BELLS BEGAN to chime, my reverie was broken, and I looked at Sarah in the choir loft off to the left, by the organ. She had already smiled at me once when they sang their way down the aisle and took their places. Now, she had her eyes closed, probably in prayer. If a Lutheran could pray in a Catholic Church, maybe an old Catholic could learn to pray in a Lutheran Church. Lots of changes going on here in the valley, but none of them more than we can handle if we work together.

When she opened her eyes, she looked at me again and smiled. I wish you could've seen that look. She's a handsome woman, always has been, but that look was special, something reserved just for me. I'm one lucky man.

"I love you," I whispered to her from fifty feet away, just moving my lips.

"I love you, too," she whispered back, without a blink.

See what I mean? About my being lucky?

AFTER THE SERVICE, I waited out front while Sarah got out of her robe. Several old friends came up to greet me, some making jokes about my converting, others just happy to see me. Sarah and I walked back to her place, waving to a few more people as we went. If the cat wasn't out of the bag before today, it certainly was now. Both churches have seen us together. It felt good, really good. Once we reached her living room, I volunteered to give her a hand, but she said that everything was pretty much ready. I sat down to read her paper, while we waited for the guests to arrive. *This could be a special day*, I thought, looking ahead, *even more special than it already has been.*

On Friday afternoon, I'd called Carl and invited him to come over to Sarah's and have Easter dinner with us, just in case he wouldn't be going to his son's, but he said he didn't think so because he didn't want to be a fifth wheel.

"How are you going to be a fifth wheel when it's just me and Sarah?"

"Hell, you know what I mean. Anyway, they give us a nice meal at the home, from what I hear, anyway."

"You won't be going to Jim's, then?"

"No, he made sure they got out of town for the day—off to her folks' place in Rawlston for dinner. Said he couldn't ask me along because their car only fit the four of them, as if I would've gone even if he'd begged me."

"Have dinner with us, Carl. I'd really like it."

"We'll see ... what time?"

"One o'clock."

I knew that was as close as I'd get to an answer, at least for the moment. After inviting Carl, the more I thought about it, the more I got to thinking about Jonathan and Miriam. Maybe they'd come too, if it didn't look like some kind of an Easter celebration. After worrying about the religious thing for a minute or two, it finally dawned on me that I'd just been over to their place for Passover, and I'd managed to get through that just fine. What difference did it make if we were having an Easter dinner? If a Christian could attend a Passover, couldn't a Jew attend an Easter meal? Jesus was a Jew, after all.

This time I figured I'd better check with Sarah before asking them. I could spring Carl on her because we'd talked about it first, but the Greens might be something different.

"Sure, Frank," she told me. "I don't see why not, unless they keep kosher."

"What do you mean?"

"I was planning on cooking a ham —"

"Oh Lord," I said, "I never even thought of that. I don't know what Jonathan eats, but she's from Israel."

"Just check on it when you ask them, will you? I can always cook a turkey instead, or even fish."

"Tuna for Easter?" I asked, surprised.

"It wouldn't come out of a can, Frank," she answered, mussing my hair on her way to the kitchen.

Since I was on a roll, I just picked up the phone and dialed Jonathan. Miriam answered, so I thanked her again for having me to Passover, then asked if I could talk with Jonathan.

"He's not here right now, Frank. He went to the City Hall to do some more research."

"Well, then I'll just ask you ... Sarah and I would like to invite you over for Easter dinner."

"Thank you. We'd be delighted, I'm sure."

"It may not be that simple, Miriam. I've also asked my old friend, Carl Markdoffer, who's the father of Jim Markdoffer. He and Jonathan are on opposite sides of the bridge debate. I just don't know how Jonathan will feel. I wanted to ask him first, you know?"

"Oh, he might be a little uncomfortable," Miriam said, "but he will be there. I'll see to it." I could almost hear the smile in her words. Jonathan had himself a handful with this woman, that's for sure.

"Okay. I'll leave the decision up to you," I said, copping out as fast as I could. Secretly, I was delighted to think of getting two of my oldest friends together like this. They had some fences to mend—at least in my opinion. "Do you eat kosher?"

I asked Miriam, remembering Sarah's concerns just in the nick of time.

"Eat kosher?" she said, the confusion apparent in her voice.

"I just knew I'd phrase it all wrong. I mean do you only eat kosher foods?"

"We're not Orthodox, but I do follow most of the rules."

"Is turkey all right?" I asked, jumping right over the ham, realizing that she probably wouldn't even know it was a traditional meal on Easter.

"I love turkey. What time would you like us?"

"One o'clock."

"Good. Tell Sarah that I'll bring a dessert."

Sarah walked back into the room just as I was hanging up the phone.

"They're coming," I told her. "Miriam said turkey would be fine and that she will bring the dessert."

"Oh, Frank. You shouldn't have let her do that. They're our guests. Oh well, nothing we can do about it now."

She walked back into the kitchen, leaving me sitting there, feeling like I'd stuck my foot in my mouth again, yet there was no reason to feel like that since everything seemed to be working out just fine, thanks to me. Everyone was coming, as I hoped, and a turkey would be good, so why was I starting to worry? Two of my oldest friends would be here for dinner, even if they were on opposite sides of the bridge issue. Maybe that was why I'd started having doubts? Now that everything was all set, I couldn't help wondering just how bright an idea it was to have Carl and Jonathan in the same room together. Maybe I really was a meddler and a big turkey.

SINCE MIRIAM HAD TOLD ME yesterday that Jonathan was at the library, I decided to stop by and ask how his research was coming along. I found his table before I found him because the pile of papers and open books could only belong to him. I sat down and waited, trying not to peek at any of the papers. Jonathan and I had not talked about his mission since that first time we got together.

"Hello, Frank."

"Jonathan, I knew this had to be your work." He had come up from behind me. "So, how's the research going?"

"Slowly, but surely."

When he didn't continue, I thought about mentioning the Easter dinner and moving on, but instead, I just blurted out what was on my mind. "It might be none of my business, Jonathan, but can you tell me anything about Carl's son and all this mess? I don't mean to pry ..."

"It's all right, Frank. I know that Carl's your friend. I can understand your concern. Actually, you might be relieved. From what I can gather, Jim is not the leader of the bridge movement. In fact, I think he is being used as a front man by others. His motives seem sincerely based on the good of the community, not on his personal gain. His name is not on any recent real estate deals."

"Really? That's actually a relief. I haven't had many good thoughts about him, lately."

"Carl's father might have been involved in the railroad business way back when, but he ended up losing money on that deal. I don't think Carl's son is involved in this bridge project, other than being in favor of it."

"Thank you, Jonathan. I appreciate knowing that." I left shortly after that, totally forgetting to tell Jonathan about the Easter dinner or that I had invited Carl. Suddenly, a big load of worry had been lifted from my shoulders.

WHEN IT GOT TO BE 12:30 on Easter Sunday, and I still hadn't heard from Carl, I thought I'd give him a call to see if he were coming or not. The phone just rang and rang without an answer. Was he on his way over, or had he changed his mind and gone somewhere else? The more I thought about it, the more worried I got about having him and Jonathan in the same room, my fears going all the way back to the schoolyard some sixty years ago. Well, nothing to do about it now. Either Carl showed up, or he didn't. We'd just have to wait and see.

I'm no kind of cook, but I did offer my services to Sarah, again. This ERA stuff has even gotten to an old geezer like me. It just never dawned on me to do that with my first wife, Ruthie. My job was to teach and earn the money, and she took care of the home. That's just the way things were back then. Sarah said no thanks, for the second time, then chased me out to the living room when I kept getting in her way. Now, I'm not so old that I don't like bumping into a good-looking woman, but she was trying to get something done. When I got back to the front room, I tried Carl's place once more, but I had no luck getting him. The countdown is on, I guessed.

JONATHAN AND MIRIAM arrived right on time, with Carl in tow. They'd met out front, walking in from different ends of the same street. My first reaction on seeing them together was, *Uh oh*, but they seemed to be doing all right, actually. Carl looked a little uneasy, being in their company, but he'd been a little uneasy about coming at all. I could just hear him thinking—"Now, I really am going to be a fifth wheel." Since we were going to be five of us, I guess it was true. Well, he was going to have Easter dinner with us, even if I had to tie him to the chair.

I shook hands all the way around, complimenting Miriam on her outfit, a spring dress with red flowers and white leather belt. The whole thing complemented her hair, and vice versa. She is a very attractive woman, but mostly it's something that comes from inside her—self-assurance, a knowledge of who she is and what she's about. But isn't that the source of real beauty anyway?

For your information, I'd already complimented Sarah on her Easter outfit. It was a yellow suit, made of linen (she told me), a little on the warmish side once the sun burned off the morning mist, but she'd needed it for the ride across on the ferry. She'd taken off the suit coat to do her cooking, and just wore a white blouse and pearls over the skirt. Shoes to match, and pearl earrings. Sarah is a mighty handsome woman, in her own right. That's why I was having so much trouble leaving her alone in the kitchen. Anyway, I'd let her know several times just how much I liked the way she looked this morning. I can be an old smoothie at times.

I told Carl that I thought he looked nice in his suit and tie, and everyone laughed. Jonathan was wearing a comfortable cardigan sweater over a shirt opened at the neck, and I had long since dumped my coat and tie. Funny, but after teaching for forty years, you'd think that I would have gotten used to wearing those things around my neck, but they always felt just like what they looked like—a hanged man's noose. I invited Carl to get rid of the tie, and he was happy and relieved to oblige me in doing so.

"That's better," he said, folding the tie and putting it into a pocket of his suit coat. "I never changed after the late service at the church."

To my knowledge, this was the first time Carl had been to the Lutheran Church since he moved back to the valley—regular time on a Sunday, I mean, because he had gone to hear his son on Good Friday. Will wonders never cease? I'd gotten the distinct impression that Carl had no use for churches. Impression, heck—he'd told me so, in just that many words. He hadn't been inside a church for years, preferring to golf on Sunday mornings, while Karen went to church by herself, without him. Now, Carl had gone to services twice in the same week. Amazing. I'll bet it would please Karen to know it. Maybe she already does?

THE DINNER WENT WELL, lots of talking and gratitude for being able to get together on such a beautiful early spring day. We steered clear of the bridge as a topic, as much as we could anyway. I still hadn't made up my mind which way to vote, not completely. I'd started out being totally against the thing, then switched to being in favor of it because it would shake up the valley, and now I was back in the middle of the road or the river, not really sure what I wanted.

For Jonathan, it was a clear-cut issue. He was still opposed to the bridge, no matter what, but I had a suspicion, if not an absolute certainty, that his reactions were based on his father's experience from years before and not so much on current events. Good grief, the man was a judge, so who am I to play amateur psychologist on him? Maybe he sees other elements involved. Guess I could ask him again before the vote. We've still got almost a week left. Seems like both sides took Easter week off to spend with their families, so it's anyone's guess what the next few days will be like. We might get back to the rallies and the speaker trucks. Who knows?

FOR CARL, IT WAS EQUALLY SIMPLE. His son was up to his eyebrows in the project. No matter what, Carl would support Big Jim. Now that it didn't look like he was a crook, I could be more generous. What real difference would it make, though? Shouldn't a family stick together? Bottom line for Carl was that his son was on the pro-bridge side of the issue. In fact, the bridge would make our lunches much simpler. Carl never had gotten around to using Ernie's Happy Valley Ferry Service regularly, preferring to drive his car all the way around to my side of the river. For that matter, the bridge would simplify my going back and forth to Sarah's, but neither of those were the issue, not for me. The extra convenience the bridge would bring to all of us in Himmelberg was a given. I was worried about other things.

"Why does the bridge make you so upset, Frank?" Sarah had asked me sometime during this past Holy Week.

"Because I don't know which way to vote."

"It would make it a lot easier for us, getting back and forth," she suggested.

"Sure, I know that. I'm just afraid it would change us—the valley and everyone living here."

"Change us how?"

"I don't know—bring in outside people, lots of so-called improvements. You know."

"It might be good for the valley."

"I know that, too. It's just that I don't know how to decide. What if we're wrong?" I asked.

"Well," Sarah said, "I guess it'll come down to the American way—we'll vote on it."

That helped me more than you can possibly know. I am proud to be an American, and I do believe in our democratic system. Perhaps I'm just an optimist, but I do believe in democracy, in the long term. We might make some short-sighted mistakes, but I wouldn't change things. Bottom line, it's not just my problem, not all by myself, anyway. We're all in this together. How come I couldn't see that before?

MIRIAM BELIEVES IN MARRIAGE. My saying that might sound a little funny to you, coming as it does from a Catholic. We look at marriage as a sacrament, but I really think Miriam would understand the significance. I think she is also very intuitive with people. But judge for yourself.

"Were you married, Carl?" she asked, out of the blue. I almost choked on a mouthful of mashed potatoes when I heard the question. I hadn't said a word to Jonathan or Miriam about Carl's history, other than his being Big Jim's father.

"Yes, I was," he said, softly, looking into her eyes for as long as he could. Eventually, he dropped his gaze to his plate in front of him. "I lost Karen just about a year ago, this very month, in fact."

"I'm very sorry, Carl," Miriam said, "I didn't know." She

reached across the table and touched him on the arm, a simple gesture of sympathy, which she ended with a consoling pat or two before putting her hand back in her lap. It was almost the touch of an older person consoling a younger.

"Thanks," Carl said, struggling to look her in the eye again. "I appreciate it."

I glanced over at Jonathan, just as he camouflaged whatever expression had been on his face. Surprise at least, I thought, but something more, too. He was looking at Miriam. What I saw in that moment was a look of love, even awe. My friend, Jonathan, really, truly loves his wife.

Jonathan did not say a word. None of us did. We just rested quiet for a minute, until conversation picked up again, slowly at first, then back to normal.

Miriam had brought two desserts—a delicious apple pie, and a plate of candied dates. I had some of each.

AFTER DINNER, I HELPED SARAH and Miriam clear off the dessert plates and get ready to carry the coffee into the front room. On one of my trips back to the dining room, I saw Carl and Jonathan standing together, talking quietly. They were outlined in the frame of Sarah's front window. I don't know what they said, but I could tell they weren't arguing.

As I loaded up another stack of plates, I watched them out of the corner of my eye. This was the longest conversation the two of them have had since the day at the school sixty years ago. It may have been the longest conversation they'd ever had. I was dying to know what they were saying, but something kept me from walking over. Let them work it out, a voice told me, not the usual voice of Frank Hessel, that's for sure. Maybe it was the voice of the new Frank Hessel?

Just as I turned to head back into the kitchen, I saw Jonathan reach up and squeeze Carl on the shoulder. It was just a simple, manly gesture. No big deal, but my heart soared seeing its happening.

LATER ON, OVER COFFEE in the front room, Carl and I got a chance to talk by ourselves for a minute.

"Have you been to see Karen's grave since you moved back?" I asked him.

"No," he said, dropping his eyes to look at the carpet. He sighed then looked back up at me before asking, "Have you?"

"Yes," I said, nodding. "My folks and Ruthie are nearby."

"Did the marker look okay?" he asked.

"Yes," I answered, "it's very nice, and it matches the ones for your folks."

Carl just nodded. Finally, he said, "Good."

Like I'd been doing all my life, I couldn't resist sticking my nose into other people's business, but this time it felt like the new Frank Hessel in action, not the old. Since I'd decided he needed to visit those graves, I would make it easy for him.

"Would you like to go and see it, sometime? Jonathan's just put up a stone for his father. Maybe we could —"

Carl looked at me, then looked over at Jonathan, who was sitting next to his wife, the two of them visiting with Sarah. Carl stared at them for a long time before speaking.

"No," he said, "no, I don't think so. Matter of fact, I'd better get going."

Against Sarah's and my protests, he was on his feet and gone before we knew it. Just a quick handshake and a thank you all the way around, then Carl grabbed his coat and was out of there. Sarah and I went with him to the door. I couldn't help feeling that I'd driven him away, somehow, that I should've just kept my darn mouth shut. On the way back from the door, Sarah took my arm and whispered something to me that I'd never considered.

"He's lonely, Frank. That's all. Carl will come around in time."

I'd been alone for so long myself, that I hadn't considered such a simple possibility. In fact, I'd begun to think that it all had to do with Jonathan's being Jewish, plus our being on the other side of the bridge, so to speak. Maybe Carl *was* just a tired old man—nothing more than that, as if that weren't enough for a person to bear all by itself.

THE FOUR OF US SAT visiting over coffee after Carl left. Some of the things I avoided mentioning were—how much younger Miriam was than Jonathan, how it seemed funny that she would be willing to settle into a quiet little place like Happy Valley after having lived internationally, Israel and New York being just a couple of the places I knew about, and the simple fact of their being Jewish in a Christian valley. Well, I should have cautioned Sarah, I suppose, because she up and asked them about each one of the topics I had decided to avoid.

"Were you actually a student of Jonathan's?" she asked Miriam.

"Yes, in Tel Aviv. I majored in Art History but I had a minor in World Politics and he was teaching law, so the two overlapped at times. Actually, I was quite shameless in pursuing the great professor."

Miriam said this with a flirtatious look at Jonathan, who blushed and moved his coffee cup around on the saucer. Other than that, the room was deathly silent.

"He is a handsome man," Sarah joined in the teasing, much to my surprise.

Jonathan could take no more of their games.

"Frank, would you like to take a walk, so I can have a cigarette?" he asked me.

"Heck, no," I said, being too intrigued to even think about leaving now. This was just getting good. Jonathan shot me a look of shock, the old "how could you betray me like this" sort of a look, but I didn't care. You couldn't have dragged me out of that chair.

"Jonathan might be old enough, but you're much too young to retire," Sarah just blurted out, looking at Miriam. I tried to warn her with a quick glance, but she wasn't paying me a bit of attention. "Did you have a career while Jonathan was teaching?"

"Mostly I raised the children, but they're grown now, so for the past five years I worked as an art curator in New York."

"Really? Will you go back to that, or are you and Jonathan planning to stay in Happy Valley?"

In a mere five minutes, Sarah had managed to hit two out of the three taboo topics. On top of everything else, she had just pointed out how little there would be for Miriam—a sophisticated woman of the world—to do in this sleepy little valley. Now all Sarah had to do was comment on their being Jewish and she'd have made a clean sweep.

"We've just decided in the past few days that Jonathan is going to write a book, and I will handle the art work for him. I'm looking forward to designing the book. It will be half pictures, photographs, actually, and half text."

"About the law?" Sarah asked, glancing at my friend, Jonathan, the retired judge. I looked at him, too, mystified over what he would choose to write a book about. What topic could he come up with that wouldn't be dull or lifeless, stuffy as a court room? Of course, it should be obvious to you by now that everyone these days is writing books, even me. Why should Jonathan be any different?

"No," said Miriam, answering for Jonathan. "It will be about Judaism in America."

That put Sarah at three for three. She was batting a perfect thousand.

"Will you do the writing here, then?" Sarah asked, ignoring every psychic warning I could send, though they'd grown pretty feeble as I got fascinated with what I was hearing.

"Yes," Miriam answered, "it will mean some commuting to New York, and perhaps to some other collections around the country, but that's not so bad now that Jonathan's retired. We'll have the time, finally."

"Then Happy Valley will be your permanent home?" Sarah

said. I was looking right at her, but I couldn't read anything into the question other than curiosity.

"We've talked about moving back to Israel, but that would put us so far away from the kids here. We'll have to see."

Miriam said this while looking at her husband, her head slightly cocked to the side, as if she were curious to see his reaction. Jonathan was back to spinning his cup on the saucer. He didn't say a word, nor had I said a word for a good five minutes—some kind of a record for me.

"We are committed to the area," Miriam continued, "for a while, at least, because we've taken steps to begin a synagogue here in the valley."

"That's wonderful," Sarah responded, simply and sincerely, as only she can do. Without complications or hesitation, just a joy for someone else's journey.

THE FOUR OF US sat around and talked for another hour, I guess. Not always so heavy duty, just nice and friendly. The women cleaned up after a while, and I really did ask and offer to help, two or three times, even. Honest. But they tossed us out on our ears. So Jonathan and I went for a walk down to the river where I could work off some of the dinner and he could finally have two or three cigarettes, smoking being absolutely forbidden in Sarah's house.

We just talked, nothing important, nothing major. We tried to stay away from the bridge vote, seeing as how each of us "knew" we were on the same side, except that I'd never told him I might go the other way, maybe. Heck, I still don't know which way I'll vote. If the vote were today, I would vote yes on the bridge, just to force some change. Maybe it is time, past time. Meanwhile, Jonathan and I were just two old friends strolling quietly along the river, until he laid something on me.

"Did I tell you that the cemetery called me yesterday afternoon?"

"No," I said. Jonathan had already told me on Thursday

that he was going ahead with the burial, symbolic as it was, just as I'd hoped he would.

"My father's marker is finished and placed by now. Their crew was just on their way to set it in the ground when they called."

"That's great. You haven't seen it, yet?" I asked.

"Not yet. I'll go later this afternoon."

"It's a beautiful setting up there, the whole valley laid out like a tapestry."

"Will you go with me?"

"Me?"

"Yes, you."

"Shouldn't you go with Miriam? Or something?"

"This is an event a man does with his immediate family," he said, turning to look at me directly. "I would like you to be there."

The implications of what Jonathan told me were stunning. Fancy that! Have we come a long way these past six weeks or what? For once in my life, I kept my mouth shut. Instead of botching it up, asking too many questions, or making an ass out of myself, I kept it simple.

"I'd be honored to go with you, Jonathan."

AFTER THE GREENS left for home, Sarah decided to lie down for a nap, having gone to the early service with me and then cooked the whole meal before we went off to her church, so I just poured another cup of coffee and sat down in her front room to think. Jonathan was going to come by for me in his car; then we'd go over to his father's grave. So, here I was on the Lutheran side of the river, sitting in my lady friend's front room. We hadn't talked about it yet, but I guess we'll have to decide on which of our places we'll actually choose for a home. Maybe we should sell them both and start from scratch in a new house? How would that be? On which side of the river would we live?

While I sat there thinking, the phone rang. I grabbed for it quick-like, hoping it wouldn't disturb Sarah.

"Hello," I said.

"Frank, it's Carl. I just wanted to thank you and Sarah for having me over."

"Our pleasure, Carl. Anytime."

"Sorry about taking off the way I did. Everything just dammed up inside me for a minute. I really got to missing Karen and, well, you know."

"Sure, Carl."

"Hey, guess what?"

"What's that?"

"My boy called from his in-laws' place to wish me a Happy Easter. I guess it really was the car being so small. He wasn't trying to ditch me or anything. He just thought I wouldn't want to drive there by myself for over a hundred miles."

"I'm glad, Carl."

"Yeah, well, thanks again, and I'll see you during the week."

"Hey, Carl?" I said, real quick, hoping to catch him before he hung up the phone.

"Yes."

"How about going to the cemetery with us, me and Jonathan? We'll be leaving in a little while?"

"I don't think so, Frank," he said after a long pause. "I'm just not ready for that, not yet. Maybe some other time."

That's the way we left it. I was glad he called because it made me feel better about his taking off so quickly. I guess he's just a lonely old man, after all, the same as I used to be.

WELL, IF THIS IS EASTER, I thought to myself, sitting there on Sarah's couch, *then the Lenten season is officially over*. No telling how I'm feeling about that just yet. A lot has happened over the past six weeks, some good, some bad, some indifferent or yet to be determined. I wish that Carl had stayed longer, but I'm glad that he came for a while, and I really enjoyed having Jonathan and Miriam over for Easter dinner. Sarah did a bang-up job on the meal, and we all sat around afterwards getting to know each other better. The women hit it off just fine, which goes to show how little I know about the fairer sex. I was afraid that Miriam would be too worldly and sophisticated for Sarah's taste, but they chatted away like they'd known each other for years. In fact, I hadn't seen Miriam laugh so much before, though in all fairness, we haven't been meeting in social settings. The few times I'd been over to their house had been pretty serious affairs, besides which Jonathan could stand with a little loosening up. I will admit that he didn't do much to hold up his end of the conversation after dinner.

This is all leading up to my telling you about my Lenten Resolution, not the business about Sarah because that's been resolved, but the resolution I've been trying to keep secret. You'll remember that Carl was bugging me to tell him what I gave up? Well, it isn't anything so simple. If you remember, I was pretty depressed at the start of Lent, and I had been for a year, ever since my cancer was diagnosed. Well, I was tired of feeling like that, so I decided to stop feeling sorry for myself, over the leukemia and all, plus the general problems of getting old alone and all the rest of the stuff I've been laying on you for the past two hundred pages or so. But giving up a feeling like that isn't quite the same as giving up smoking, though it was just as tough at times, so what I decided to do was a little different—I decided to do something nice for someone else, every day or at least every week of Lent, and never tell them about it. Sound easy? Well it's anything but easy, believe me.

I got this great idea from reading some newspaper column a while back, maybe Dear Abby. Anyway, that was the suggestion for getting past depression—doing something nice and taking no credit for it. I think Abby took the idea from a book called *The Course in Miracles*. Now that Lent's over, I can tell you about it without jinxing the promise.

Let's see how I did—Ernie wasn't even on my list six weeks ago, but I snuck down to his ferry early this morning and hid a new rope for him in his shed, just to say thanks for all the times he's taken me across the river. You'll remember that his old one was getting a little frayed. I also put in a word for him at the high school. The current principal was just coming in as the assistant when I retired. He and I got along well, so I put out a feeler about Ernie's picking up some custodial work there if the vote next week goes against him. You know what I mean—if the bridge thing passes, Ernie will be out of work.

The thing with Jonathan and his father's grave just happened. It wasn't anything I planned or thought about for Lent. It turned out pretty well, though, even if I do say so myself. I know Jonathan feels a lot better about Happy Valley, now. His father's gravestone will be here, where it belongs. Maybe his soul—father and son's, both—will rest a little easier, I don't know. Maybe their spirits will help this valley do some changing, some healing? I think Jonathan will stay here long enough to see that the synagogue is up and running, but I don't know if he and Miriam will settle here for good. Thanks to our dinner conversation, Jonathan knows just how much she misses Israel. They may have to write that book in Jerusalem, who knows?

My friend Carl was difficult for another reason. Neither he nor Jonathan were on my list at the start because I didn't know either one of them were living in the valley when I made the resolution. You know about all the ups and downs Carl and I've had, so you can see the problem. What to do for him? I couldn't just promise to have lunch with him once a week because I was already doing that and would have done it, anyway. No, it had to be something different, something special. That's when I got the idea of the poker game. I knew that Carl's son, Jim, was a poker fanatic, so all I had to do was suggest that Carl find us another player or two. That made it look like it was his idea the whole time. Thank God, it seems to be working out. Jim said okay, and we will start playing in a week, just before the vote, in fact. At least for one night every two weeks, Carl and his son will be together. Who knows what might happen over the course of time? I might go broke, that much I do know, because I'm not much of a card player, but we'll see.

Sarah says she'll come over and help me set up for the card game. She's planning on sandwich snacks, dips, that kind of stuff. I told her that I could handle it fine all by myself, but I didn't argue with her because it's something she wants to do to help. I did get a little irritated when she said that I wouldn't be able to open a bag of potato chips, as if I didn't have any experience with cooking. I didn't do too bad on those casseroles for my neighbor, Ed Shrader, though I will have to admit that Sarah did the actual cooking on those, too. All I did was reheat them. She is quite a woman. I even asked her if she might want to stay and play a hand or two of cards with us, but she just laughed. "Not on a bet," she said. "I'm going to leave before your guests arrive."

Sarah is a mystery. She was first on my list, but nothing happened the way I'd planned it. As I've already told you, at one point early in Lent I had decided that my resolution concerning her was to let her go, to stop tying up all her time. Nobly, I would stop seeing her, so she could meet someone else and live with him happily ever after, while I would just crawl off and die from my cancer, celebrating my humble sacrifice. Now, you understand that I was doing all this so I wouldn't feel depressed. Instead of anything like that happening, now it looks like were going to get married. Go figure it—I can't.

And what about me? Francis J. Hessel? My name wasn't even on my own list, yet I am the one to get all the benefits. It's enough to make a man believe in God and miracles, don't you think?

A FEW MINUTES LATER, Jonathan came by for me and we drove to the end of the valley and around, and then up to the cemetery. His father's stone had been laid the day before, but as we drove, what a thought struck me! Why hadn't I seen it till just now? On the Saturday before Easter, his father's tombstone had been placed. The day before Christ rose. Is that spooky or what? I didn't know what most Jews believe about the afterlife, so I asked Jonathan on the drive to the cemetery. He was vague about it, saying it varied from person to person, sect to sect. According to him, there was no consistent belief about heaven within Judaism.

"Most Jews leave heaven in God's hands," he'd told me. "Our policy—our religion, if you will—is to live as decent a life as we can here on earth and leave eternity to Him. God has promised us that swords shall be turned into plowshares, and that Jerusalem will replace Rome—not your Catholic Rome," he added with a smile, "but the military Rome, the symbol. There will be peace in the world, but whether that means *this* world, for our children, or a heavenly next world ... we just don't know."

"I'll settle for either one—or both," I said.

"So will I, old friend. So will I."

WE REACHED THE CEMETERY and made the long climb to his father's grave. It was a beautiful day, a little crisp but clear and sunny. I couldn't help being surprised when I saw the stone. Below the Star of David, I read, "Aaron Green."

"Green?" I asked without thinking.

"Yes."

"Not Greenbaum?"

"Green was always our name. I changed it back in my twenties."

"How did that happen?"

"When my grandparents came through Ellis Island, they spoke no English, so when asked his name, my grandfather said, 'Green, Noam,' but what got written down was Greenbaum."

"I didn't know. I wondered why you changed it."

"You aren't the first to wonder. Many people assume it was to be more American and less Jewish."

"I heard that many people changed their names coming here."

"Or had them changed for them. Anyone from Poland or Czechoslovakia, even Russia, anywhere with the Cyrillic alphabet, ran that risk. Americans could not pronounce names with cz's and the like, so new immigrants became Carpenter and Collins, instead."

"Why didn't your grandfather or father change it back?"

"Anyone from the Old Country, Jews especially, had little trust for the authorities. It was better to just live with the new name."

"Will that be in your book?"

"That and many other stories like it."

"I'm sorry, Jonathan. I didn't know."

"For some people it might not have mattered so much. You can look at it both ways. One, your identity was stripped away, so you did not know who you were anymore. Or, two, America gave you a new name and new life. For me it was important to regain my sense of myself, my heritage. Especially so after the Holocaust. My entire family was wiped out, except for the American branch."

"I had no idea, Jonathan."

We stood there for quite a while, lost in our own thoughts. Then Jonathan turned back to the headstone and recited some Hebrew words. One of these days, I will ask him what they mean, but there's no rush. All I did was live in the moment, thinking back on those friends and family who were already dead and gone beyond this world into whatever is to follow. Honoring the dead might seem a little old fashioned, today, but I've always believed in the old adage: If we forget the past, we are doomed to repeat it. My time with Jonathan was a good, close moment between old friends.

Out of the corner of my eye, I caught a movement to our left. Glancing over, I saw a figure coming up the hill, slowly making its way through the cemetery. Because of my own vision problems, I couldn't be sure it was Carl until he got closer. He had his hands thrust deep in his pockets, but nodded when he saw me looking. I glanced back at Jonathan, but he was staring out over the valley, in the other direction. I followed his gaze and again saw the beauty of Happy Valley. When I looked back at Jonathan, he had closed his eyes, in prayer, I assumed.

Carl paused and was looking down at his feet. Judging from how I remembered the positioning of the plots, he had to be at the section I'd visited the other day, meaning that he was probably standing right over the graves of his parents and his wife, Karen. For a moment, he just stood there looking down, until he moved one hand up to his eyes, obviously to wipe away his tears. Then he was really crying, deep, wrenching sobs, letting loose all the pent up grief he'd carried for the past year, if not for many years before that. When I looked back at Jonathan, he too had turned and was watching Carl. By mutual assent and without a spoken word, we moved down the hill to join our childhood friend.

Together, the three of us stood on the side of the hill overlooking the valley—old friends reunited at last. As the sun began to move toward its setting, the light on the horizon shifted into a lovely shade of lilac, moving toward a deeper shade of red. I put my arm around Carl's shoulders, finding Jonathan's hand already there. He and I reached out, putting our free hands on each other's shoulder, so all of us together formed a loose triangle of sorts. In my mind, I saw the famous sculpture of the Three Graces, a trinity frozen in mid-step during a moment of their dance. We hardly matched their young and vibrant figures, but I liked the symbolism. Just one more of the countless memories I carry in my mind, stored up for all eternity.

I don't know how the bridge vote will turn out next week, but the valley will change, one way or another. It already has. Sometimes change happens quickly. Sometimes it takes a lifetime. This year, Easter turned out very well, after all, thank God. As my friend, Jonathan, has taught me to say in Hebrew—*l'chaim* ... to life!

Kyrie eleison
Lord, Have Mercy

Made in the USA
Charleston, SC
24 March 2014